CW00780958

WINNING THE BENEVOLENT CUP AND REACHING FIRST BASE

ALLEN NICKLIN

For Janet, Rachel and Esther

To Windmill

Best Wishes

Allen Nickli

CONTENTS

PROLOGUE 1

PART 1 NO HIDING PLACE 5

PART 2 A CHRISTMAS STORY 32

PART 3 THE MAN WITH AN UMBRELLA 39

PART 4 IT'S A CRUEL WORLD 75

PART 5 THE MONDAY CLUB 113

PART 6 THE BEAT GOES ON 161

REFERENCES 222

PROLOGUE

Monday 11 August 1963

James Bond took cover from the searing mid-day sun under a majestic oak tree; he checked his Timex watch; it was 11.58 pm He pulled a handkerchief from his pocket and wiped the sweat from his face. What he wouldn't give for a cool refreshing glass of Tizer. A rustle from behind interrupted his thoughts.

'I'm not late am I?' asked the newcomer.

'No, you're dead on time. Good to see you again, John,' replied James.

John Drake smiled, 'It's good to see you too. I'm looking forward to working with you again.'

'The feeling's mutual and this is the big one.'

'Excellent, so what's the assignment?'

'Our intelligence tells us that a top Russian spy is holding out at Leatherslade Farm.'

'Do we know his name?'

'Yevgeny Ivanov.'

'Him!' exclaimed John. 'We've been after him for years. What are our instructions?'

'Simple: locate and eliminate.'

'Understood: how far away is the farm?'

James took out his compass, 'about half a mile north-east.'

John looked at James, 'this is it, James; we're doing this for England.'

'Death to all Ruskies; this will be another nail in the coffin of communism.'

'Once more unto the breach, dear friends, once more.'

They looked at each other, stood to attention, saluted and said, together, 'For England.'

Leatherslade Farm is situated off the B4011 near the sleepy village of Oakley on the Beds/Bucks border. James and John jogged along the track that led up to the farm. As they approached the farm buildings, they crawled through the hedgerow so that their approach would be undetected. John took out his binoculars to get a better look. There seemed to be a lot of activity around the farm. They saw a Land Rover and men carrying out bags from a badly painted yellow lorry.

James and John observed for a while before John said, 'There's more than one, James. Should we abort?'

'Not sure,' replied James. 'Obviously our intelligence was flawed, but I think we need to have a closer look before we call for back up.'

'Do you think this could be a KGB training camp?'

'It certainly looks like it, but we need to be sure.'

'A closer look then?'

'Absolutely, are you armed?'

'Of course, are you?'

James pulled out a catapult, 'made this one last week.'

'Wow,' said John. 'What wood did you use?'

'I found a nice forked branch in a holly tree and I used a tongue from an old shoe my dad threw out.'

'Nice job; I've got my trusty pea shooter.'

'There's no-one better than you with one of those.'

'Thanks.'

Just as they started their approach they heard a twig crack.

'And what do you think you are doing?' Bellowed a voice behind them.

The two boys turned, looked up at the rough looking stranger; he looked about thirty, short, stocky, and had maybe done a bit of boxing.

'Nothing,' they said together.

'This is private land and you are trespassing.'

The boys just stared.

'Cat got your tongue; what's yer names?'

'I'm Nick Allen and this is Don Patrick. We didn't know we were trespassing; we thought the farm was empty.'

'Well, it's not, as you can see. My friend bought it about two months ago'.

'Sorry.'

'Okay, lads,' said the stranger smiling. 'I didn't mean to frighten you. It's just that we're on a very important government mission. You know: Top Secret.'

'We understand,' replied Don. 'So are we. We're looking for a top Russian spy.'

'That is a coincidence; so you understand how important it is that you tell no one what you have seen today.'

'Haven't seen a thing all day,' said Don. 'Have you, Nick?'

'Not a thing; bloody boring afternoon,' replied Nick, shaking his head vigorously.

'That's good, lads,' said the stranger, fishing in his pocket. 'Take these, call it expenses. I'm sure you'll find something to spend it on.' The stranger gave them each a grubby one pound note.

'Thanks, mister,' the boys said in unison.

'By the way,' said Nick. What's your name?

'My friends call me Buster.'

'Like the comic,' said Don.

Buster laughed. 'Yeh, just like the comic, but my surname ain't Capp.' The boys laughed.

'Well we'll be on our way,' said Don, 'nice to meet you.'

'Okay,' replied Buster, 'and remember Mum's the word.'

'Never heard of Leatherslade Farm, Nick, have you?'

'Where?..... Bye Buster.'

The boys ran as fast as they could back down the lane. They stopped when they reached Thame Road. After catching their breath, they looked at each other and Nick said, 'He's a crook.'

'Absolutely,' replied Don. 'Let's tell my uncle and he can call the police.'

Nick and Don returned to the home of Don's uncle, a small cottage on a farm adjacent to Leatherslade Farm. Don's uncle Fred and his auntie Betty had invited the boys to stay for a few days during the summer holidays. Uncle Fred was a farm worker and rented the cottage from the farmer. Nick thought they were a lovely couple and they treated the boys as if they were their own. Unfortunately, they hadn't been blessed with any children, so they always made a fuss of them when they came to stay.

Uncle Fred had promised to take the boys to the cinema that evening to watch *The Great Escape*, but said, 'I'll have to nip up to the farmhouse and use their phone. I expect the police will want to talk to you, so we'll go tomorrow. Anyway I think you've had enough excitement for one day.

Let's just hope they've gone before *The Archers* starts; Betty will be upset if she misses that.'

The boys stayed at the farm for the rest of the week. Uncle Fred was good to his word and took them to see the film the next day. So, for the rest of the week, James Bond and Danger Man were forgotten as the boys planned their escape from Stalag Luft III. On the Wednesday the boys were disappointed after reading the morning paper that their names had not been mentioned.

PART 1

NO HIDING PLACE

Wednesday 18 September 1963

Nick Allen is a thirteen-year old boy who attends the Sandridge Grammar School. He has a mop of light brown hair, is of average height and build, has a nice smile and twinkling blue eyes. He is a hardworking, conscientious student whose ambition is to become a professional footballer. Our story starts one Wednesday afternoon in September 1963.

Mr Freeman, the Sports Master, a tall athletic man in his mid-thirties; although his main sport is basketball he has a great passion for football. Looking at his watch, he gives a long blow on his whistle, and then shouts, 'that's it lads, game over, well played. Collect in all the balls, leave the nets up, and don't walk over the cricket square.'

It was upper 3A's weekly games period and the blue team had just beaten the red team 5-2 in an extremely competitive football match. Nick Allen, who had scored a hat-trick for the blue team was walking back to the changing rooms with his friend Keith Nevin when Mr Freeman called him over.

'Nick, can I have a word?'

'Certainly, Sir,' replied Nick.

'The first eleven are playing Batchwood Boys School tomorrow in a friendly and I would like you to come along as a reserve[1]. If things go okay, you should get a run out in the second half.'

'Gosh,' exclaimed Nick. 'But Sir, I'm only 13; I hope I won't let you down.'

'You won't let me down,' laughed Mr Freeman. 'You have a lot of talent and I think you can hold your own against the older boys.'

'Thank you, Sir,' replied Nick. 'I'll jolly well do my best.'

'I know you will; the match kicks off at 2.30 pm so I'll see you in the changing room at 2 o'clock. Don't be late.'

As Mr Freeman jogged back to the changing rooms, Keith looked at Nick and said, 'Congratulations. Not many third years get picked to play for the first eleven.'

Keith was Nick's closest friend at school. He was a good two inches taller than Nick and had dark brown hair and a slight oriental look due to his mother being Vietnamese.

'Thanks,' replied Nick. 'I just hope I get a run out, but I don't want anyone to get injured.'

'I expect it will be a tactical move. He obviously wants to find the best team; a lot is expected of them this year.'

'Who usually plays centre forward, because that is my best position?'

'Ah,' said Keith, apprehensively. 'That would be Alan Prince. You know him… …..the school bully. I don't think he'll be too pleased if you replaced him.'

'I think he would understand if it was for the good of the team.'

'Well, I wouldn't like to be in your shoes if it happens.'

'Spurs did well Monday night; beat Villa 4-2 away,' said Nick, quickly changing the subject.

'You're avoiding the issue, Nick.'

'Jimmy Greaves scored twice.'

Nick and Keith walked solemnly back to the changing rooms.

Nick lived in a two-bedroom council house on an estate to the west of St Albans. He lived with his mother, father and his nine-year old brother, Richard. He parked his bicycle outside the back door and entered the kitchen where his mother was cooking the evening meal.

'Hello dear,' said Mrs Allen, a pretty petite woman in her late thirties. 'Have a good day?'

'As it happens, I did,' replied Nick, throwing his school bag down and slumping into a kitchen chair. 'I've been selected to play for the school football team tomorrow.'

'That's good, but I didn't think they had a third year school team.'

'They haven't; it's for the fourth year team. And if I play two games I can apply for the Sportsman Badge at the Scouts. You only have to play a couple of games for the school team and answer a few questions on sport and it's yours. Anyway, what time's tea? Shall I get changed for Scouts now or after? What have we got, I'm starving?'

Well, there has been … erm … how shall I put it … .a development.'

'What do you mean, Mum?' replied Nick, kicking his shoes off under the table.

'Hang you school blazer up and let me explain. Would you like a cup of tea?'

'Yes please, two sugars.'

Mrs Allen quickly poured out two cups of tea, whilst Nick hung his blazer up on the Newel post on the bottom of the stairs and came back and sat down at the kitchen table opposite his Mum.

'Well, Mr Bowden, your Scout Leader phoned me today.'

Nick didn't like the sound of this and just said, 'Oh.'

'He thinks it would be best if you resigned from the Scouts, due to a number of complaints.'

Nick started to fidget and said, 'It wasn't my fault, we just made the fire too close to the scout hut and then the wind changed direction. There wasn't much damage done.'

'It wasn't that.'

Nick took a sip of his tea, and then said, 'How was I to know that the Hangman's Noose wasn't on the list of knots we had to learn? And I was only showing that kid the right position to place the knot round his neck for the quickest death. Not my fault he keeps having nightmares.'

'That was mentioned, but the main complaint was about last Saturday.'

Nick was feeling agitated and put two more spoonful's of sugar in his tea and stirred it vigorously.

'That definitely was not my fault; how was I to know that there was a Pimlico in Hertfordshire? The instructions said - start at the Swan Public House in Pimlico and make your way to the Swimming Baths in Watford. Which is what we did; admittedly, we never made it to Watford.'

'Maybe, that's because you went to Pimlico in London.'

'Easy mistake to make, but we did find the Swan pub in Pimlico.'

'It was the White Swan. Surely you must have realized that Pimlico in London is more than eight miles away from Watford. You left at ten o' clock in the morning and were supposed to meet the others at the swimming pool at one o' clock; plenty of time to walk eight miles. You arrived home at eight o' clock in the evening; Ronald's parents were frantic. And to make matters worse, you hitched-hiked home and Ronald is only twelve years old.'

Nick shrugged his shoulders and said 'Ronald seemed to enjoy it; he's never been in an articulated lorry before and the lorry driver did treat us to a bacon roll and a mug of tea in that roadside café.'

'That didn't go down that well either; you know Ronald has a delicate stomach and has to watch what he eats.'

Nick laughed, 'I realized that when he asked the lorry driver if he could have another bacon roll. He said that he had never tasted anything so delicious. You should have seen him, grease running down his chin and grinning like the Cheshire Cat.'

'That may be so, but his parents were not impressed and he also said that you were a bit rough with the younger boys.'

Nick huffed, 'that's a bit of an exaggeration; I'm just over-competitive. If they get in my way and get a bit hurt, it's not my fault. Anyway, they need toughening up a bit; they're just a load of wimps.'

'That may well be the case, but that's why Mr Bowden phoned.'

'Oh well,' said Nick, finishing his cup of tea. He sat thinking for a while before he said, 'Know anyone who wants to buy a second hand scout uniform? What did you say was for tea?'

'Toad-in-the-Hole.'

Thursday 19 September 1963

At 2.00 pm the next day Nick Allen walked nervously into the changing room; the rest of team were already assembled and getting changed.

He was greeted by Mr Freeman. 'Hello Nick,' he said. 'Let me introduce you to the rest of the team. Lads, quiet please. If you don't know him already this is Nick Allen and he will be our reserve today.'

Danny Fooks, the stocky captain of the football team, with a mass of uncontrollable curly hair, approached Nick and shook his hand. 'Welcome to the team.'

'Thank you,' replied Nick nervously.

'Who wants a snotty third year in our team?' said a voice from the other end of the changing room.

'Quiet, Prince,' said Mr Freeman.

'Take no notice of him,' whispered Danny. 'If he had his way only his friends would be in the team.'

'Is that Alan Prince, the school bully?' asked Nick looking at the ginger-haired boy at the opposite end of the changing room.

'That's right,' said Danny. 'But don't worry; his bark is worse than his bite.'

Nick found himself a quiet corner and changed alone.

The game commenced with Batchwood Boys having the majority of play and this was rewarded by a goal on the stroke of half-time. The second half saw an improvement in the Sandridge Grammar's play, but all the good approach work was wasted by the Sandridge forward line who squandered many chances. With twenty minutes left, the Batchwood boys scored a second goal against the run of play. Then Mr Freeman said the words that Nick had been waiting to hear: 'Nick, get warmed up. You're going on.'

Nick started his special warm-up routine, which consisted of lots of stretching and jogging on the spot.

'Next time the ball goes out,' said Mr Freeman. 'It'll be a straight swap.'

Nick removed his track-suit top. 'This is my big chance,' he said to himself as he bounced up and down on the touchline.

The ball went out of play on the far side of the pitch.

'Ref,' shouted Mr Freeman, 'I'd like to make a change.'

'Okay,' said Mr Hamilton, the music teacher who was today's referee.

'Prince!' yelled Mr Freeman, 'Off you come.'

As Prince ambled off the pitch, with his ginger hair and crooked mouth, he gave Nick an evil stare that sent shivers down his spine.

Nick entered the field of play and took up his normal position of centre forward. It was a full five minutes before he touched the ball. A long clearance by the Sandridge goalkeeper, Simon Francis, was beautifully controlled but before he could turn he was brutally fouled by the Batchwood centre half; a free kick to Sandridge. Eddie Lee, the blonde, wiry, rat-faced Sandridge Grammar right half walked up to take the kick. Nick stood beside Eddie whilst the rest of the attacking players took their position on the edge of the penalty box.

'Try chipping the keeper,' said Nick. 'The ball's greasy and he's not wearing any gloves.'

'Piss off brat,' replied Eddie. 'Leave the set pieces to me.'

Charming, thought Nick as he walked away. Batchwood had formed a four man wall, which Eddie's shot hit and the ball rebounded straight into the path of Nick Allen. He looked up, noticed the Batchwood keeper had strayed off his line, and hit a delightful chip towards the Batchwood goal. Seeing the danger, the Batchwood keeper frantically scurried backwards towards his goal. All the players stared in anticipation. The keeper just managed to grasp the ball from under the bar but his feet got in a tangle and he stumbled backwards into the goal.

Sandridge Grammar 1, Batchwood Boys 2

The school bell sounded and a few pupils started to wander towards the playing field to form a small crowd on the touchline.

'Show them how it's done, Nick!' cried a voice from the crowd.

One down, two to win with only ten minutes remaining, thought Nick. It's an impossible task.

Sandridge Grammar had started to believe in themselves and were pressing hard for the equalizer. Nick felt he still wasn't seeing enough of the ball, even though he was creating space and constantly calling. Andy Graham, the Sandridge Grammar outside left, a long-haired lad who styled himself on George Best, was causing a lot of problems on the left wing but his final crosses were very erratic. With five minutes remaining Graham received the ball just inside his own half by the touchline, and set off on another mazy run towards the corner flag. Nick noticed that all the other attacking players were making their way to the near post. It was a slim chance, but Nick ghosted his way to the far post. Eventually after getting in a bit of a tussle with two defenders, Graham crossed the ball. The crowd groaned as the ball sailed over the Sandridge attackers, but the groans turned to cheers as Nick stole in unmarked at the back post to head the ball firmly home. The crowd went wild and a few players patted Nick on the back as they jogged back towards the half-way line for the re-start. Batchwood kicked off but Sandridge soon regained possession and Nick, who had created some space for himself, received his first direct pass. He turned and made his way towards the Batchwood goal. A drop of the left shoulder and a change of pace took him past the last defender and gave him a clear run at goal.

'Go for it,' a voice cried from the line. This time Nick recognised the voice as belonging to his friend, Keith Nevin.

As Nick reached the penalty area, he noticed the keeper was still rooted to the line. Time seemed to go into slow motion as Nick balanced himself for the shot, but he was rapidly brought back to reality by a clumsy tackle from behind which left him face down in the mud.

'Penalty!' the crowd roared.

'Let Nick take it!' screamed Keith from the touchline.

Nick picked himself up and dusted himself down as Eddie Lee placed the ball on the penalty spot. All went quiet as Eddie Lee strode up to take the penalty. The kick was firmly struck, but too near the keeper who pushed the ball away. The crowd groaned but before the Batchwood defenders could clear the danger, Nick, whose reactions were second to none, had sprinted in to slide the ball into the net. Before Nick had time to regain his feet the final whistle had blown. The crowd, mostly Nick's class mates, rushed onto the pitch and chair-lifted him back to the changing rooms. The rest of the team was jumping up and down congratulating each other. Nick noticed that one boy stood alone on the touchline, his face very solemn - the boy, Alan Prince.

After showering and changing, Nick walked to the bicycle shed with his friend, Keith Nevin.

'That was a magnificent game,' said Keith, 'and a superb hat-trick. You certainly changed the game'.

'One man doesn't make a team,' replied Nick. 'We just needed a bit of luck. The team just needs to believe in themselves, and luckily I was in the right place at the right time'.

'Three times,' laughed Keith. 'Sometimes, Nick, you're just too modest'.

The world was at peace as Nick and Keith cycled home that evening. Late September; the sun was low in the sky and there was a chill in the air. Little did they know what effect the following events would have on their lives.

'Who's that little lad over there,' asked Keith, 'the one pushing the bike with two flat tyres? He looks as if he has been crying.'

'That's Jock; he's in the first year. I don't know his real name, but he lives round the corner from me.'

'What's up, Jock?' shouted Keith.

'Two flat tyres. That's rotten luck,' said Nick. 'Have you tried pumping them up?'

Jock sniffed.

'Where is your pump?' asked Keith.

'Don't know.'

'Great conversationalist,' said Keith sarcastically.

'Come on, Jock. Sit on this bench and tell us all about it,' said Nick trying to comfort the boy.

Nick opened his duffle bag and pulled out a bag of crisps. 'Here, Jock, have these,' said Nick, smiling at Keith and saying, 'he'll do anything for food'.

'Well,' said Jock, frantically searching for the little blue bag of salt, 'I can't be sure, but I think it might be the same boys who wanted a shilling.'

'What do you mean, Jock?' gasped Nick.

'Well, on Friday, I had to stay behind after class to clear up all the litter off the floor, just because I dropped a sweet wrapper. A spangle wrapper, I think. Anyway, when I went to get my bike from the bicycle shed, everyone else had gone. As I was unlocking the chain on my bike, three boys wearing masks approached me.'

'What kind of masks?' interrupted Nick.

'Guy Fawkes masks. Anyway, they said that first-year students were very vulnerable to bullying and that they could provide protection. They said if I paid a shilling no harm would come to me. They told me to leave it in my desk after last lesson on Monday. Well, I didn't, and thought no more of it; that was until today. I watched the end of your game and when I went to get my bike both my tyres were flat and my pump had disappeared.'

Nick looked at Keith.

'Are you thinking what I'm thinking?' asked Keith.

'I think so,' replied Nick. 'We have a protection racket in our school.'

'You don't think it's the Kray twins do you?' asked Keith.

'I don't think their operation reaches this far from the East End.'

'Thank goodness.'

'But it's not going to be easy for us to crack it.'

'Us?'

Nick and Keith left Jock eating his crisps.

'What do you think we should do?' asked Keith.

'I'm thinking,' replied Nick.

'Well, I suggest we tell the Headmaster,' interrupted Keith.

'No, we have no evidence; we need concrete proof before we report it.'

'What do you suggest?'

'We'll have to catch the villains ourselves.'

'Oh dear,' said Keith wondering what he was being conned into.

'It's my guess that other first-year boys are also being threatened. We don't have time to interview all the boys individually and it might look suspicious. We need to get a group of boys together,' pondered Nick.

For the next few minutes the boys pushed their bikes in silence.

'Eureka!' exclaimed Nick. 'I've got it.'

'Well, don't give it to me,' mumbled Keith.

Nick explained, 'as you are well aware, first-year students don't play football, they play rugby. If we organise a training session for the first years, say in the lunch hour, we could talk to the boys and we'll be away from prying eyes.'

'Excellent idea,' exclaimed Keith.

'But, we'll need to get permission from the Headmaster. I'll talk to Mr Freeman first; I'm sure he'll help swing it for us.'

'Super,' said Keith now bubbling with enthusiasm. 'We could pin a poster on the notice board inviting all the first-year students interested in football to come along'

'That's the way and I think we should ask them to bring a ball as well; the school is a bit short of footballs.'

'I agree' said Keith. 'Young players need as much ball work practice as possible.'

'Once we have gained their confidence we can probe them about the bullying. After that we'll lay our master plan.'

'What's that?' replied Keith.

'Wait and see; the game is afoot,' said Nick with a smug look on his face.

Nick was totally engrossed in *A Study in Scarlett* by Arthur Conan Doyle when his father entered the living room that evening and announced that he was off to play darts.

'Where are you playing tonight, dear?' asked Mrs Allen.

'We're away to the George and Dragon in Frogmore,' replied Mr Allen, a slim gentleman in his late thirties who has more than a passing resemblance to Tyrone Powell.

'Good luck then; is Tom picking you up?'

'Yes, he should be here in a minute. What are you up to Nick, now you have been dishonourably discharged from the Scouts?'

Nick slowly looked up from his book with a disdainful expression on his face.

'I was going to resign anyway; I think I had outgrown the Scouts.'

'You could join the Sandridge Youth Club,' said Mrs Allen 'I hear that the council has voted to make it a mixed youth club now. You might meet a nice girl.'

'I've far more important things on my mind than youth clubs and girls.'

'Such as?' enquired Mr Allen, suppressing the urge to start laughing.

'I'm thinking of becoming a consulting detective, like Sherlock Holmes.'

This time Mr Allen did start laughing.

Nick gave his dad another dirty look.

'What's funny? After all, who was it that solved the Great Train Robbery?'

'You just struck lucky: in the right place, at the right time,'

'You could say that; on the other hand, I succeeded where the whole of the British Police force failed. So, put that in your pipe and smoke it.'

'When you put it like that, so what is your next case Mr Sheer-luck Holmes?'

Before Nick could answer, a voice shouted out, 'Are you ready, Stan?'

'That's Tom,' said Mr Allen. 'I'll see you later.' With that he put on his blazer, picked up his darts, kissed Mrs Allen and left the room.

'He thinks the world of you really,' said Mrs Allen picking up a copy of *Weekend*.

Friday 27 September 1963

Permission was granted from Mr Mills, the Headmaster, for Nick and Keith to organise football training for the first years during the lunchtime. Posters were placed on the various notice boards around the school inviting all first-year students to attend football training that Friday lunchtime.

Friday came and Nick and Keith took eighteen first-year students onto the playing field. Nick started the session with some warm-up exercises and stretches. This was followed by a vigorous session on passing. A small game of 9-a-side followed; then Nick sent the lads on a warm-down run around the pitch.

'There are some good lads there,' said Keith.

'Yes,' replied Nick 'I like the look of Jock. He's got bags of skill, but look at him now; he's last in the run.'

'He eats too many crisps if you ask me.'

The boys finished their run and Nick made them sit down in a circle whilst he had a chat with them. After outlining his ideas for future training sessions, he decided to mention the protection racket.

'I know some of you lads are being bullied into giving up a shilling and we want to help you, but I need to know how many of you are involved.'

No one moved.

'Come on, lads,' encouraged Keith. 'Put your hands up; Jock, I know you are.'

They all looked at Jock and slowly, one by one, the hands went up. In all, twelve lads admitted being bullied. Further questions revealed a similar pattern. All the lads left a shilling in their desks after the last class on Mondays.

'Okay, this is what we intend to do,' said Nick. 'On Monday, leave the money in your desks as requested; Keith and I will hide in that empty old wooden cupboard at the back of upper1A's classroom. When the villain comes to collect, we'll nab him. Simple.'

Keith looked at Nick, shaking his head.

Nick smiled and said, 'Trust me.'

Saturday 28 September 1963

Nick had promised to take his brother, Richard, to the Saturday morning pictures. Normally; Nick enjoyed these excursions, but today he had other things on his mind. He questioned his own decision to become a consulting detective, thinking that perhaps he was just lucky with the Great Train Robbery. He thought about all the things that could go wrong and that he could make a complete fool of himself. But then again, if you don't try these things you will only regret them in the end. Careful planning, that's the key, careful planning.

They met Don outside the Peahen Hotel and together they walked down London Road towards the Odeon Cinema.

'Whose turn is it to pay?' asked Don.

'I believe it's your turn as you know full well,' replied Nick.

After visiting Mrs Joseph's sweet shop, in which Nick bought four ounces of liquorice allsorts, Don four ounces of sweet peanuts, and Richard opted for blackjacks, fruit salads and some coconut tobacco, the boys separated. Don joined the small queue whilst Nick and Richard made their way down the steps to the rear of the cinema. After paying the sixpence entrance fee, Don made his way to the front of the stalls and made himself comfortable in the end seat three rows from the front. Inside the cinema, boys and girls aged between five and thirteen were running up and down the aisles. Don smiled to himself, because nobody would notice him as he left his seat and quietly made his way through the exit doors to the toilet which was to left of the screen. Next to the toilet, a single bar locked the exit door. Trying not to make a sound, he forced the bar up. As the crack in the door became wider and the sunlight burst in, he heard Nick say 'where have you been, we've been waiting ages?'

Nick and Richard pushed their way through and Don quietly shut the door behind them.

'Okay,' said Nick, 'where are we sitting?'

'Usual place, third row back,' replied Don.

'You go first, bruv, and try not to be noticed.'

Richard strolled into the auditorium and made his way to the seat. He noticed the usherettes trying to calm the other children down and get them seated. A minute later Nick appeared and sat next to Richard. Both boys looked anxiously at the exit door waiting for Don, but just as he appeared, the manager came walking down the aisle and grabbed Don before he reached his friends.

'Have you got a ticket?' he asked.

'Of course I have,' replied Don trying not to appear frightened.

'Well, show me then.'

Don fumbled in his pockets until he found his ticket stub.

'There you are,' said Don, sighing a breath of relief.

'Okay then, sit down. But I can't be too complacent; I know kids are sneaking in without paying.'

'That's terrible, who would do such a thing?' replied Don as he took his seat next to Nick.

All three boys watched as the manager disappeared through the exit door to check for any non-paying guests.

As the lights went down and the screaming subsided Nick noticed the smell of stale cigarettes and remembered how the red sort of velveteen on the seats used to make his legs itch before he wore long trousers. The show started with some community singing which was followed by the audience singing happy birthday to any unfortunate kid whose birthday it happened to be that week. This was followed by the cartoons, and then some serial designed to make you come back next week. The main feature this week was Zorro, one of Nick's favourites. Zorro, which is Spanish for fox, was the secret identity of Don Diego de la Vega, a nobleman and master swordsman living in nineteenth century California. He defended the people against tyrannical governors and other villains.

When the show had finished, the boys made their way home walking back up London Road towards the town centre.

'You look a bit thoughtful today, Nick,' said Don.

'Got a few things on my mind,' replied Nick.

'Anything I can help you with?'

'Not at this stage, but I may need your help in the future.'

Don looked at Richard with a what's up with him look.

'He's got a new hobby; he's fancies himself as a consulting detective. He's working on his new case,' said Richard.

'Sounds exciting. Are you sure you don't need my help?' enthused Don.

'It's a school thing, but if I crack it I'm sure I'll get lots more cases and your help will be invaluable.'

Monday 30 September 1963

Monday came and as soon as the classes had ended, Nick and Keith made their way to upper1A's classroom and hid in the old cupboard at the back of the classroom and waited. After about twenty minutes the classroom door opened.

'Someone's coming,' whispered Keith.

'Let's just wait a while, and then we'll catch them red-handed,' replied Nick.

Nick opened the cupboard door just a little to see what was going on. He could see two boys but couldn't recognise them as they both wore masks.

'What's happening?' whispered Keith.

'Quiet,' replied Nick. 'One's coming this way.'

Nick pulled the door shut as the masked intruder approached the cupboard. Nick and Keith held their breath. There was a loud click.

'What was that?' whispered Keith.

'I think he's locked us in,' answered Nick.

'What?' screamed Keith, as he banged on the door. 'Let us out.'

'That'll stop you interfering,' said a voice outside the cupboard.

All of a sudden the cupboard tumbled forward.

'Ahhhhh!' cried the boys as the cupboard crashed to the floor.

The boys thrashed about trying in vain to escape from the fallen cupboard.

'What's going on?' said a loud voice. 'Give me a hand to get this cupboard up.'

Nick and Keith lay still as they felt the cupboard being returned to its proper upright position.

'The cupboard's locked,' said the voice, which they now recognised as belonging to Mr Munt, the school caretaker. 'Stay here, I'll go and get my tool-bag.'

The boys heard him walk off and return a minute later. They heard noises as Mr Munt prised the cupboard doors open with the use of a large screwdriver. The two boys, totally distressed, emerged from the cupboard. Blood was trickling from Nick's nose and Keith was sporting a large bump on his forehead.

'Bloody kids, always fooling around,' said Mr Munt, a slightly built man in his late fifties with fair hair recently cut in a traditional short back and sides. He was escorted by two overweight female cleaners both wearing headscarves.

'But we were locked in' said Keith sheepishly.

'Less of your lip,' shouted Mr Munt. 'I'm reporting you to the Headmaster, now what are your names?'

'You know who we are,' sighed Nick.

'Of course,' said Mr Munt, 'you'd better get yourselves cleaned up and get off home and don't let me catch you fooling around here again.'

'No, Sir,' said Keith.

'Thank you, Sir,' said Nick.

Nick and Keith scrambled quickly out of the classroom and into the toilet.

'Well, that was a brilliant idea,' said Keith sarcastically as he examined the bump on his head in the mirror.

'Mmmm,' replied Nick.

'I hope your next plan is better.'

'We've got a mole.'

'Don't change the subject.'

'Not that sort of mole, stupid. They knew we were in the cupboard, one of the first years must have told them.'

'Gosh!' gasped Keith. 'That means we're on our own.'

'It looks like it.'

'So what are we going to do now?'

'If we lie low for a while, they'll think we have given up.'

'You haven't got another plan have you?'

'Afraid not.'

Monday 7 October 1963

A week had passed since the cupboard incident; Nick and Keith had just finished their free school milk and were walking past the school gymnasium.

'Look,' said Keith 'Mr Freeman's putting something up on the notice board.'

'It could be the team for the forthcoming cup match,' replied Nick rushing to have a look. 'Hey, Keith, you're reserve.'

'Gosh, I didn't expect that. Are you playing?'

'Yes, I'm inside right. Alan Prince is playing centre forward.'

'Who are we playing?'

'St Stephens Catholic Grammar School.'

'Doesn't your friend Don Patrick go to that school?'

'That's right but I don't suppose he will be playing, he's only in the second year.'

'But he's a good player?'

'He's an excellent all-round footballer. But you never know, they may bring him along as reserve. He's big for his age.'

Thursday 10 October 1963

On the day of the match Nick and Keith were walking around the playground during their afternoon break. Kick-off was at 3.30 pm; it was now 2.30 pm.

'I'm looking forward to this game, Keith. Aren't you?'

'Certainly; if we win this one we'll be in the quarter-finals,' replied Keith. 'Do you think you'll be alright playing alongside Alan Prince?'

'I hope so. I know he doesn't like me and he's not keen on third years playing in the school team; but he's not a bad player and he wants to win as much as anyone.'

Their conversation was interrupted by someone shouting out Nick's name.

'Nick' said Walter Roberts, a cheeky first-year student who attended Nick's lunchtime training sessions. 'Mr Bilk, the Rural Science teacher, wants to see you urgently in the potting shed.'

'Thank you, Walter. I'll be right there.'

'What's that about?' asked Keith.

'No idea. I definitely cleared up my station after re-potting those plants this morning. What were those plants?'

Keith shrugged his shoulders.

'I'll pop along and see him,' said Nick 'and I'll meet you in the changing room.'

'Okay, but don't be long,' replied Keith. 'And give me your kit, I'll take it with me.'

Nick walked behind the Science block through the small vegetable patch that led to the main potting shed. Looking round he thought I can't see anyone. He opened the potting shed and looked in.

'Hello, Mr Bilk. Are you there?'

Getting no reply he stepped into the potting shed. As he stood there he heard a small creak that made him turn round. But before he could complete the move a sack was thrust over his head.

'Hey, who's put the lights out?' screamed Nick.

But before he could react he was forced to the floor; his hands and feet were bound together and a gag was tied around his mouth. After receiving a couple of kicks in the ribs he was dragged and dumped unceremoniously in a corner. He heard the attackers walk away and lock the door.

Someone doesn't like me thought Nick as he struggled to make himself comfortable. After the initial shock Nick pulled himself together and started to think about what to do, and then he remembered that he always carried a penknife in his pocket. It took a while but he finally managed to extract it from his pocket. Opening the blade was not a problem but it took him at least twenty minutes to cut through the ropes around his wrist. After freeing himself from the rest of the bonds, Nick looked at his watch: 3.15 pm; only fifteen minutes to kick-off. The door was still locked but he managed to climb through a window and ran straight to the changing rooms.

As Nick rushed into the changing room, everybody turned and looked at him.

'Nick,' shouted Mr Freeman, 'you're late! Where have you been?'

'Sorry, Sir,' he replied. 'Got a bit tied up.'

Nick saw Keith and went to change next to him.

'Where have you been?' asked Keith.

'I'll tell you later,' replied Nick, 'but someone didn't want me to play.'

It was the second Round of the St Albans and District Benevolent Cup and Sandridge Grammar and been drawn at home to St Stephens Catholic Grammar School. The first half was a dour affair and ended 0 – 0. The attacking striking force of Alan Prince and Nick Allen was very ineffective. Nick had not received a single pass from Alan Prince and on many occasions both players had collided going for the same ball. Mr Freeman was well aware that his tactics were going drastically wrong.

'If there isn't a marked improvement this half,' said Mr Freeman, looking at Nick and Alan, as they sat on the edge of the pitch sucking their orange quarters, 'then one of or both of you will be dropped for the next game; if there is another game. You two must work together, like Bobby Smith and Jimmy Greaves.'

'It's not my fault,' interrupted Prince. 'I can't play with that upstart.'

'More like you don't want to' interrupted Keith.

'Put a sock in it Nevin or I'll re-arrange you features,' snarled Prince.

'Cut that out now,' screamed Mr Freeman, 'or I'll put you on detention.'

'Well,' said Prince 'why do we have to have third years playing?'

'Why?' asked Mr Freeman trying to control his temper. 'Because this is a school team and I pick who I consider to be the best players. What you seem to forget is that it has taken me three years to persuade the Headmaster to allow us to have a football team. You know this is traditionally a rugby-only school and he only gave us permission on the proviso we win this cup, otherwise its back to rugby. If we win this cup we can enter the league competitions and have teams at every year. So you can see how important it is that we win. Now go out there and forget your personal vendettas and play football.'

The game re-started and Sandridge Grammar settled into some sort of pattern. Alan Prince took the role of target man with Nick feeding off him. It soon became clear to Nick that Alan Prince either couldn't pass a ball or was trying to make him look bad as every pass was either over or under hit. With fifteen minutes left, Alan Prince received the ball on the half-way line and made a strong run towards the opposition's goal. The St Stephen's defenders were closing in on him, but Nick had an idea. He ran right across Prince's path taking the ball with him. This sudden change of direction wrong footed the defenders and left him with a clear run at goal. The keeper tried to close him down but Nick coolly slotted the ball home.

Sandridge Grammar 1, St Stephens Catholic Grammar 0.

Jogging back for the re-start Nick met Prince. 'Well done, Alan' said Nick. 'The old cross-over routine always works.'

Nick's goal had knocked the stuffing out of St. Stephens Catholic Grammar School. Straight from the re-start, Sandridge regained the ball and went in search for a second goal. A fine shot from Nick was deflected for a corner. Andy Graham took the corner kick and sent a peach of an out-swinger to the far post. Both Nick and Alan went for the ball but just as Nick was about to head it, he felt a push in his back and stumbled when he landed. Before he could regain his feet a knee came crashing into his face. Tears filled his eyes and blood spurted from his nose. Mr Freeman rushed on the field to attend Nick. 'Are you alright, lad?' he asked.

'I fink my dose is bwoken,' replied Nick.

'Right, my lad, let's get you to hospital.'

Nick walked off the pitch holding his head back, a sponge soaked in blood covering his nose.

The St Stephen's sports master came over to see how Nick was. 'You can put your reserve on if you want,' he said. 'I think it's only fair.'

'That's very sporting of you,' replied Mr Freeman. 'Thank you; Keith, get ready.'

Keith looked on anxiously as he removed his tracksuit top. 'Will he be alright, Sir?'

'I'm sure he'll be as good as new; now, on you go and don't let this game slip.'

Friday 11 October 1963

It was the following evening; Nick was sitting watching *Ready Steady Go!* on the television, and feeling slightly sorry for himself. His nose had been re-set and he had spent the night in hospital. Brian Poole and the Tremeloes were singing their Number One song *Do You Love Me* when the doorbell rang. Mrs Allen, answered it. 'Hello, Keith.'

'Hello, Mrs Allen', replied Keith. 'How's Nick, may I see him?'

'Of course you can; come in. Nick,' said Mrs Allen. 'Keith's come to see you. Go on through.'

Keith walked into the living room. 'Hello Nick, how are you feeling?'

'A bit groggy,' replied Nick. 'How did the match finish?'

'We won 1-0. Oh, I've bought you a present,' said Keith, handing Nick a bag which he looked inside and found a 7 inch single record. 'It's a new female singer called Cilla Black. It's her first release; it's called *Love of the Loved*; your sort of thing, soppy music.'

'Thanks very much. I'll play it later.'

Keith took a long look at Nick's nose and said, 'nasty accident.'

'It was no accident; it was deliberate.'

'Gosh!' exclaimed Keith, 'Who did it?'

'I'm almost certain it was Alan Prince.'

'Oh dear,' said Keith as he sat down next to Nick.

'Don't worry, Keith; he won't get away with it.'

Nick managed a smile and there was a twinkle in his bright blue eyes, even though they were surrounded by yellow and purple bruising.

'What do you intend to do?' enquired Keith, remembering how Nick's plans have a tendency to go wrong.

'Listen carefully,' said Nick. 'After leaving the pitch yesterday, Mr Freeman and I went into the changing rooms. He left me for a while to make a phone call. I was so annoyed at being hurt that I kicked Alan Prince's sports bag, it went flying and all the contents fell out. I quickly calmed down and started to put the stuff back in the bag, and guess what I found?'

'Go on' said Keith inquisitively.

'Well it was a list of first year students with dates and amounts of money.'

'We've got him,' said Keith. 'Did you tell Mr Freeman?'

'Of course not,' replied Nick. 'I want to catch him red-handed.'

'Do you have a plan?'

'Not yet. I want to get this one right. It has to be thoroughly thought out. We don't want to make the same mistake as last time.'

Saturday 12 October 1963

Nick was feeling a lot better Saturday morning and decided to go out for the day. Spurs were not playing today as England were playing away to

Wales in the Home International Championship, so he asked his mum if he could go to London for the day.

'As long as you're back before it gets dark. Do you want me to make you a packed lunch?' she replied as she finished washing up the breakfast plates.

'Thanks, Mum. That will be great,' said Nick and went over and gave her a big hug. 'I love you, Mum, you're the best.'

'Oh, don't be silly now.' she replied blushing. 'Will cheese be okay in your sandwiches?'

'Great, Mum.'

Nick took the 330 bus to the train station, bought his ticket and made his way to St Pancras. From there he took a tube on the Circle line for his intended destination, Blackfriars. He always enjoyed the walk along the Thames; he found it peaceful and it allowed him to think. By the time he reached the Embankment he was feeling a little peckish; he decided to find a bench and eat one of the cheese sandwiches his Mum had made for him. Most of the benches were taken up by families also enjoying their packed lunches. Then he spotted a bench that was only occupied by a young woman. He approached it and asked, 'May I sit here?'

The woman, about twenty, pretty with long brown hair, turned her head. She smiled and said, 'It's a free country.'

Nick sat down and gazed at the Thames. After about two minutes the woman asked, 'What happened to your nose?'

'I broke it in a football match.'

'It looks painful.'

'It hurt at the time, but just aches now.'

'How did it happen?'

'I'm not sure, but I think it was done on purpose.'

'Why would anyone want to hurt you?'

'It's a long story, but there's a protection racket at my school. I'm trying to find out who's running it and someone's trying to stop me.'

'Right little Inspector Lockhart[2], aren't we?'

'I like him,' said Nick enthusiastically, 'and there will be no hiding place for those yobs when I get back to school.'

The woman smiled and took off her sun glasses.

Nick looked at her and smiled back, and said, 'Hope you don't think I'm being rude, but your eyes are red, have you been crying?'

'You're very observant,' she replied, taking a long look at him. 'What's your name, kid?'

'My name is Nick Allen and I'm from Hertfordshire.'

'Pleased to meet you, Nick Allen from Hertfordshire; I'm Christine from London.'

They shook hands.

'So,' said Nick, 'what's troubling you?'

'You're not backward in coming forward are you, Nick Allen?'

'You can call me Nick,' he replied. 'My Mum, she's from the East End you know, believes in straight talking. 'Say what you mean; don't beat about the bush'.

'Well Nick, she's right, so I'll tell; like you said, it's a long story, but I'm not having a very good time at the moment. A friend of mine called Stephen[3] killed himself recently and I might have to go away soon.'

'And I take it you don't want to go away?'

'You're right there. Anyway, it might only be for a few months.'

They sat there for a moment, both gazing at the Thames, when Nick heard the familiar sound of an ice cream van. 'Oh look,' he said. 'A Tonibell van; can I buy you an ice cream?'

'You certainly know how to treat a lady; yes, I'd love one.'

'Great, what would you like?'

'Surprise me.'

Nick ran over to the van and purchased two ninety-nines at a cost of one shilling and six pence. He returned to Christine and gave her the ice-cream.

'Thank you, kind Sir' she said.

'My pleasure,' replied Nick, giving her his biggest smile.

They sat there eating their ice-creams, taking in the last of the autumn sunshine.

'Do you have a girlfriend?' asked Christine.

'Not yet,' replied Nick. 'I'm not really into girls; I don't think I'm ready for a girlfriend. Can't really see the point of one; I mean, what can you do with them? Apart from a bit of kissing; you can't really talk to them. They just giggle all the time. I mean, it would be nice to get a female point of view on the proposed changes to the LBW rule or the like. But when I do get a girlfriend, I hope she looks like you. You know you are very pretty; you should be a model and you're easy to talk to.'

'Well, Mr Smoothie, when you are eighteen come and look me up and we'll go for a drink.'

'How will I find you?'

'I'm sure you will have no problem.'

She opened her handbag and took out a photo.

'You're right; I have done a bit of modelling.'

She wrote on the back of the photo and gave it to him.

'See you in a few years,' she leaned over and kissed him on the cheek.

Nick looked down at what she had written.

To my favourite boy Nick. All my love, Christine [4] xx.

When he looked up she had gone. He turned the photo over and thought - that's different. He put the photo carefully in his duffel bag and pulled out his sandwiches. As he sat there eating his cheese sandwich with Daddies sauce, he thought if that's all there is to getting a girlfriend, I can't see what all the fuss is about.

When he had finished his sandwich he took a deep breath, smiled and said to himself, 'Alan Prince, I've got you.'

Monday 14 October 1963

Nick returned to school on Monday wearing dark glasses to hide his black eyes. Keith was waiting at the school gates when he arrived.

'How are you feeling today?' enquired Keith

'Not too bad,' replied Nick.

'That's good; so have you thought of a plan yet?'

'As it happens I have. This is what I want you to do. I borrowed my aunties typewriter and spent yesterday typing up some affidavits for the first years to sign, stating that they have been bullied into paying protection money. All you have to do is quietly see each of the kids individually and get them to sign them; simple, eh?'

'What happens then?' asked Keith

'Well, I need them signed before Friday's lunchtime training session; then I'll reveal phase two.'

Friday 18 October 1963

By Friday, Keith had obtained signatures from of all the boys they knew to be paying protection money. During the training session Nick sent Walter Roberts back to the changing rooms to collect the training bibs. When Walter was out of sight he called the boys in and sat them down in the far corner of the field.

'Right lads,' said Nick. 'I think you should know what is happening. As you know, you have all signed an affidavit. I have put them along with some other evidence into an envelope and given it to the Headmaster, so now all your problems are over.'

'But the Headmaster's been away all week,' said Jock as he opened another packet of crisps.

'Ah yes,' said Nick. 'I knew that. That's why I gave the packet to his secretary who will give it to him first thing Monday morning.'

At that moment Walter Roberts came back carrying the training bibs.

'Right lads,' sighed Nick. 'Get yourselves sorted onto two teams and let's get a game going.'

The boys obeyed without question and soon the red team was attacking the yellow team. Keith approached Nick with a confused look on his face. 'I thought you wanted to catch Prince red-handed.'

'That's right,' smiled Nick.

'Come on Nick, you haven't told me everything.

'Alright,' laughed Nick. 'Listen carefully; if things go according to plan, Alan Prince will try to retrieve the evidence this weekend. I've phoned the police and told them to expect a break-in at the school this weekend. With any luck they will catch him red-handed.'

'But how will Prince know the secretary has the evidence?'

'The mole will tell him.'

'But I thought Walter Roberts was the mole'

'No,' laughed Nick. 'He's a red herring; I want the real mole to think we suspect someone else. Trust me.'

Monday 21 October 1963

Nick felt excited as he made his way to school the following Monday morning. As usual, Keith was there waiting for him.

'Do you think your plan has worked Nick?' asked Keith.

'I do hope so; I haven't slept a wink all weekend thinking about it,' replied Nick.

'Well, we'll soon find out.'

After parking their bikes they walked through the school grounds in complete silence, both deep in thought. Nick, ever the optimist, was thinking that he'll be hailed a hero. Keith, the pessimist, was thinking about all the trouble they could get in. They didn't have to wait long; their tranquillity was broken by Graham Brett, editor of the school magazine. Graham was in the fifth form and one of the school's brightest students. Everyone expected him to go to Cambridge.

'Nick, have you heard?' gasped Graham holding a notebook in one hand and a pencil in the other.

'Heard what?' replied Nick expectantly.

'There was an attempted break-in at the school. The police were here and everything,' said Graham bursting with enthusiasm. 'Would you like to comment?'

'Did they catch them?' asked Keith.

'I think so,' replied Graham. 'Rumour has it they had a tip-off and caught the villains red-handed.'

'Anyone we know?' asked Nick casually.

'No names at present, but I'm working on it' said Graham, 'I'll keep you informed.'

Nick smiled at Keith as Graham rushed towards a group of boys talking to the Science master.

'He'll make a good journalist one day,' stated Nick.

'I never thought it would work,' said Keith. 'You're a genius.'

He waited for a reply but one never came. He turned to look at Nick, who had turned as white as a ghost. 'Nick, talk to me,' said Keith.

'Look,' replied Nick, struggling to get his words out, 'it's Prince and he's coming this way.'

'Hello Nick,' said Prince. 'How's the nose? It's looking better. Are you alright? You looked surprised to see me.'

'Don't know what you mean; it's always a pleasure to see you, Alan.'

'Of course it is. You heard about the break-in then, a couple of local villains trying to steal the petty cash. Apparently, they have done a few other schools but the strange thing is, the police had a tip off about this one. Can't imagine who would have done that.'

'And how come you know all this then?' asked Keith.

'The school secretary told me. She's my aunt. Didn't you know?'

Alan Prince walked back towards the school leaving Nick and Keith standing there, stunned.

Keith was the first to move putting an arm around Nick's shoulder and saying, 'Don't worry, Nick; it will soon be over. Once the Headmaster sees the envelope you left him with the affidavits and the other evidence your troubles will be over.'

'Afraid not; I didn't leave any envelope with the Headmaster. It was all a bluff; I have no evidence to connect Prince with the crime.'

'Oh dear,' said Keith as they walked to their classroom.

After school on Mondays, Nick and Keith normally went for a 5 mile run. But this Monday, Keith told Nick that he was going straight home as he was behind with his homework. Nick was not too disappointed as he was in no mood for company and was glad to run alone. So Nick set off on his own, running at a faster pace than normal, making his limbs hurt to take away the pain from the disappointment of failure. How could he have been so stupid? What made him think that his silly plan would work? Why didn't he just report what he knew; was he getting too big for his own boots. He returned back to the school in record time, covered in mud. Mr Munt the caretaker always left the dressing rooms open on a Monday for the badminton club, so Nick could always take a shower. After removing his muddy clothes he stepped into the communal showers. Nick loved showers, at home, like most houses, they only had a bath. He found them so refreshing that he usually stayed there for about fifteen minutes, allowing the hot water to caress his body. On this occasion he felt he could stay there forever but his Mum would have his tea ready and he didn't want to be late. Stepping out of the shower, he reached for his towel. I'm sure I put it there, he thought.

'Lost something?' a voice asked.

He couldn't see anything because of all the steam, but as he stepped out of the shower he could make out four boys standing there. Each was wearing a Guy Fawkes mask and wielding a rounders bat.

'You've caused us enough trouble,' said the boy in the front. 'It's about time we taught you a lesson.'

'Come on lads,' pleaded Nick as he stepped back into the shower. 'Let's talk about this.'

'Nothing to talk about.'

'A beating won't stop me talking. I know all about your little racket and I know who your leader is.'

'You know very little and even if you did, it wouldn't stop us giving you the beating you deserve.'

Nick was cornered in the shower and the boys were getting closer.

'Okay, but before you start, just one question,' asked Nick.

'Make it quick.'

'Who's been telling you my movements?'

The four boys started laughing.

'Don't you know?' said the leader.

'No,' replied Nick with a puzzled look on his face.

'Well, we're not going to tell you,' said the second boy, taking a swing at Nick and just missing him.

'That's enough,' said a loud voice behind them.

All the boys turned around; standing there was the Headmaster, Mr Mills - a tall, distinguished looking man with a good crop of grey hair and a neatly trimmed moustache; the sports master Mr Freeman; and the caretaker Mr Munt.

Mr Mills was the first to speak: 'I think I've heard all I need to hear. Now take off those silly masks and let's see who we've got.'

The first boy to remove his mask was Eddie Lee; Nick didn't recognise the next two boys, as they were not Sandridge Grammar students. As expected the last boy to remove his mask was Alan Prince.

'Right, you four follow me to my office, and Prince take a good look at these changing rooms because it's the last time you'll ever see them,' said Mr Mills as he led the four culprits away.

'Put some clothes on, Allen,' said Mr Freeman to Nick, who was standing there in all his glory.

'How did you know they were coming to get me?' enquired Nick as he frantically rubbed himself dry with a towel.

'Your friend, Keith, told me everything,' replied Mr Freeman.

'But how did he know they were coming?'

'I think you'd better ask him,' said Mr Freeman as he turned and walked out of the changing room.

As he left, Nick noticed Keith standing outside looking very sheepish. Keith stepped into the changing room.

'So you are the mole,' said Nick, trying to control his anger.

'Sorry,' replied Keith.

'And I thought you were my friend.'

'But you don't understand,' interrupted Keith. 'I had to tell them.'

'Oh yeh,' said Nick, who had finish dressing and was putting the last of his muddy clothes into his duffel bag.

'Listen, Nick, this protection racket is being run in other schools as well, even in the Girls Grammar. They threatened to hurt my sister Anna. What could I do?'

'Whatever,' said Nick, as he walked out of the changing room, leaving Keith standing there all alone.

PART 2

A CHRISTMAS STORY

Tuesday 24 December 1963

Nick Allen and Don Patrick stood outside the Town Hall in St Peter's Street, St Albans, singing carols with the Salvation Army Band. It was Christmas Eve; Nick and Don had completed their last minute shopping. The shops were closing and the market stall holders were crying out, trying to sell the last remnants of their stock. As the large crowd finished the last verse of Good King Wenceslas, Nick said 'This is what it is all about. I love Christmas Eve. It is definitely my favourite day of Christmas.'

'Even more than Christmas day;' replied Don, 'when you open all your presents?'

'Absolutely; to me it's not about receiving presents. Don't get me wrong. I love receiving presents but there is a real atmosphere on Christmas Eve which is like no other. Can't you feel it? Look around. Everyone is smiling; that sense of anticipation; good will towards men, and all that.'

'I'm not sure it's natural for a 14-year old to be thinking this way,' said Don scratching his head.

'Perhaps you're right. I worry about myself sometimes with the strange thoughts I have. So what are you getting for Christmas?'

'I'll tell you after this carol; it's my favourite.'

The band started playing Silent Night, which coincidently was one of Nick's favourites, so both boys sang their hearts out. Nick looked around at the crowd, looked at the Christmas lights down the St Peter's Street and thought it doesn't get better than this. When they had finished, the band leader announced that they were taking a small break and invited the assembled crowd to join them for a mince pie and a glass of mulled wine. The boys didn't need asking twice, and with the speed of a pair of cheetahs they managed to be first in the queue.

An elderly lady dressed in her Salvation Army uniform looked over her National Health glasses, smiled, and wished Nick and Don a merry Christmas and presented them with a warm mince pie. Next, a tall thin gentleman, also wearing a Salvation Army uniform, looked down at Nick and Don and handed them a half-filled plastic cup with mulled wine. Nick looked up at the man, put on his doleful face and said in his best Oliver Twist voice: 'It's very cold sir, just a little more.'

The man, trying to suppress a large grin, dipped his ladle into the hot wine and filled both cups to the brim.

'Thank you, kind sir,' said Nick and Don in unison, as they walked away.

'So,' asked Nick, 'what are you getting for Christmas?'

'Not sure. I made a list some time ago but I can't remember what I put on it. I definitely need some new football boots and a board game, perhaps Monopoly or Cluedo – and, of course, my annuals.'

'Of course, which ones have you asked for? Hopefully I'll get *Roy of the Rovers* and the *Victor*.'

'*Roy of the Rovers* is a must, but I also asked for the *Beano* or the *Dandy*. I still like them.'

'That's good; then I can borrow them when you've read them.'

'What are you up to tonight?' asked Don, looking at his watch, aware that it was getting late and that he needed to be home by five o' clock.

'Well, Mum and Dad like to have a drink down at the Waverley Club, so I'll have to baby sit my brother Richard for an hour or two. Then I'll be in bed by ten. What about you?'

'As you can guess, being Catholic, we'll have to go to church. I think the Family Mass starts at seven o' clock.'

'That's nice,' replied Nick licking his fingers. 'Fancy another?'

'That's being greedy,' replied Don. 'Won't they recognise us?'

'Don't be silly. Look, let's change hats. That'll fool them.'

So Nick and Don helped themselves to another mince pie and a cup of mulled wine. Now feeling suitably refreshed with a warm glow inside, Don said 'I'll have to go now and catch the bus. Are you coming?'

'No,' replied Nick. 'I think I'll hang around and sing a few more carols,

I can't get enough of this.'

'Okay' said Don. 'Well, have a great Christmas and I'll see you on Friday. Don't forget, you're coming round for tea.'

'How could I forget; merry Christmas, Don.'

Nick watch Don make his way up St Peter's Street towards the bus stop, before throwing himself in singing Oh Little Town of Bethlehem. When the singing was finished Nick, ventured down Market Place. He stopped and looked in Jeffersons shop window, thinking that he might buy some new fashionable clothes with any Christmas money he might receive. His plan was to walk down French Row, turn right, and then make his way down George Street into Fishpool Street. If you were looking for a part of St Albans that had that Dickensian feel, this was the route to take. He walked past the Tudor Tavern, looking through the leaded windows, seeing all the customers enjoying their steak meals. Closing his eyes, he could imagine the smell and taste of cream sherry that his Mum let him try the last time they had eaten there. As he passed the antique shops that lined George Street, he tried to imagine what it would have been like a hundred years ago. He continued down Romeland Hill, looking left and staring in awe at the magnificent cathedral. A group of carol singers were gathering on the corner, singers of all ages, complete with lanterns, all wrapped in colourful scarves and hats. As Nick wandered down Fishpool Street, he peered in all the windows, admiring the Christmas trees and the fairy lights that adorned the windows. He stopped outside the Lower Red Lion public house, formally a 17th century coaching inn. At 5.30 pm the doors had just opened and the first drinkers were sipping their frothy pints. The bar was tastefully decorated and a big log fire was blazing in the hearth. He looked forward to the day he was old enough to drink in a pub and made a mental note to definitively visit that pub on Christmas Eve 1967.

As Nick walked down Fishpool Street he remembered what his father had once told him. Fishpool Street is one of the oldest roads in St Albans, first documented around 1250 and was originally part of the medieval route from London to Chester. Many of the buildings date back to the 16th and 17th century and many were re-faced in the 18th century in order to keep up with the changing styles of the time. There are also some fine examples of Victorian Terraces and a high proportion of the building are statutory listed. His father also told him that around 1880 there were ten public houses in Fishpool Street; now there are only three.

It was about six o'clock when he stood looking down St Michael's Street. He thought this scene should be on a Christmas card. A row of Victorian terraced houses on the left, a Victorian School on the right, followed by two even older public houses. As he admired the view, his solitude was broken by a voice behind him.

'Hello, Nick Allen.'

Nick turned around to see a young girl standing there. He recognised her as Jenny Reynolds, a pleasant girl who lived on his estate. She was the same age as Nick and they had been in the same class during their time in infant and junior school. Nick had always had a soft spot for Jenny; unfortunately, she wasn't a very popular girl. She was bullied a lot, not only by boys, but girls as well. Nick thought this was because she was slightly different from the rest of the children. Jenny came from a large family. She had four brothers and three sisters and they all squeezed into a three bedroom house. Some people called them gypsies and Nick had to admit she did have a Romany look to her. Two of her older brothers had been in trouble with the police and rumour had it that the eldest sister was a prostitute. But Jenny was a quiet girl, kept herself to herself and as she stood there in front of him he thought how sad she looked. She had a pretty face beneath a mass of long curly black hair that needed a good comb through.

'Will you walk with me?' she asked.

Although his Mum would be expecting him home for his tea, he felt he could not refuse her invitation.

'This way,' she said, and Nick followed her through the entrance to Verulamium Park. Verulamium Park is set in 100 acres of parkland which was purchased from the Earl of Verulam in 1929. They walked in silence till they reached the bridge that separated the two man-made lakes. The smaller of the two lakes was a boating lake and Nick had spent many a Sunday afternoon watching the radio controlled boats whizzing around the water.

'This is my favourite spot,' said Jenny as she gazed over the largest lake.

'It's certainly a fine spot,' replied Nick nervously as he started to wonder what he had let himself in for.

She turned and looked at him 'You've been good to me over the years.'

'Have I?' he replied.

'You've never bullied me like the other kids. Do you remember that time in Miss Hall's class when they were calling me names and you took me outside and comforted me? And the time I was walking home and that gang of boys were throwing stones at me.'

'Oh yes, I remember that time,' commented Nick. 'I've still got the scar on the back of my head. Three stitches I had to have.'

Jenny giggled, 'and do you remember that time we went for a walk round the golf course.'

Nick did remember and he could feel himself blushing. He was eight years old and had decided to go golf-balling around Batchwood golf course. Lots of boys his age would walk around the edge of each hole looking in the rough for lost golf balls, then try to sell them to any passing player. He was just about to climb over the fence when Jenny walked by. She enquired as to where he was going and asked if she could join him. It was a hot afternoon and after about 20 minutes they had reached the edge of the 12th green. They laid down on the edge of the bunker that protected the green. It was there that Nick had his first kiss.

'You're not blushing are you Nick Allen?' Jenny asked.

'Of course not,' retorted Nick. 'I'm just a bit warm.'

'You are funny, Nick Allen. It's bloody freezing.'

She was right; it was a clear crisp evening, the moon was in its first quarter and the frost was creeping in.

'That was my first kiss as well,' she said. 'And you never forget your first kiss. Are you still not talking to Keith Nevin?'

Christ, thought Nick, where did that come from?

'That's right. What of it?' he asked.

He's a good friend to you; I think you should forgive him. It doesn't do to hold grudges.'

'Huh,' said Nick, 'if I want to hold a grudge, I'll hold a grudge. In fact, one day I will be a champion grudge holder. Is that why we are here - did he send you?'

'Don't be silly and stop being aggressive; it doesn't suit you. Of course he didn't send me. I haven't seen him for ages. I just think that it's the season of good will that you should forgive him.'

'Do you know what he did to me? He betrayed me. Friends don't do that.'

'But he was protecting his sister; remember blood is thicker than water.'

'And you can choose your friends but not your family.'

'What's that got to do with anything?

'I don't know; it was the first thing that came into my head.'

They both burst out laughing.

'But promise me you will think about forgiving him.'

'Okay I'll think about it, just for you, but I'm not promising anything.' She smiled.

He looked at her as she gazed over the lake. There was something different about her that could not put his finger on. She looked a little pale, but he put that down to the falling temperature; but she looked contented. She was pretty in a strange sort of way. If I had lots of money I would have taken her into town and treat her to some nice clothes and take her to a decent hairdresser, he thought.

She sensed he was staring at her. 'What are you thinking?' she asked.

'I was just thinking how much I would like to kiss you,' he replied, thinking why did I say that?

'That's nice.' She smiled, and then replied, 'not a good idea at the moment.'

'Sorry,' he said, feeling embarrassed.

'No,' she turned to him. 'I'm flattered and I would love to kiss you, but it's just not the right time.'

He didn't push it and just asked, 'What are you doing for Christmas?'

'Not sure yet,' she replied.

Nick looked at his watch; it was getting late. 'I think I'd better be going. Mum will wonder where I am.'

'Okay,' she said 'What are your plans for the future?'

'What do you mean?'

'Oh it doesn't matter. You had better go; I don't want to get in trouble.'

'Okay, it's been nice talking to you. Do you want me to walk you home?'

'No thanks, I think I'll stay here for a while. It's so peaceful. Have a wonderful Christmas, Nick Allen, and remember me occasionally.'

'Bye Jenny,' said Nick, blowing her a kiss before he started to jog back to the entrance.

He reached the gate at St Michael's Street and stopped to get his breath. Perhaps I'll take her to the pictures in the New Year, he thought; yes, I'll make that my New Year's resolution. He then started a brisk walk and arrived home fifteen minutes later. His Mum and Dad and little brother Richard were already sat down eating their tea.

'Where have you been?' asked Mrs Allen. We were getting worried.

'Sorry, Mum.' replied Nick. 'Met an old friend, got talking, lost track of time.'

'Well never mind. Sit down and eat your tea before it gets cold.'

Nick sat down and took a large mouthful of shepherd's pie. 'So,' he asked, 'have I missed anything?'

'Well,' said Mrs Allen. 'Did you hear about the Reynolds girl - what's her name, Jenny, I think?'

Nick looked up.

'She died this morning; apparently she fell in the lake on Saturday and caught pneumonia, poor thing.'

Nick Allen wept.

PART 3

THE MAN WITH AN UMBRELLA

Wednesday 8 January 1964

Nick Allen looked a forlorn figure as he sat alone in the school changing room shivering and covered head to foot in mud. It was half-time. The Sandridge Grammar School under-15 football team were playing Cottonmill Boys School in the Quarter final of the St Albans Benevolent Cup and were 0-1 down. Nick had missed a penalty. To make matters worse, no-one was being particularly friendly towards Nick. Recent events had made Nick a little unpopular, especially with those involved with the school football team. Before Christmas Nick had uncovered a protection racket in the school and numerous first-year students were being bullied into giving away a shilling. The result was that the two main culprits had been expelled; unfortunately, they were both very good footballers and the main stay of the school football team. Just to make matters worse, Sandridge Grammar School was traditionally a rugby playing school and the Headmaster, Mr Mills, under pressure from the Sports Master Mr Freeman, had agreed to let football be played, at all levels, only if the under-15 side won the Benevolent Cup. Also Nick wasn't talking to his friend, Keith Nevin, whom he felt had betrayed him during the investigation.

'Well,' said Mr Freeman, a tall athletic man in his mid-thirties. Although his main sport was basketball, he had a great passion for football: 'a repeat of that performance will not see us through to the semi-final, will it?'

'No, sir,' replied Danny Fooks, the stocky captain of the football team, with a mass of uncontrollable curly hair. 'But they're a very good side and very strong, and no disrespect, but we are missing a couple of our best players.'

'I know that, but what's done is done and we can't change it. Alan Prince and Eddie Lee were bullies and the Headmaster had no alternative but to expel them. So let's not hear any more about them, is that understood?'

Two or three of the team mumbled, 'Yes sir.'

'Now, what we have got to do is to find a way of beating this team. Oh unlucky with the penalty, Nick: just a little too close to the post. I know it sounds obvious but if we keep possession of the ball, we'll have more chance of scoring. It's very muddy out there so try to keep our passes short and crisp; and Nick, put away your personal vendettas and work with Keith. With the skill you two possess we should walk this game. So come on lads,' shouted Mr Freeman, clapping his hands, 'get out there and show me what you can do.'

As the two teams emerged from the changing rooms, Danny Fooks yelled: 'Come on you lot. I don't know about you but I don't fancy playing rugby again next year.'

It was a cold murky afternoon, slightly warmer than it should be for January, which made the ground rather muddy after some recent rain. As a spectacle the game was very poor with most of the play centred round the middle of the pitch, which had cut up quite badly and most of the passes were going astray. The wings, however, still had plenty of grass and Nick thought that if Sandridge could get the ball out wide, their wingers could make some head way. Mr Freeman had selected a new player to play outside right; his name was Mick Parsons. Although small in stature, he was very fast and had good close control. Being new to the team, he hadn't seen much of the ball and Nick was also being starved as well. With time ticking away, Nick had estimated that there were only about fifteen minutes remaining when, after finding some space he received the ball. He turned, looked up, and sent a delightful ball down the right wing. Parsons was like a greyhound out of a trap chasing the ball. He reached it just on the half way line and sprinted down the right wing. He easily avoided a couple of hearty challenges and just before he reached the corner flag he sent a delightful cross which Keith Nevin met firmly with his head to score the equalizer.

It was clear to all the Sandridge players that Parsons was the player to win this game and they pumped the ball to him at every occasion. After about four runs down the wing which had all resulted in good scoring chances, Cottonmill responded by putting their two fastest players to mark him. This resulted in Parsons being sent flying as the two defenders tackled him simultaneously. Whilst receiving treatment from Mr Freeman, Nick ran over to have a quick word.

'Mick', said Nick, 'you're playing brilliantly but they think you are a one trick pony. The next time you get the ball cut inside and have a run at goal.'

'Okay, Nick,' gasped Mick, still trying to get his breath. 'I'll give it a try.'

'How long to go, sir?' asked Nick.

'Only a few minutes,' replied Mr Freeman, 'and I don't think the light will hold for extra-time.'

Play resumed with a free kick which was easily defended by the Cottonmill defence. Their attack was broken up by an excellent tackle by Danny Fooks who then passed the ball to Keith Nevin. Nevin received the ball in the centre circle; Nick who was ten yards to his right, called for the ball. Nevin looked up; there were other players in better positions. He looked at Nick, smiled and said 'all yours' and passed the ball to Nick.

Nick strode forward looking for Parsons; he spotted him hugging the touchline with his two markers in close proximity. It was a chance; he chipped the ball over the defenders into the space behind them. Before they could turn Parsons was away, but instead of running down the wing he cut inside and made his way towards the goal. His two markers were chasing in his wake but were never going to catch him. The centre half was left flat-footed and the rest of the defenders were slipping as they tried to turn in the mud. Nick just watched as Parsons easily rounded the goalkeeper and stroked home the ball to put Sandridge Grammar into the semi-final of the Benevolent Cup.

After showering and changing, Nick started to make his way home. He hadn't cycled far when Keith Nevin caught up with him.

'That was a close game,' gasped Keith, pulling alongside Nick.

'S'pose,' replied Nick.

'Oh, for god's sake, I've said sorry a million times. When are you going to forgive me?'

'I'm sorry, but I find betrayal a little hard to forgive.'

'I thought you were supposed to be a Christian. Isn't forgiving one of their main things? I mean, it's not like I kissed you in the garden or anything.'

Nick found that amusing and tried to suppress a laugh.

'That's better,' said Keith. 'You can't be angry forever.'

'Okay, okay, I'll think about it.'

Then after a short pause Nick said, 'What are you doing Saturday? Thought I might go and watch Spurs play; fancy it?'

'Can't this week; got my Auntie coming round for tea. That's a shame, would have been nice.'

'Never mind, another time.'

'So what else have you been up to? Bought any new records lately? 'said Keith, trying to keep the conversation going.

'As it happens, I had some money left over from Christmas, so I popped to the Record Room and bought *Glad All Over* by the Dave Clark Five, *Secret Love* by Kathy Kirby and *Sugar and Spice* by the Searchers.'

'Good choice, did you see that new programme last week - *Top of the Pops* - I thought it was brilliant.'

'Fantastic, can't wait to see it next week.'

So Nick and Keith cycled home together, the friendship maybe still a little strained, but it was on the mend.

Saturday 11 January 1964

Tottenham Hotspur were playing Blackburn Rovers at White Hart Lane and Nick decided this was just the tonic he needed. Even though his friendship with Keith was on the mend he still wasn't 100% happy. The events of last term were still hanging over him and he felt people were always staring at him. What he needed was a boost and seeing his favourite team thrash Blackburn Rovers would certainly fit the bill. He left home early to watch the match, catching the train to St. Pancras and then a tube to Finsbury Park where he would catch a bus to the ground. He knew a nice little café in Seven Sisters Road, just opposite the Astoria Theatre. He always stopped there for something to eat. The café was quite crowded but he noticed there was one empty bay in the corner. He ordered his food then sat himself down with his mug of tea and decided to start an essay that he had been given for homework and was due for submission on Monday. The essay was entitled "My Thoughts Today". He had just written two sentences when the door to the café opened and four young men in their early twenties burst in.

'Four teas and four bacon sarnies please, Mabel,' shouted one of the men with a broad Liverpool accent.

The four looked around and saw that the only space available was next to Nick and without hesitation squeezed in the bay next to him.

'Don't mind if we join yer, lad?' asked the man who had ordered their food. 'My name's John. What's yours?'

Before Nick had a chance to answer, John grabbed Nick's exercise book and said 'What yer writing?'

'Just doing my homework and my name's Nick.'

'Well, Nick, you haven't done much have yer? Oh, this is Paul; he's, George, and the ugly one's called Ringo.'

'Nice to meet you,' gasped Nick.

'What's he written?' asked Paul.

'Not a lot' exclaimed John, 'but it's a good start: Yesterday all my troubles seem so far away, now it looks as though there are here to stay.'

'Sounds a bit depressing to me,' mocked Ringo.

'Could be the first line of one of your songs[5], Paul,' laughed George.

'Yer never know,' exclaimed Paul.

'So, what are you doing in London?' enquired Nick.

'It's our last night at the Astoria. You mean yer not coming to see us?'

'Afraid not. Going to see the Spurs play, but I am a big fan of yours; bought all your records.'

'Ham, egg and chips and four bacon sarnies,' yelled Mabel.

'Over 'ere luv' replied Ringo, making room on the table.

Mabel brought over the food, laid out the cutlery and Nick along with the four lads from Liverpool ate their meals, shared jokes and told stories until it was time for Nick to catch his bus. Nick hadn't enjoyed himself so much for a long time and felt on top of the world as he arrived at the ground just in time for kick-off. Surely the day couldn't get any better he thought, as he found himself a decent view at the Paxton Road end of the ground. But it did, as the Spurs demolished Blackburn Rovers 4-1 and Nick's favourite player, Jimmy Greaves, scored a hat-trick.

Nick arrived back at St Albans station at around 7:00 pm and was in such a good mood that he decided to walk home instead of getting the bus. From the station he walked up Victoria Street and turned right into St Peter's Street. To save a few minutes he turned into Adelaide Street, a poorly lit side road which ran adjacent to his old infant school[6]. Still humming to himself *I Wanna Hold Your Hand* and totally oblivious to his surroundings, he was set upon by four youths. First, he was pushed quite hard in the back; he stumbled but managed to keep his feet. When he turned round a fist struck him in the mouth. He could taste the blood trickling from his cut lip. Before he had time to react he was punched in the stomach and then his legs were kicked away. He fell to the floor; he instinctively brought his knees up to his chest as more kicks rained in on him.

'Stop that,' he heard a female voice cry.

'This is just the beginning,' a familiar voice snarled.

Nick heard the assailants run off as the female voice asked: 'are you alright?'

'Not really,' he replied. 'Could you call an ambulance? There's a phone box at the end of the road.'

An elderly lady came out of her cottage and said, 'What's all the noise? I'm trying to listen to the wireless.'

'Sorry, love,' said the female voice. 'This young boy has just been attacked; I think he's badly hurt. Could you phone for an ambulance?'

'Oh dear, I'll go straight away. Do you have any pennies?'

The female voice opened her purse and gave the old lady four pennies. 'Here you are and please hurry.'

Nick managed to say, 'You don't need any money for a 999 call.'

'Silly me,' laughed the elderly lady running towards the phone. Nick noticed that she didn't return the money.

'Try not to move,' said the female voice as she comforted him in her arms.

Nick tried to get comfortable but he was hurting all over. He wiped away the blood from a cut above his eye that was impairing his sight so he could see the girl. When she came into vision, he thought she must be about nineteen years old. She had dark brown hair in a bouffant style, big beautiful brown eyes and reminded him a bit of Elizabeth Taylor.

'I hope I haven't stopped you going somewhere,' he asked.

'Well, I'm meeting some friends at the Jazz Club but it won't matter if I'm a bit late.'

'You're very kind, what's your name?'

'My name is Jane, Jane Goldberg, and whom do I have the pleasure of attending to.'

'I'm Nick ....' he said as he fell unconscious.

Sunday 12 January 1964

When Nick regained full consciousness he found himself tucked up comfortably in a hospital bed. He felt very sore, his head was thumping, his ribs were aching, and his mouth was very dry.

'Ah, you are awake at last,' said a very pretty nurse who introduced herself as Nurse Hickey. 'We've been worried about you.'

Nick rubbed his eyes and stared at the vision in front of him. He guessed she must be about eighteen years old, five foot five inches tall and immaculately dressed in her uniform, consisting of a white starched bib-front pinafore dress and cap and a blue elasticated belt with a crest on the buckle. Her grey/green eyes shone out from her heart-shaped face and a smile that would melt many a heart.

'What happened?' asked Nick, still a bit confused.

'You've had a bit of an accident. Now don't try and move. The doctor will be here soon and he can explain everything to you.'

'Can I have a glass of water please; my mouth is as dry as the desert.'

'Certainly,' said Nurse Hickey, as she helped Nick sit up and put the glass to his lips.

'Thank you,' said Nick. 'You're very kind and if you don't mind me saying, very pretty.'

'Thank you' said Nurse Hickey, feeling her cheeks blushing. 'Ah, here comes the Doctor.'

A tall handsome man in a clean white coat appeared at the end of the bed. He picked up the clipboard and looked at the medical notes attached.

'Good morning, Nick,' he said. 'My name is Doctor Wilson and it looks like you have been in the wars.'

'Just a little trouble with the natives, nothing to worry about,' replied Nick.

'Two busted ribs, a broken tooth, five stitches plus multiple bruising and he says nothing to worry about. Someone doesn't like you young, Nick Allen.'

'Can't please everybody,' said Nick very sheepishly.

'You're right there, but Nick, you have been very lucky; it could have been a lot worse. I've spoken to the police and they will be along later to interview you. We can't have this type of thing happening on our streets. Now you need to rest; anything you want just ask Nurse Hickey, she's one of our finest nurses.'

Nick noticed that Nurse Hickey was blushing even more now.

The police came about one o'clock that afternoon and Nick made a statement giving the facts as best he could remember. Asked if he could identify his assailants he stated that although it was dark he recognised one of the voices as belonging to Alan Prince. The policeman made a note of this and said he would be looking into it. Visiting time in the hospital was between two and four o'clock and Nick's parents were the first through the door followed by his younger brother Richard. Richard, who insisted on being called Dick, was four years younger than Nick and looked bored as soon as he entered the ward. Mrs Allen, a petite woman in her late thirties, started crying as soon as she saw Nick and kept repeating 'my poor boy, my poor boy,' and stroking his hair. Mr Allen, who a lot of people said looked like Tyrone Powell and a year older than Mrs Allen, kept a stiff upper lip and said 'this sort of thing wouldn't have happened in my day. They shouldn't have abolished National Service.' Although Nick loved his parents to bits he felt a bit uncomfortable and was struggling to keep a conversation going. As luck would have it, on the stroke of three o'clock his friends Keith Nevin and Don Patrick walked in the ward. Mr Allen, who was eager to see some programme on the television, said 'Well, I think it's time for us to leave and let Nick talk to his friends.' Mrs Allen started crying again and Nick said, 'I'm alright Mother, I'm coming home tomorrow, and then you can fuss over me all you like.' So Mr and Mrs Allen and young Dick bade their farewells and left Nick with his friends.

'I thought they would never go,' gasped Nick.

'Well, it's good to see you,' said Don. 'Are you in much pain?'

'Quite a lot,' replied Nick, 'but I can take it.'

'You took one hell of a beating,' said Keith, taking a serious look at the bruises on Nick's face.

'It would have been a lot worse if I wasn't saved by some beautiful girl,' replied Nick.

'Oh do tell us; what was she like?' said Keith excitedly.

But before Nick could answer Nurse Hickey approached his bed and stuck a thermometer in his mouth, grabbed his wrist and started counting to herself. After a minute she removed the thermometer, looked at it, gave it a shake and said 'All done.' After writing the details on the chart she went to attend another patient.

'Wow,' exclaimed Keith. 'She's a little cracker.'

'I know; she's gorgeous and very efficient' agreed Nick, as they admired the shapely rear of Nurse Hickey

'I say, chaps' interrupted Don, who was a year younger than Nick and Keith. 'Are you two interested in girls all of a sudden?' Don, who was the same height as Nick, had short black hair neatly cut Boston style and attended a Catholic school.

Nick and Keith both blushed. Nick was first to answer, 'Well, I suppose I must be. You see I been getting these funny feelings whenever a pretty girl walks by.'

'Have you?' gasped Keith. 'So have I. Do you think it's normal?'

'I didn't come here to listen to you two talk about your funny feelings. I want to know all about the beating and who the culprits were,' interrupted Don.

Nick laughed, 'Sorry, Don, but you'll be getting them soon enough.'

'I don't think so,' said Don, 'I'm a catholic; we're not allowed those sorts of feelings.'

This time Keith laughed, 'It won't be long before you're looking at the women's underwear pages of your Mum's Littlewoods catalogue.'

Don blushed.

'And then you'll be playing "tents" in the morning like the rest of us,' said Nick.

'You're disgusting, both of you,' replied Don, trying to suppress a laugh.

Then all three burst out laughing. They laughed so loud that Nurse Hickey rushed over to them.

'Quiet, boys; you are disturbing all the other patients' she shouted.

But try as they might they couldn't stop laughing.

'I'm going to have to ask you two to leave. Nick needs his rest.'

Keith and Don managed to contain themselves for just enough time to say goodbye to Nick before running out of the ward in a fit of hysterics. Nick managed to suppress his laughter and looked up at Nurse Hickey who was standing, hands on hips with a serious look on her face.

'Are you quite finished?' she inquired.

'Sorry about that,' replied Nick, looking rather sheepish. 'Can I ask you a personal question?'

'And what might that be?'

'Do you have a boyfriend?'

'No I don't,' she replied. Nick smiled. 'But I have a fiancé.'

'Lucky fellow,' muttered Nick feeling despondent.

'I think so,' she said, smiling at Nick before turning away to attend another patient.

Nick sighed, looked through the pile of comics his mother had brought in and decided on The *Victor* and turned straight to Tough of the Track featuring Alf Tupper. He was just finishing the latest episode of Gorgeous Gus when the bell sounded for the end of visiting time. Automatically he looked up and saw a girl, who looked vaguely familiar, talking to Nurse Hickey. He couldn't make out what they were saying but the nurse was smiling and then she pointed to Nick and the girl walked towards his bed.

The girl approached Nick and said, 'Hi, handsome; how are you feeling?'

'I'm fine,' Nick sputtered. 'On the mend.'

'Well, I'm glad to hear it; you gave me quite a fright when you passed out like that.'

Nick, now realising who the girl was, quickly said, 'it could have been a lot worse if you hadn't come along.'

'Well, I couldn't see a sweet young boy like you being beaten to a pulp.'

'Absolutely not,' Nick was struggling for words in the presence of this beautiful girl. 'I'm very sorry but I've forgotten your name.'

'It's Jane.'

'Well Jane, thank you very much for coming to my rescue and thank you for coming to visit me in hospital.'

'My pleasure, but I was a bit worried; so my boss let me finish early this afternoon to come and visit you.'

'Well, thank him for me as well,' replied Nick who was struggling to find things to say.

'The Nurse said you can go home tomorrow, so you must be on the mend. Anyway, I better be off, it's gone past visiting time.'

Jane bent down and kissed him gently on the cheek. 'Now you be a bit more careful next time.'

'Okay,' Nick croaked.

With that, she smiled at him turned and walked away.

Nick sat there, mouth open, not realising that a tent was slowly being erected under his sheets.

Monday 20 January 1964

Nick was released from hospital the following day and spent the following week convalescing at home; he returned to school the following Monday. First period after lunch was gym which Nick was excused due to his injuries, so he decided to go to the library. He found an interesting book entitled *The Young Footballer* by Robert Bateman, and sat down to read it. After a few minutes the new school caretaker, Mr Campion, a tall, strange man with a scar on his right cheek, approached him. The old caretaker, Mr Munt, had recently retired due to ill health. Nick guessed that Mr Campion was about middle to late 40s with jet black hair swept straight back and had a military look about him.

'May I join you?' he asked.

Nick looked around to make sure it was him he was addressing; he felt uncomfortable as he had never spoken to the man before.

'If you like,' he replied.

'Heard you've had a bit of bother,' said Mr Campion, as he sat down opposite Nick.

'You could say that,' replied Nick, a little wary of this strange man.

'What you need is some self-defence lessons.'

'I don't really believe in violence.'

'So you would rather get beaten up, eh?'

'Of course not, but I ...'

Before Nick could finish his sentence Mr Campion stood up and said 'Meet me in the gym after school and don't be late.' With that he was gone.

What was that all about? thought Nick, unable to concentrate on his book; but being a curious chap Nick was outside the gym within minutes of the school bell being rung. He was greeted by Mr Freeman, the Sports Master, who said, 'He's in there waiting for you.'

Nick entered the gym with some trepidation. Mr Campion was standing in the middle of the gym; arms folded wearing a white tee-shirt and camouflaged trousers.

'So, how many attacked you?' he asked.

'I think there were four,' Nick replied.

'Okay, first thing you need to know is that these types of attackers are basically cowards.'

'Oh, that's comforting,' replied Nick sarcastically.

'So that's why you need to be prepared.'

'Oh, so you're saying it's going to happen again? This just gets better.'

'Listen Sonny-Jim, cut out the back chat, because next time it could be worse.'

'Sorry,' said Nick.

'And I hear you were rescued by a girl.' A smirk appeared on Mr Campion's face.

'That's right,' muttered Nick. 'And she was a real cracker.'

Mr Campion laughed, 'well, stick with me lad, and you'll win the lady.'

All of a sudden Nick relaxed, looked Mr Campion square in the eyes and said, 'Let's do it.'

The next hour was taken up by Mr Campion explaining all the weapons that Nick had at his disposal: his feet, knees, elbows, hands and most important, his head. He first explained what to do if he was attacked from behind. 'If your back is to your assailant, you can bring your knee up without impediment and think for a moment of how a mule kicks with his rear legs. He will bring his leg up with the hoof close to his underside and then kick straight back. In some styles of martial arts, bringing your knee and foot up and also kicking straight back just happens to be termed a "mule kick." Ideally, as you slam your heel backwards, you will hit the assailant's knee, a very unstable, vulnerable joint. Regardless if you hit the knee or the shin, the rest of the technique requires you to allow your heel to slide down the assailant's leg and onto the bones of the instep or toes. If you have been lucky enough to hit the knee or break the bones of the foot, don't stop there. Use your head as a battering ram against your assailant's nose and mouth If your arms are pinned but your hands are free, attempt to step backwards as close to your assailant as possible, use your strongest hand to reach back and grab a handful of testicles or pinch as hard as you can on the inside of the thigh as close to the groin as possible. To get the idea of how light a pinch can cause pain, reach down and pinch the inside of your own thigh.'

Nick tried it, and yes, it did hurt.

After trying various techniques of escape, and learning how to punch and kick properly Nick gasped, 'I think I've had enough for one day. I should be getting home for my tea.'

'Sorry,' replied Mr Campion. 'I didn't realise the time. Mrs Campion will be wondering where I've got to. Wait outside and I'll walk you to the school gates. Just give me a minute to get my things.'

Mr Campion lived in a small bungalow by the entrance to the school. As they walked Nick asked, 'Were you in the army?'

'Oh yes,' replied Mr Campion, 'Special Ops in France and Holland.'

'Sounds exciting.'

'At times; I'll tell you about one day if you're interested.'

'I'd like that.'

They had reached the school gates. Nick thanked Mr Campion, mounted his bike and rode home. Nick had agreed to have a lesson every night that week as he wasn't allowed to train with the school football team until his ribs were healed. The doctor told him that it would take between 6 and 10 weeks for them to heal. Nick was hoping that he would be fit for the Cup semi-final, if he was selected. The draw had not been made yet nor a date set. With all the cold weather and the frozen pitches Nick guessed that it would be played some time in February.

Towards the end of January, life seemed a lot rosier for Nick, apart from not being able to train with his football team, everything else was going well. He really looked forward to his self-defence lessons, which after the first week were reduced to twice a week; they somehow seem to have given him a lot more confidence. Nick was finding Mr Campion very good company. After each lesson he would tell Nick stories about the war, his adventures in France and Holland and the D-day landings. In the evenings, after he had finished his homework, he met up with his friends, Keith and Don. They had become inseparable; some nights, especially when the weather was bad, they would meet at one of their houses and listen to records, play games, or watch television. Their favourite programmes were *The Saint, Ready Steady Go, Top of the Pops, Dr Who* and *The Avengers*. Keith had a crush on Cathy Gale who was played by Honor Blackman; Nick was smitten with a pop singer called Cilla Black. Don said he was too young to fancy girls, but both Nick and Keith had noticed a large poster of Kathy Kirby on his bedroom wall.

Monday 3 February 1964

Good things always come to an end, and life decided to change Nick Allen's fortunes in the first week of February. Still being excused from gym, Nick met Keith in the library during afternoon break.

'Guess what?' said Keith

'Do you have to say that? Just tell me,' replied Nick.

'We're been drawn against Camp Boys School in the semi-final of the Benevolent Cup. It's being played the week after half-term.'

'That's good. Hopefully, I'll be fit enough to play.'

'There's something else.'

'Go on, don't keep me in suspenders.'

'Alan Prince and Eddie Lee will be playing. That's where they were put after being expelled from here.'

'Oh dear! But you don't know for sure that they will be playing; they might not get selected.'

'Dream on.'

'Ah, I've just thought. They can't play because they are cup-tied.'

'Get real, Nick; this is not professional football. I don't suppose it's in the competition rules. After all, how many people change schools in the middle of a year?'

'Oh well, it will be nice to see him again.'

After his last lesson Nick made his way to the gym for his self-defence class. I wonder if Mr Campion has any tips on dealing with enemies on a football pitch, thought Nick. He entered the gym but it was empty, which had never happened before. Strange thought Nick and went to see if Mr Freeman was in his office. He was.

'Excuse me, Sir,' said Nick. 'Have you seen Mr Campion?'

'Not since break. He said he was helping Mr Bilk in the rural science classroom.'

'Thank you, Sir, I'll just wait for a while.'

Nick waited for five minutes; this is not like him he thought, I'd better go and look for him.

The rural science class was away from the main buildings, next to the tennis courts. The door to the classroom faced the garden which was divided into small plots, each allocated to a class for growing their plants. As Nick approached the class room the door, it burst open and a strange man wearing a black raincoat, a bowler hat, and carrying an umbrella came out and scurried away. Nick didn't think the man saw him as he disappeared in the opposite direction. Nick ran to the classroom, entered it and found Mr Campion lying on the floor. He rushed over to him and lifted his head. He was still breathing.

'Mr Campion!' Nick screamed. 'Are you alright?'

Mr Campion opened his eyes and in a shallow voice he whispered 'Nick, my boy, look under the Rhod… ..….' then passed out.

'Mr Campion, Mr Campion,' shouted Nick. 'Wake up, wake up!'

At that point Mr Bilk, the rural science teacher appeared. An amiable, bald, overweight man in his late forties, wearing a brown warehouse coat and carrying a small bag of peat, 'What's happened?' he asked.

'I don't know, Sir,' replied Nick. 'I just found him like this. Is he going to be alright?'

'I hope so, boy. Quickly run to the secretary's office and get her to phone for an ambulance.'

'I think he was attacked, Sir. I saw a man coming out of the classroom.'

'Nonsense boy, I've been here all afternoon, I haven't seen anyone. Now, run along and get that ambulance and no more silly stories. I think he's just had a heart attack.'

'Yes, Sir,' and Nick ran as fast as he could to the secretary's office.

Mrs Kelley dialled 999 straight away, and then informed the Headmaster. Nick rushed back to the Rural Science block to find Mr Bilk had covered Mr Campion in an old blanket.

Five minutes later the ambulance arrived and took Mr Campion away.

Thursday 6 February 1964

Three days later it was announced in assembly that Mr Campion had died the previous night of a suspected heart attack. Nick decided then that he should visit Mrs Campion after school and pay his respects. Keith offered to go with him but said he thought it best to go alone. It was a miserable February day; the sky was full of clouds and the rain had drizzled down all day. Nick had never known a day to drag so much. All he wanted to do was go home, cuddle his Mum and have a good cry. When the final school bell sounded he packed his bag, making sure that he had all his homework, grabbed his coat and cap and made his way to the caretaker's bungalow. Nick knocked on the door and waited. Eventually the door opened and a stern faced woman dressed head to foot in black. Black skirt, black cardigan buttoned up to the neck, thick black stockings and black shoes. She had black hair with lots of grey showing tied in a ponytail, her face showed no trace of make-up.

She looked at Nick. 'What do you want?' she asked with an accent Nick didn't recognise.

'Sorry to disturb you, Mrs Campion, but I just wanted to say how sorry I am to hear about your loss.'

'Are you that kid that Arthur has been seeing after school?'

'Yes, miss, and I was the one who found him and called for the ambulance.'

'Well you better come in, but I'm very busy.'

Mrs Campion showed Nick through to the living room. It was a dingy room with a dull brown two-seater settee and one matching chair, a small dining table covered with a thick brown and gold cloth, and an old sideboard. There was also a couple of tea chests which Nick assumed were filled with ornaments and photographs that had previously adorned this room.

'Are you moving?' asked Nick.

'Well, they will be looking for a new caretaker so I might as well get packed up now. Do you want a cup of tea or something?'

'No, thank you,' replied Nick thinking that this might be a mistake; she doesn't look like a grieving widow to me. 'Mr Campion was a wonderful man. He taught me a lot, and he made me laugh with his stories of the war and such like.'

She turned to him, her dark eyes staring hard, and said, 'They were just stories; Albert was never in the army. Do you hear me?'

'Yes, miss.' Nick was now physically shaking.

'The nearest he got to the army was the Home Guard - flat feet, or something like that.'

'Well,' said Nick, 'I better go; my Mum will wonder where I am. No need to show me out.'

Nick grabbed his bag and rushed to the door. 'Bye,' he shouted and quickly left the bungalow.

That evening Nick met Keith and Don outside the Blacksmiths Arms public house and made their way down Hatfield Road towards the Pioneer Youth Club, which was situated in the old fire station. They bought themselves a bottle of Coca Cola each from Ma's Bar and found themselves an empty table.

'How did you get on at Mrs Campion's?' asked Keith.

'Not very well,' replied Nick. 'She was very scary.'

'What did she say?' asked Don.

'Not a lot; I didn't stay long. She said that Mr Campion wasn't in the army, which I don't believe, and she didn't seem very upset either. I got the impression it was all a bit of a nuisance him dying. She had already started packing.'

'It all seems a bit fishy to me,' said Keith. 'Didn't you say you saw someone leaving the classroom before you found Mr Campion?'

'That's right, but Mr Bilk told me I was mistaken.'

'What does old F.B.I. know?'

Mr Bilk had the nickname F.B.I. which stood for Fat, Bald and Ignorant.

'I'm confused,' confessed Nick. 'I can't believe Mr Campion died of a heart attack. He seemed so fit and I definitely saw someone come out of the classroom. And Mrs Campion knows more than she's telling.'

'Do you think,' said Don excitedly, 'that Mrs Campion hired a hit man to kill Mr Campion?'

'Don't be silly, Don,' said Keith looking up to the heavens.

'Wait a minute,' said Nick. 'He could be right. Mr Campion tried to tell me something as I held him in my arms, but for the life of me I can't remember what it was. And why would she lie about his military record, saying he was never in the army?'

'I think,' said Keith, 'that we need to check a few things out. First, we need to confirm whether he was ever in the army.'

'How do we do that?' asked Don.

'I don't know. I'll have to ask my dad,' replied Nick.

Friday 7 February 1964

Next morning Nick was sitting down to breakfast with his parents and little brother.

'Dad,' he asked, 'where can I find out someone's military record?'

'Well,' his dad replied, 'depends. Was the person killed during the war or did he survive?'

'He survived.'

'Okay, in that case you will need to contact the National Archives. Why don't you phone them? You can get their number from directory enquires. Is it for a school project?'

'Yeh; something like that.'

As soon as Nick returned home after school he phoned directory enquiries, obtained the number and then phoned the National Archives and asked them for details of Albert Campion's military record. They said it might take a while, so they took his phone number and promised to call him back. Whilst at school Nick had asked the Headmaster if he could miss school one day next week to attend Mr Campion's funeral. Permission was granted as long as he caught up with the school work he would miss. When Nick returned home from school the following day, his mother told him that the National Archives had phoned and left a message. It said that they had no record of an Albert Campion ever doing military service.

Wednesday 12 February 1964

The following week Nick attended Albert Campion's funeral. He was to be cremated at the Garston Crematorium at 2:00 pm. Nick wore his school uniform with his best white shirt and a black tie which he borrowed from his dad. The crematorium was situated in High Elms Lane, Garston which is between Watford and St. Albans. Nick decided to bike there. There were two chapels available for funerals. Nick checked the notice board, and then made his way to the smaller of the two. Just as well they choose this one thought Nick as the chapel was virtually empty. At the front was seated Mrs Campion accompanied by another woman who, Nick recognised as the head cleaner at the school. Behind them were two more cleaners; to the right of the aisle sat the Headmaster, Mr Mills, and his secretary. The only other mourners were two serious looking middle-aged men dressed smartly, all in black, sitting at the back.

After the service Nick made his way back to the car park where he had left his bicycle chained to the fence. He was just unlocking when he was approached by the two men he had seen sitting at the back in the chapel. Both men, in their late forties, spoke with posh accents. They were well dressed and didn't look too intimidating.

'Nick Allen?' one of them asked.

'Who wants to know?' Nick replied.

'We do,' replied the other one. We would like to have a word. Come and sit in our car.'

'My mother told me never to speak to strange men.'

'We're not strange,' said the taller of the two, grabbing Nick by his collar and dragging him to their car which was parked not far away. 'Now less of the lip, and get in there.'

Nick was bundled into the back of the car, followed by the taller of the two whilst the other went round the other side and got in.

Nick was the first to speak. 'If you wanted me to get in the car, aren't you supposed to offer me sweets?'

'Very funny,' said the tall guy.

'Okay,' said Nick who surprisingly wasn't feeling scared. 'Who are you and what do you want?'

'My name is Arthur Martin[7] and this is Peter Wright[8]. We work for British Intelligence and we know all about you, Nick Allen.'

'What does that mean – you know all about me?' replied Nick sarcastically.

'We have a file on you,' said Arthur.

'A file on me; I'm only fourteen - why would you have a file on me?'

'You helped solve the Great Train Robbery.'

'I did solve the Great Train Robbery, not that I got any thanks.'

'Well, we're grateful,' said Arthur.

'Cheers.'

'And we know that you've been corresponding with Christine Keeler, who at present is spending time at Her Majesty's pleasure,' said Peter.

Nick chuckled. 'Yes, nice girl, totally mis-understood.'

Then in a serious voice, Arthur said, 'You've also been enquiring about Albert Campion's military record.'

'That's right, but without much success; seems he was never in the army.'

Arthur looked at Peter. Peter nodded. 'How much can we trust you?' he asked.

'100%,' replied Nick. 'I'm the soul of discretion.'

'This is serious, lad,' said Arthur. 'We might need your help.'

Nick sensed this was not a game. 'You can trust me and I'll help you in any way I can. Do you want me to sign the Official Secrets Act?'

Arthur looked at Nick and raised his eyebrows.'

'Sorry,' said Nick.

'Okay,' said Arthur, 'first we need you to answer a few questions.'

'Go ahead.'

'You found Albert Campion when he collapsed.'

'That's right. When he didn't turn up for my self-defence lesson, I went looking for him. Mr Freeman said he thought he was in the rural science block. That's where I found him.'

'Did you see anything out of the ordinary?'

'As I told Mr Bilk, I saw a man leaving the class room, but he didn't see me.'

Arthur looked at Peter then said, 'Nobody told us this. What did he look like?'

'I didn't see his face. He was quite tall, broad, wearing a black raincoat, a bowler hat and carrying an umbrella.'

'Interesting, did Albert give you anything or say anything?'

'He certainly didn't give me anything; he tried to say something but I couldn't catch what he said.'

'Okay, Nick, you've done well. If you remember anything else, you'll let us know.' He took out his wallet, extracted a business card and said, 'Call me on this number; you can go now.'

'Just a minute,' interrupted Nick. 'I've a few questions I need to ask. If I'm going to help you, I need a bit more information.'

'Like what?'

'To start with, who is Albert Campion, if that's his real name?'

Arthur smiled, 'It didn't take you long to figure that out.' Again Arthur looked at Peter. Peter nodded. 'Okay, I'll tell you what I can. You're right, Albert Campion was not his real name, but you don't need to know his real name. We'll still call him Albert.'

'Okay,' said Nick.

Arthur continued: 'Albert was a member of the SAS during the war. After that he was recruited into MI6 and worked as a double agent in Russia. Ever heard of Guy Burgess?'

'Vaguely, he was a spy wasn't he?'

'That's right; along with Donald Maclean and Kim Philby they passed information to the Soviet Union during World War II and into the early 1950s. We believe that there are two other members of this ring. Arthur was working in Moscow trying to find out who they are. Unfortunately, he was betrayed and fled back to England. Our intelligence informs us that there is a contract out on him; so we gave him a new identity but it looks like they may have found him.'

'But they said he died of a heart attack,' interrupted Nick.

'That's what it looked like, but your information changes everything. We'll have to do another post-mortem.'

'Might be a bit difficult since they have just cremated him,' said Nick looking up at the black smoke coming out of the chimney. Nick looked at

Arthur, then Peter, 'That wasn't Albert in that coffin, was it?'

'You're learning fast,' replied Peter.

'Okay, I won't ask the obvious. But I think Mrs Campion has something to do with it. She didn't seem the grieving widow to me.'

'Right again; but she wasn't Albert's wife; she worked for us, keeping an eye on him while he was in hiding; anything else?'

'I think that's all; that's a lot to take in.'

'Okay,' said Arthur. 'Off you go, and not a word to anyone, not even Keith or Don.'

'My lips are sealed,' replied Nick, hoping that they wouldn't see that he had his fingers crossed.

Wednesday 19 February 1964

The following week was half-term and with his ribs now feeling a lot better, Nick set himself a training programme hoping to get himself fit enough for the cup semi-final next week. It was late Wednesday afternoon. Nick was just finishing a vigorous 5-mile run which included Batchwood Golf Course. He was on the road which ran between the 2nd and 4th hole when he spotted three lads walking towards him. He immediately spotted the ginger hair of his arch-enemy, Alan Prince. Oh no not again, thought Nick.

'Well, if it isn't my old mate Nick Allen,' said Prince, with that crooked smile that Nick despised. 'You're looking good. All your injuries seemed to have healed up nicely.'

'Yes, I'm fine. Thank you for your concern. Now if you don't mind I'd like to get on with my run.'

'Not so fast. I think we have some unfinished business to attend to.'

'And what might that be? You've already given me one good beating.'

'Well that's not enough,' screamed Prince. 'You got me expelled and they've sent me to that bloody dump of a school.'

Before Nick could answer, Eddie Lee jumped out of the hedge and grabbed him from behind pinning his arms to his body.

Prince smiled. 'I think one more beating should do, just enough to stop you playing us in the semi-final next week. Nick dropped his chin on his chest; he could feel Eddie Lee's hot breath on his neck. Then with all the strength he could muster, he jerked his head backwards. A sickening crunch was followed by a piecing scream as Eddie released his grip raising his hands to his face. Nick spun around and kicked him between the legs. Lee fell to the floor doubled up in pain. Nick turned around to face the others and screamed: 'Come on then who's next?'

Alan Prince turned and ran, followed closely by his two friends. Nick chased after them screaming 'Aaaaahhhhhh.'

After about twenty yards Nick stopped, totally exhausted, and bent forward placing his hands on his knees gasping for breath. He then slumped down on the side of the road and looked back. Eddie was just getting to his feet, blood pouring out of his nose. Eddie looked down the road and seeing Nick jump to his feet, he ran off in the opposite direction. Nick jogged the final mile home, had a bath and his tea, and settled down to a quiet night in front of the television.

It was about 7:30 pm when the doorbell rang.

'I'll get it,' said Mrs Allen, who had just finished the washing up.

'Wonder who that is?' enquired Mr Allen, looking up from the *Daily Mirror*.

Nick just shrugged.

The door to the living room opened and a very worried Mrs Allen came in followed by a policeman. 'He wants a word with Nick.'

'Sorry to bother you, but I need young Nick to accompany me down to the station,' said the policeman who Nick recognised as PC Adams, the older brother of Dave Adams who was in the same class as him.

'What for?' asked Nick.

'I'm afraid there has been a serious complaint of assault,' said PC Adams.

'Nick,' asked Mr Allen, looking at his son. 'What have you done?'

'It was self-defence,' pleaded Nick.

'Well you can make your statement to the sergeant down at the station,' replied PC Adams.

'I'm coming with you; I'll just get my coat,' said a worried Mr Allen.

A blue and white Morris Minor was parked outside. Nick and Mr Allen made themselves comfortable in the back seat. The Police station was situated in an old Victorian brick building in Victoria Street. Nick and Mr Allen were led in and introduced to the custody sergeant.

'So this is the little thug,' said the sergeant, whom Nick took an instant dislike to. The sergeant was about fifty, overweight, small piggy eyes and greasy grey hair.

'My son is not a thug,' protested Mr Allen.

'Of course not; that's why some poor lad is in hospital with a broken nose and severe damage to his nether regions. I reckon it'll be Borstal for you, lad.'

'What happened to "innocent until proved guilty?"' asked Mr Allen.

'Well, three witnesses have sworn it was an unprovoked attack.'

Nick could feel his blood boiling, but he could hear the words of Mr Campion in his head. 'Never lose your temper; stay calm. That way you will always be in control'.

'Councillor Lee has made it his crusade to get scum like you off the streets and make St Albans a safer place,' smirked the sergeant.

'What's it got to do with Councillor Lee?' asked Mr Allen.

'Don't you know anything; it's his son that thug of yours put in hospital.'

'I'd like to make a phone call,' demanded Nick.

'What?' gasped the sergeant.

'A phone call; the law clearly states that I'm entitled to one phone call.'

'You've been watching too many TV cop shows. Anyway, who are you going to phone, your solicitor?' laughed the sergeant.

'Why would I need a solicitor? I'm innocent; now can I make that phone call. Please.'

'I suppose so. Come this way.'

The sergeant led Nick to an empty office. 'You can use that phone.'

'Thank you,' said Nick looking at the sergeant. 'You can go now, this is a private call.'

The sergeant left. 'And don't be long.'

Nick pulled a card out of his wallet and dialled a number and made his call. When he had finished he came back out and sat down next to his father.

'Alright son?' asked Mr Allen, giving Nick a nervous look.

Nick smiled. 'Give it five minutes and we'll be out of here,' he whispered to his dad.

Two minutes later Nick heard a phone ringing in a distant office. Another two minutes passed. The door of the office opened and an important looking plain clothes policeman came out, took the sergeant aside and started talking softly to him. Nick couldn't hear what they were saying but the sergeant wasn't looking too happy. A minute later the sergeant came over to Nick and his father and said, 'You can go now. All charges have been dropped.'

'That's it? No apology or explanation,' asked Mr Allen.

'Looks like your son has got friends in high places,' replied the sergeant.

Nick smiled to himself, turned and walked over to the sergeant. 'And when I tell my friends in high places how I've been treated by you in this poor excuse for a police station, I wouldn't want to be in your shoes. I hear that they are looking for shelf stackers in Woolworths. Come on, dad. Let's go. I think we've outstayed our welcome.'

Nick and Mr Allen left the police station and walked round the corner to St Peter's Street to catch a bus home.

'So who are these friends in high places,' asked Mr Allen.

'MI5,' replied Nick.

'Ask a stupid question . . . . .'

Wednesday 26 February 1964

The semi-final of the Benevolent Cup between Sandridge Grammar School and Camp Comprehensive was scheduled for a 2:00 pm kick off on the Wednesday, first week after half term. Nick had recovered enough to convince Mr Freeman, the sports master, that he was fit enough to play, and also that he had repaired his friendship with Keith, so they were both raring to go. Although both boys were still in their third year, Mr Freeman had no hesitation of playing them in this important match even though the majority of players would be a year older. Keith, who was tall for his age and at least two inches taller than Nick, would play centre forward whilst Nick would play inside right. Nick was a bit worried about playing against Camp Comprehensive. The school had a bit of a reputation as it was situated in a tough area of St Albans. The catchment area of the school included a council estate called Dellfields, not a place you would visit after dark. But luckily Sandridge had been drawn at home; unfortunately, this home advantage hadn't helped Sandridge as they walked off the pitch at half time trailing by two goals to nil. It was clear to all that Camp school were all-round a better team than Sandridge. As a spectacle, it was an enjoyable game and with a large slice of luck and some fine goalkeeping by Simon Francis, Sandridge were only two goals down. Even Nick had to admit that Alan Prince was playing out of his skin. He was everywhere. He definitely had a point to prove, and he had scored both goals.

As the downcast Sandridge players sucked on their half-time oranges, Mr

Freeman called Nick over. 'I think we've got a problem, Nick,' he said.

'I know,' Nick replied. 'What do you think we should do? They are a much better side then we are.'

'Alan Prince is their star player. Everything evolves from him. We need to neutralise his threat.'

'Do you want someone to man-mark him, sir?'

'That may work, but we are still two goals down. We need something else.'

Mr Freeman went silent for a moment, deep in thought, and then he said, 'Listen Nick. What I'm going to ask you to do is something that goes against everything I believe in; I shudder just thinking about it. But sometimes the needs of the many outweigh the needs of the few.'

'What is it, sir; what do you want me to do?' pleaded Nick.

Mr Freeman took a deep breath, then said, 'Take out Alan Prince.'

Nick smiled to himself. 'It's not a thing I agree with sir, but I'll do it for the school. As you quite rightly said "the needs of the many outweigh the needs of the few".'

'Good boy. I know I can rely on you.'

Mr Freeman went back to the team and said, 'Right lads. We have a difficult half ahead of us, so I'm going to make a tactical change. Nick Allen will drop back to right-half and Barry Dudley will play alongside Keith at inside right. Nick will man-mark Alan Prince and try to reduce the threat he is causing. This way, perhaps we will see more of the ball; all clear?'

'All clear,' the team shouted as they made their way back onto the pitch.

The whistle blew and Nick made his way straight to Alan Prince.

'Well, well, if it isn't my old mate Nick, come to mark me. I am honoured.' laughed Prince.

'It's nice to see you to,' replied Nick, 'but we can't let you continue playing as well as you did in the first half.'

'I'm flattered.'

'No. Give credit where it's due, even to a scum-bag like you.'

'There's no need for names now. After all, it's just a game.'

'Sorry, force of habit. By the way, how's your mate, Eddie?'

'Nasty break, but he's on the mend. How did you get away with that? I thought we had you good and proper.'

'Good will always overcome evil, didn't they teach you that at Sunday school?'

Prince laughed. 'Well it's been nice talking to you, but I need to score my hat-trick.' And with that he went in search of the ball.

Nick needed to act fast, remove the threat of Alan Prince and inspire his team to score three goals. He knew what he had to do; by keeping close to Prince, it made him drift out to the wing to find space. Nick let him wander, keeping about ten yards away. Then it happened: Prince received the ball wide on the left and started to make progress down the wing. Nick chased him, and as soon as he was in catching distance he executed a perfect sliding tackle. Perfect, except a fraction too late, and a fraction too high. Prince felt the full force of Nick's studs as they broke his Fibula.

Prince screamed in agony. The referee, Mr Burridge the English teacher, came running over. 'I say, young Nick. That was a bit late.'

'Sorry sir,' replied Nick. 'I got there as soon as I could.'

Mr Freeman, who was a trained first-aider, rushed over to examine Prince. 'It looks broken; we'll need to call an ambulance.' He looked at Nick, shook his head and said, 'Terrible accident.'

An ambulance was called and the game was suspended for 30 minutes whilst they waited for assistance. Prince was then taken to hospital and the game continued. Losing Alan Prince and being reduced to ten men had the desired effect and the Camp team looked a shadow of their former selves. It didn't take long for Sandridge to score, a fine through ball from Nick set up Keith for his first goal. Barry Dudley scored the second, Keith headed the third and Nick sealed victory with a well taken penalty. Sandridge won 4-2 and were in the final of the St Albans Benevolent Cup.

As they cycled home Keith said, 'I can't believe we won that, talk about the underdog coming out on top.'

'Well, that's the second time it's happened in the last two days,' replied Nick.

'What do you mean?'

'Well, didn't you hear? Cassius Clay beat Sonny Liston to become the World Heavyweight boxing champion last night.'

Keith laughed, 'well, he took out an ugly bear and so did you.'

Friday 28 February 1964

The following Friday, Nick, Keith and Don were sitting in Nick's front room watching *Ready Steady Go*. Nick was particularly excited because his favourite pop star, Cilla Black, who was currently number one in the charts with her song *Anyone Who Had a Heart,* was performing tonight.

When the programme had finished, Keith started moaning about the rural science lesson he had had that morning.

'It was so boring,' he exclaimed. 'Old F.B.I. went on and on about the beauty of rhododendrons. Did you know there are over 1000 species and they can be evergreen or deciduous?'

'Not interested,' said Don.

'Sorry,' said Nick. 'What did you say?'

'He was talking about boring rhododendrons,' interrupted Don.

'And did you know that it has been reported that the plant has anti-inflammatory and hepatoprotective functions against related diseases?' continued Keith. 'Anyway where were you during that lesson?'

'Had a doctor's appointment - that's it!' exclaimed Nick, jumping from his seat. 'At last I've remembered what Mr Campion said.'

Together, both Keith and Don said 'What?'

'Nick, my boy, look under the rhododendron,' blurted out Nick. 'That's what he said.'

'What does that mean?' enquired Don.

'I think he must have hidden something there and I think he wanted me to find it.'

'Is there something you haven't told us?' asked Keith with a very inquisitive look.

'Well, yes,' replied Nick dying to tell them everything, 'but I'm sworn to secrecy'.

'I know I'm going to regret this, but what happens now?' asked Keith.

'Let me think,' said Nick standing up and looking out of the window. 'We need to find the rhododendron bush he was referring to. Keith, you seem to be an expert. Do you know what a rhododendron bush looks like?'

'Of course I do. F.B.I. showed us one in the school garden.'

'That's it; that must be the one Mr Campion was referring to.'

'So what do we do now?' asked Don.

'Simple,' said Nick. 'We go and dig it up.'

'And when do you intend to do that?' asked Keith.

'We shall go tonight, right away, once we've assembled the equipment,' replied Nick.

'What do you mean – we?' enquired Keith.

'Listen chaps, as I've said: I'm sworn to secrecy, but I can tell you - this is of national importance. Think of it as an adventure. We might even get a medal.'

'Okay,' said Don. 'I'm always ready to serve my country. Tell me what to do.'

'I know I'm going to regret this, but I'm in,' said Keith reluctantly.

'Good lads. This is the plan; go home and get your bikes and a flashlight. We'll also need some digging tools. I'll get my dad's spade. Can you two bring a trowel each? Meet back here at 20:30.'

Nick was waiting outside his house mounted on his bike, holding his dad's garden spade when Keith and Don returned.

'Okay, lads,' Nick said. 'We'll cycle to the school, leave the bikes where no one can see them, just follow me and I'll show you. We'll climb over the fence there and make our way to the garden. They haven't employed another caretaker yet so nobody should be about.'

'What about Mrs Campion?' asked Keith. 'Is she still living in the bungalow?'

'I'm not sure,' replied Nick. 'We'll ride past and see if there is a light on, but I don't think she will be wandering around the school grounds.'

There were no lights on in the bungalow when the three boys cycled past. To the right of the school there was some waste land adjacent to the bike shed. They left their bikes there, out of sight from anyone passing by and climbed over the adjacent fence. Using their flashlights they made their way to the school garden where Keith identified the now famous rhododendron bush.

'Right, chaps,' said Nick, as they gathered round the bush. 'The ground looks reasonably soft so this shouldn't take long.'

Nick was holding his dad's spade, which hadn't been that easy to carry whilst cycling his bike. 'Shine your torches down there and I'll start digging.'

'I was thinking,' interrupted Keith. 'We don't know what we are looking for and to start digging away with that thing might damage it. I suggest we use the trowels and dig carefully.'

'Good point,' said Nick. 'Okay, well I don't have a trowel, so you two start digging and I'll hold the flashlight and keep watch.'

Keith and Don got down on their knees and started carefully digging around the base of the bush.'

Keith looked at Don and whispered, 'How did he do that?'

'I heard that,' chuckled Nick. 'Less talking and more digging.'

It was a full five minutes before Don said, 'I think I've found something'.

Nick dropped to his knees and said, 'Show me.'

Don carefully scraped away some earth to reveal an old Golden Virginia tobacco tin.

He picked it up and shook it, then said, 'There's something inside.'

'Okay,' said Nick, snatching the tin from Don. 'Quickly, fill the hole in and let's get out of this place.'

Nick put the tin in his rucksack, grabbed his spade and started pushing the soil around the bush. When he was satisfied he said, 'That will do. Let's go.'

It didn't take them long to climb back over the fence and cycle back to Nick's house. In their rush to get home they failed to notice the light in a window of the caretaker's bungalow, and the outline of Mrs Campion.

Without saying hello to anyone, the three boys ran upstairs to Nick's bedroom. They sat in a circle on the floor looking at the rusty tobacco tin which was placed in the middle of them.

'I think we should open it, because it's getting late and I should be home,' said Don.

'You know how Nick likes to be dramatic,' replied Keith.'

'Okay, I'll open it,' said Nick grabbing the tin and prising the lid off. Inside the tin they found a small key wrapped in a piece of paper. On the paper was written

REX+5!-1

'What does that mean?' asked Keith.

'Well,' said Nick, 'We have a key, so this must be a clue to what the key opens.'

'No shit, Sherlock, I know that. What does the code mean?'

'No idea, but Don's right, it's getting late. Let's meet up tomorrow when are minds are fresh and I'm sure we'll crack the code.'

Saturday 29 February 1964

Nick had suggested that they needed an early start so he invited Keith and Don for breakfast. Mrs Allen liked to entertain, and she always made a fuss of her guests. So the three boys sat down to enjoy a full English breakfast. First course was a bowl of prunes which Mrs Allen insisted they had because 'it would make them regular'. This was followed by a plate of egg, bacon, sausage and fried bread. Toast and marmalade was available if they had any room left. Nick explained to his Mum that this was a business breakfast and they had lots of things to discuss. Mrs Allen thought how good it was to see the lads playing nicely.

As they sipped on their tea and nibbled on their toast, Nick asked, 'Any ideas on the code?'

Don was the first to answer. 'I was thinking about the REX part. Isn't REX a dog's name?'

'How silly of us,' giggled Keith. 'All we need to do is find a dog that's got a keyhole instead of an arsehole.'

Nick and Don burst out laughing.

Mrs Allen turned to her husband who was doing the washing up, and said, 'It's so good to see him happy again.'

Composing himself, Nick said, 'Let's look up REX in the dictionary and see what it says.'

'Good idea,' replied Keith.

'Dad,' Nick shouted. 'Can you get the dictionary, please?'

'What did your last servant die of' replied Mr Allen as he wiped his hand dry.

'Not doing as he was told,' laughed Nick.

'Cheeky sod,' said Mr Allen throwing the dictionary at Nick.

'Thanks, Dad.'

Nick quickly open the dictionary and turned to the relevant page. 'Here it is – Rex-Reigning king. That's it, king and the plus sign – Kings Cross. Gosh, that was easy. It must be a key to a left luggage locker and the other part must be the number.'

'Five something, take away one. I wonder what the exclamation mark means?' asked Keith.

'Never seen that before; I'll have to ask Dad. He is good at maths. Dad' shouted Nick, 'you're needed again.'

'And what is it this time, Your Highness,' asked Mr Allen.

'Sorry to bother you ol' chap' said Nick, putting on his posh voice. 'What does an exclamation sign mean in mathematics?'

'An exclamation sign means factorial. For example – six factorial means six times five times four times three times two times one; easy.'

'Thank you, Jeeves. You may go now.'

Mr Allen smiled and gave Nick a playful slap on the head.

'So,' said Nick. 'Five factorial must mean five times four times three times two times one, which is one hundred and twenty.'

'Therefore,' interrupted Keith. 'One hundred and twenty minus one is one hundred and nineteen. That's the number of the left luggage locker at

Kings Cross station. Elementary, my dear chap,' he smiled and shouted, 'more toast, Mrs Hudson.'

The boys finished their breakfast, thanked Mrs Allen and then made their way to the back garden.

'What happens now?' asked Keith.

'We take a trip to London, recover whatever is hidden in the left luggage locker and crack the case,' replied Nick. 'But I'll tell you one thing; supposing we unravel the whole matter, you may be sure that someone else will pocket all the credit. That comes of being an unofficial personage.'

Permission was granted and all three boys were allowed to go to London on the pretext of train spotting. They purchased their tickets and made their way to platform one. As they stood there Don asked, 'is this going to be dangerous?'

'Shouldn't be, all we are going to do is collect whatever is in the locker,' replied Nick.

'And then?'

'Well, that depends what's in the locker. We'll take it home, examine whatever it is, then make a decision.'

Keith, who was taking this journey very seriously, was scouring the platform. Suddenly he said, 'Nick, I think we have a problem.'

'What is it?' asked Nick.

'Look,' pointing down the platform. 'Isn't that your friend, Mrs Campion.'

'Do you think see has seen us?'

'I wouldn't be surprised; do you think she's following us?'

'Not sure, but we can't take the risk. Tell you what, let's sit on that bench and pretend we are actually train spotting, and then we'll get the next train.'

Being prepared for every eventuality, each boy took out a note book and pencil and sat waiting patiently for the next train. The eleven fifty to St Pancras was on time, and the boys duly took its number and watched as Mrs Campion boarded it. As the train chugged out of the station the three boys all waved at Mrs Campion as she contemptuously looked out of her window.

'How long till the next train?' asked Don.

'Fifteen minutes; just enough time to grab a cup of tea,' replied Nick.

The journey to St. Pancras was uneventful; the boys took a few train numbers just to pass the time. Once they arrived, they left the station, took the short walk to King Cross station, and quickly found the left luggage room. Nick had an uneasy feeling about this. Perhaps he should have phoned Arthur and Peter; was he getting carried away again thinking he could do it all himself. No, he thought; he would recover whatever is in the locker, check it out and if it was important then he would phone them.

'Do you think we've been followed?' asked Keith.

'Not sure,' replied Nick, now getting extremely nervous.

'What's the plan?'

'Okay, this is how we play it. I'll go to the locker and remove the contents. You two keep watch from a safe distance. If you see anything suspicious, warn me or create a scene or something. Okay?'

'Good plan. I'll go in first and stand the other side of the locker. Don, you stay this side. That way Nick's covered from both sides. When you've retrieved whatever is in the locker, make your way back here. I'll be covering your back. Then we'll make a bolt back to St Pancras.'

Nick was surprised and impressed by how calm Keith was and Don just looked as if he was enjoying himself.

Keith entered the room and casually walked past locker 119 and parked himself about twenty yards away. Nick had a good look around before he went in. It looked safe enough. He approached the locker, breathing heavily as he inserted the key. Closing his eyes he gave it a turn. Click. It opened. He looked inside. There was an old briefcase. He took a deep breath, took out the briefcase, closed the door, locked it and walked away. Keith, whose eyes were everywhere, waited a few seconds then followed Nick out. Nick stopped when he reached Don, looked at him and nodded. Don nodded back. A few seconds later Keith reached them and said, 'All clear. Let's just take it easy and not draw attention to ourselves. So they casually walked back to St Pancras.

It was 2:00 pm when the boys arrived back at St Albans station.

'What are we going to do now?' asked Don.

'We can't really go home; it's too early. Let's pop along to the cinema and see what's on.' replied Nick.

'I think they are still showing *From Russia With Love* at the Gaumont,' said Keith.

'Excellent,' said Nick, 'and very appropriate.'

Monday 2 March 1964

'What did you do with the briefcase?' asked Keith as he walked with Nick after parking their bicycles in the bike shed the following Monday morning.

'I've hid it safe at home,' replied Nick.

'I thought you were going to give it to those men you know.'

'I will, in a few days. I still think Mrs Campion's involved somehow, and I'm a bit suspicious about Mr Bilk.'

'Do you think they're in it together?'

'Could be; now listen, if anything suspicious happens to me today or I give you the nod, I want you to phone this number and ask for Arthur Martin. He'll know what to do.'

'Do you think someone else is after the briefcase?'

'We'll soon find out.'

Just before the end of their last period, whilst Nick was trying to solve a particularly difficult simultaneous equation, the school secretary, an efficient woman in her mid-fifties with permed white hair, came into the class and whispered something to Mr Asher, the maths teacher. He nodded to her and she left.

'Nick,' he called, 'Mr Bilk would like to see you after school in his class room.'

'Okay, sir, thank you,' replied Nick, turning to Keith and giving him the nod.

When the school bell rang for the end of the day, Keith packed his things away very quickly and rushed out of the classroom; Nick needed to kill some time to allow Keith to contact the authorities. First, he had a word with Mr Asher, asking him to explain how to solve the equation he was struggling with. Following that he paid a visit to the toilet and then walked very slowly to the rural science classroom. When he entered, Mr Bilk was waiting.

'Ah, there you are, young Allen, thought you weren't coming,' he said. 'Come in, come in. I expect you are wondering why I wanted to see you.'

'It had crossed my mind,' replied Nick putting his bag down and leaning against a cupboard.

'Well, just wait here a moment. Someone wants a quiet word with you.'

Nick smiled to himself; no points for guessing who that will be, he thought.

Three minutes later Mr Bilk returned with Mrs Campion.

'Hello, Mrs Campion, or whatever your name is,' said Nick.

'You think yourself so smart,' replied Mrs Campion with that accent Nick couldn't place. But it could be Russian he thought. 'Where are those papers, I know you have them?'

'Sorry,' said Nick. 'Don't know what you are talking about.'

'And where is the money?' demanded Mr Bilk.

Nick looked confused. 'Definitely know nothing about any money.'

Mr Bilk looked crossly at Mrs Campion. 'You said he had the money.'

'There is no money, you fool; it's the papers I want,' she snapped as she pulled out a small revolver from her handbag.

'There is no need for that; I'm getting out of here,' said Mr Bilk as he made for the door.

'You're going nowhere,' she said as she aimed the gun and fired. Mr Bilk fell to his knees. She quickly turned, pointing the gun at Nick and said, 'You see. I'm not mucking around. Give me those papers.'

As she came closer to Nick, he quickly grabbed the wrist holding the gun with his left hand. At the same time he grabbed the barrel with his right hand pushing it towards her, rolling it against her thumb. She seemed to freeze as the barrel pointed towards her. Nick saw his chance and head butted her straight on the nose. She screamed as the blood sprayed out. Nick grabbed the gun and threw it down the classroom then caught her with a beautiful right hook to the chin. She was out cold before she hit the ground. Nick looked around and found some garden string and quickly tied her hands and feet. He then went to attend Mr Bilk who wasn't badly injured. The bullet had hit him on the shoulder. There was no exit wound which meant there wasn't much blood. Nick pulled out his handkerchief and told Mr Bilk to hold against his wound. At that point, Arthur Martin burst in followed by four uniformed policemen and Keith Nevin.

'Looks like you've got it all under control,' said a smiling Arthur Martin.

'The things I do for my country,' replied Nick, with an even bigger smile on his face.

'You've got the papers?'

'Yes, sir, they're safe.'

'Good, well you better get off home and let me clear up here. I'll meet you tomorrow after school; I believe there's a nice little coffee bar at the top of the town called Sally's. I'll be there about 4 o'clock, and don't forget those papers.'

Tuesday 3 March 1964

Arthur Martin was already seated when Nick entered Sally's the following day. Arthur was sipping a double espresso, and a delicious looking strawberry milkshake with ice cream was waiting for Nick. Nick handed over the briefcase which Arthur immediately examined. After about five minutes, Arthur said, 'it's exactly what we thought: Anthony Blunt is the fourth man; it's all here.'

'So why didn't Mr Campion give you the papers, and who was Mrs Campion, and how is Mr Bilk involved?'

Arthur laughed, 'One question at a time. Now listen and I'll tell you all; well, what I can. Politics and ideologies are a strange thing; it's difficult to believe 100% of what a political party stands for, and the same goes for an ideology. When you are a double agent, you can see bits of good in both sides, which can confuse you. Sometimes, if you are a double agent, you can even forget whose side you are actually on. Mr Campion was a good friend of Anthony Blunt so he was a bit reluctant to turn him in. Mrs Campion, who was in love with Blunt, wanted to destroy the evidence.'

'Was Mr Blunt in love with Mrs Campion?' asked Nick.

'Hardly, you see he batted for the other side.'

'What does that mean?'

'You'll find out one day.'

'Anyway, Mrs Campion is well, ugly.'

'Apparently she was a bit of a looker in her day.'

'If you say so; now what about Mr Bilk?'

Arthur laughed. 'Well, he was in love with Mrs Campion. She told him that Mr Campion was hiding a lot of money which really belonged to her and she needed his help to find it. She promised that they would run off together and live happily ever after.'

'The poor deluded fool. So was Mr Campion murdered?'

'That's the sad part – he was.'

'That's awful. How was it done?'

'We have you to thank for that. The person you saw leaving the class room wearing a bowler hat was a top Russian assassin. We don't know his name.'

'Gosh, how did he kill him?'

'We think he used an umbrella gun. An autopsy was performed and it was found that Mr Campion's lungs were full of fluid - due to heart failure - and that his liver was damaged due to blood poisoning. His intestines, lymph nodes, and heart were riddled by small haemorrhages, and his white blood cell count was shockingly high. During the autopsy, a large block of tissue was cut from around a 2 mm diameter puncture wound on Mr Campion's right thigh. In it, the examiners discovered a strange 1.52-mm wide metal pellet, about the size of the head of a pin. The pellet was actually a jeweller's watch bearing, used in precision watch making. This pellet had been drilled and filled with a poison called Ricin.'

Nick sipped his milkshake.

'So what will happen now?'

'Well, Mr Wright and I will be having a quiet word with Anthony Blunt[9] very soon.'

'I suppose this will go in my file.'

'I expect so.'

'No medals then?'

'Not this time.'

'I still can't believe that old Bilky fancied Mrs Campion.'

'Not everyone has your impeccable taste in women, Nick. By the way how is Christine these days?'

'She seems okay. I think she likes receiving my letters. They cheer her up.'

'That's good. You're a kind and thoughtful lad. Now I better be going. Oh I've bought you some comics and magazines; I think you'll find them educational.'

With that he stood up, shook Nick's hand and said, 'Goodbye for now Nick, but I think we might be meeting again soon.'

That evening Nick was telling Keith and Don about the events in the rural science class room. When he had finished and had answered all their questions, Keith said 'What shall we do now?'

'I think,' Nick replied, 'we shall do some revising.'

'Revising what?' exclaimed Keith.

'Human biology. Mr Martin gave me a new text book, see?' He handed a magazine to Don.

'Wow,' said Don opening the centrefold of the latest edition of *Parade*. 'That's what I call a nice Catholic girl.'

PART 4

IT'S A CRUEL WORLD

Friday 6 March 1964

'What the hell are you supposed to be?' asked Mrs Allen, a pretty, petite woman in her late thirties, trying to suppress a giggle.

Nick Allen, a fourteen-year old schoolboy of average height, with a mop of light brown hair and twinkling blue eyes, stood there wearing black plimsolls, his black school trousers, a black V-neck sweater over a black t-shirt and a black balaclava. On his face he had smeared black boot polish.

'We are on a special operation tonight,' he replied, feeling a little self-conscious.

'And what would that be, Nick?' she asked, biting her bottom lip to stop herself from laughing.

'I'm afraid I can't reveal that information. If I did, I would have to kill you.'

Before Mrs Allen could reply there was a knock on the back door.

'I'll go,' said Mr Allen who was a year older than his wife and looked a lot like Tyrone Powell. 'Hello, Keith. Go through, they are in the living room.'

'Hello,' said Keith, who was one of Nick's best friends; they were in the same class at school. Keith was a good two inches taller than Nick and had black hair and a slight oriental look due to his mother being Vietnamese.

The sight of Keith was too much for Mrs Allen and she burst out laughing. She had to leave the room for fear of wetting herself in front of her family.

Keith was dressed similarly to Nick; he was wearing his best black shoes, a black track suit zipped up to his neck, a black balaclava and he also had black boot polish on his face.

'I think we'd better be going,' said Nick, slightly embarrassed. 'I'm glad we've amused you but we have important business to attend to.'

'Have fun and don't get into trouble,' replied Mr Allen who was now used to Nick's strange behaviour.

With that, Nick and Keith disappeared through the kitchen and out of the back door. Mrs Allen re-appeared in the living room, streaks of mascara running down her cheeks.

'Don't you think it's a bit strange that Nick is still dressing up and playing army games at fourteen?' asked Mr Allen.

'Perhaps, but we don't want him to grow up too quickly. It won't be long before he's smoking and chasing girls and think of all the problems that will bring,' replied Mrs Allen. 'Let him play for a little while longer.'

Nick Allen lived on a council estate consisting of approximately 300 brick-built houses. This estate was built after the war in the early 1950s and situated in a valley between Batchwood Golf course to the north and some waste ground at the back of the hospital to the south. There was a track between the back of the houses and the waste ground. This track was commonly referred to as "the Lane". It was wide enough for a single small vehicle; anything bigger would get badly scratched by the thick hedgerows on either side. There was access to the back gardens of the houses from the Lane. Nick and Keith were rendezvousing with an older boy called Charlie Roberts at the end of the lane. Charlie was an ordinary looking lad of about sixteen years of age; average height, brown hair and a plain face, not the sort of lad who would stand out in a crowd. But Charlie's one outstanding feature was coming up with bizarre money-making ideas.

'Good,' said Charlie as Nick and Keith approached him. 'You're on time. What have you done to your faces?'

'You told us to wear dark clothes so we won't be seen, so we went the whole way.' replied Keith.

Charlie shook his head, 'whatever, as long as you are here. Have you got the money?'

Nick and Keith each gave Charlie a shilling.

'This better be worth it,' said Nick.

'It will be,' replied Charlie. 'All part of your education.'

Charlie led Nick and Keith along the lane for about 100 yards.

'Here we are,' said Charlie, standing beside the back gate to one of the houses. 'The show should start in about five minutes.'

Nick and Keith quietly entered the garden through the back gate and climbed onto the brick shed situated to the right. There was a steep gradient down to the house which was about 80 feet away, and from the top of the shed you would get a good view into the back bedroom. As they climbed onto the roof of the shed, they noticed that two other boys were already there lying down facing the house. Nick was not familiar with the boys, but they looked about the same age and dressed all in black.

'Hi,' said Nick. 'I'm Nick and this is Keith.'

'Hello,' said the boy nearest to Nick. 'I'm Chris and this is Julian.'

'Been here before?' asked Keith.

'Fourth time,' replied Chris. 'Worth every penny.'

So the four boys lay there looking towards the house. Nick and Keith had brought their binoculars. Nick noticed that Chris had an expensive looking pair whilst Julian had a large brass telescope.

'What's the format?' asked Nick.

'Well,' replied Chris. 'She normally gets home in about five minutes, goes to the kitchen, puts the kettle on and then goes upstairs to change.'

They waited for about ten minutes before the kitchen light came on.

'Here we go,' said Chris excitedly.

They put the binoculars to their eyes and watched. The lady in question was in her mid-thirties with long brown hair and a very large bosom. The boys watched as the lady disappeared. Moments later the bedroom light was turned on and the lady entered. The boys were drooling as the lady stood in front of the window and slowly unbuttoned her blouse, which she then removed and tossed on her bed.

'Warm tonight, isn't it?' remarked Nick.

'Quiet,' said Julian. 'This is the best bit.'

The lady, still standing looking out of the window put her hands behind her back and unclipped, then removed her bra.

'Wow,' said Keith. 'They are magnificent.'

The lady just stood there, completely naked from the waist upwards staring out of the window.

'Is this heaven or what?' asked Chris.

Their tranquillity was broken when a voice shouted, 'You bloody perverts.'

Nick recognised the voice straight away. It was PC Adams, the older brother of Dave Adams, who was in the same class as Nick.

'Run for it,' shouted Chris.

Nick and Keith jumped off the shed roof and ran towards the house; Chris wasn't far behind. Unfortunately Julian, who was slightly overweight and didn't fancy jumping off the shed, was apprehended by PC Adams. There was an alley between the house of the garden they were in and the next house. As they headed towards it, Nick looked up at the bedroom window. He saw the lady, bosom and all, waving as they made good their escape.

When they thought it was safe to stop running they stopped, gasping for breath and laughing nervously.

'That was fun,' said Nick.

'That's never happened before,' said Chris. 'Well, it's been nice meeting you.' And with that he was gone.

'Fancy a hot chocolate back at my place?' asked Nick.

'Why not?' replied Keith. 'By the way who is that woman?'

'Don't know her real name, but she is fondly referred to as "the body". She's an Avon rep, often comes round our house. Mum always sends dad to the living room while they talk in the kitchen.'

It took only a couple of minutes for Nick and Keith to jog back to Nick's house. As they entered the back door Mrs Allen shouted out, 'You're back early.'

'We achieved our objective quicker than expected,' replied Nick.

'Didn't get caught then?' smirked Mr Allen.

'It was close, Mr Allen, very close,' replied Keith.

'Go and wash that muck of your faces and I'll make some hot chocolate,' said Mrs Allen.

The boys ran up the stairs to the bathroom. When they had finished they came down to the front room where Mr and Mrs Allen were waiting with their hot drinks.

'What's wrong with your face?' enquired Mrs Allen looking at the red blotches that had appeared on Nick's forehead and cheeks.

'Think I'm allergic to boot polish' replied Nick.

This time Mrs Allen, who had a wicked sense of humour, did have a small accident as she burst out laughing again.

Saturday 7 March 1964

It was about 10:00 am when Keith and Don, Nick's other friend who was a year younger and attended a Catholic school, called for Nick. The three boys liked to visit the market on Saturday mornings, browse the record shops and generally enjoy the hustle and bustle.

'How did you get on last night? Did you see much? I wish I could have come' said Don, as they walked up Folly Lane towards the town centre.

'You didn't miss much,' replied Nick, playing down the excitement of last night so as not to upset Don too much for missing the event. 'The police turned up so we had to leg it.'

'Okay; so, have you got much to buy today?'

'As a matter of fact I have. Don't forget its Mother's Day tomorrow and I want to get Mum something special,'

'Expect I'll buy my Mum a bunch of flowers. She'll like that,' said Keith.

'I would normally, but she's been a bit stressed lately, what with me keep getting beaten up and having to go to hospital,' replied Nick.

'Good point,' said Keith, 'Any ideas?'

'Thought I'd have a look in that gift shop in St Peters Street, Kings I think it's called. They do some nice stuff, but first we must buy a card.'

Keith and Don agreed and the three of them popped into Heading and Watts, the newsagents in Catherine Street, which stocked a large selection of greetings cards. Having each purchased a nice card, they continued down Catherine Street, turned right at the Painters Arms public house into St Peter's Street and the St Albans market. Nick always felt a buzz of excitement when he heard the cries of the street vendors. He remembered his mum pushing him in his pushchair to visit the cattle market on a Wednesday. She would take him to the fence so that he could watch the animals being paraded and listening to the 'bellows' of the auctioneer, which sounded like some foreign language. As soon as one cow had been paraded around the circular ring or `stall` and sold on, another would be forced in through the huge iron gates and the process repeated. And so it went on until all were sold.

Kings was situated just a few shops passed Adelaide Street. The boys entered and immediately started looking at the large selection of leather gifts on offer.

'Well, if it isn't my favourite boy, Nick Allen, come to visit me,' said a voice from behind the counter.

The boys turned round to see a gorgeous girl in her late teens with dark brown hair in a bouffant style and big beautiful brown eyes.

Nick's eyes lit up as he recognised the girl, it was Jane Goldberg; she had rescued him when he had been attacked two months earlier. His mouth went instantly dry and his tongue seemed to have swollen to twice its size. 'Hello, Jane,' he managed to say.

'Not coming over all bashful?' she asked, trying not to laugh. 'Is there anything in particular you're looking for?

Don came to the rescue as Keith had also been struck dumb. 'He's looking for something special for Mothers' Day.'

'That's nice,' she replied. 'Well, just have a look round while I serve this other customer.'

'Okay,' croaked Nick.

The boys continued to look whilst Jane sold an expensive looking handbag to an elderly gentleman.

'She's a bit of alright,' whispered Keith.

Nick just smiled. At that point the shop door opened and an attractive blonde girl wearing black boots and a short black and white dress. She had blue eyes, a button nose and Nick thought there was something vaguely familiar about her.

'Another cracker,' gasped Keith. 'No wonder you wanted to come in here'

The new girl waved to Jane. As the elderly gentleman left the shop, Jane said, 'Nick, I want you to meet my sister Veronica; you can call her Ronnie. Ronnie this is my good friend, Nick Allen, and his friends whom I don't know.'

Keith reacted first, offering his hand. 'My name is Keith and this is Don.'

'It's nice to meet you all,' replied Ronnie, smiling and shaking each of the boys' hands in turn.

'Well,' said Jane. 'This is nice. Now have you decided what to buy?'

'I quite like this purse' said Nick as he regained his power of speech.

'Excellent choice, would you like it gift wrapped?'

'That would be great, thank you,' replied Nick.

The purchase was made and the boys said their farewells and continued their way through the market.

'Let's go to the Record Room[10], I want to buy a record,' said Nick.

'Another sloppy love song I expect,' sighed Keith.

'Absolutely; *I Think of You* by the Merseybeats. It's a beautiful song.'

Don pretended to retch by putting two fingers in his mouth.

Whilst the three boys were browsing through the LPs they were approached by a tall good-looking boy with brown shoulder length hair wearing a white tee-shirt and jeans. 'Hi, Nick. Looking for anything special?'

'Hello, John,' replied Nick, who recognised the boy as John Holland, a 4th year at Nick's school. 'Just looking, can't afford LPs on my pocket money.'

'Are you going to the dance at Mandeville School next Saturday? The King Bees are playing.'

'Hadn't thought of it, never been to a dance before. I'll have to ask my parents, but they should be okay. Are you up for it, Keith?'

'Sounds great, but what shall I wear?' asked Keith.

John laughed. 'Smart casual. Try to make yourself look a little older. There should be loads of birds there; guaranteed to pull.'

John joined the boys as they shuffled through the LPs, showing each other ones they liked. 'Who are Spurs playing this afternoon?' he asked.

'Home to Everton, will be a tough game; already lost to them once this season.'

'Did you read in the Herts Ad about those girls going missing?' asked John.

'No, didn't have time last night; we were a bit busy,' replied Nick.

Keith sniggered and Nick gave him a quick kick on the ankle.

'According to the paper, three local girls all aged between 15 and 18, all blonde, have just disappeared. Apparently, they all went clubbing or to a youth club and never came home.'

'That's awful,' said Don. 'Their parents must be worried silly.'

When they'd had enough of records the three boys said goodbye to John and decided it was time for refreshment, so they made their way to Christopher's coffee shop in French Row. They found a table by the window and ordered three milkshakes.

'Strange about those girls going missing,' said Nick looking down at his empty glass.

'I know what you are thinking,' replied Keith. 'Don't get involved.'

'I don't know what you mean!' gasped Nick.

'You nearly got yourself shot a few weeks ago.'

'I know, but I just think we should be vigilant.'

Monday 9 March 1964

'Did your Mum like her present?' asked Keith as he unlocked his bicycle at the end of the school day.

'She loved it,' replied Nick. 'We had a really nice day. Dad cooked Sunday lunch and then we went for a walk round the lake in the afternoon. Did your Mum like her flowers?'

'Of course; she loves daffs. They're her favourite.'

'Excellent. Oh, have you heard where they're playing the final of the Benevolent Cup?'

'Well, rumour has it that it's being played on Good Friday at Clarence Park - the home ground of St Albans City FC.'

'That will be fantastic. Just imagine running out of the tunnel to the roar of the crowd and playing on a full size pitch with a proper referee and linesmen.'

'Clarence Park is quite a big pitch so we'll have to be really fit.'

'Absolutely, so I think we need to do some extra training.'

'Okay, what do you suggest?'

'Well, it doesn't get dark till six-thirty; so let's get home quickly, get changed and I'll meet you on the green.'

'That's a plan. I'll call for Don on the way.'

So Nick and Keith cycled home from school, changed into their football kit and met later at the playing field at the edge of the estate, commonly known as "the green"

'Right,' said Nick. 'First, we'll run a couple of laps; then we'll do some ball work.'

Nick led the run; they started with a gentle jog and then, on his command, they sprinted for ten yards. On the second lap, Nick increased the sprints to twenty yards.

'Well done,' said Nick. 'Now I think we should take turns in dribbling. I'll start by attacking you two, and then you can have a go.'

Nick took the ball and started running with it towards Keith, then swerved his body to his right. Keith thought he was going to pass him that side but Nick then swayed back to the left and leaving him off-balance, slipped the ball past him. He repeated the same procedure as Don tried to make the tackle.

Feeling pleased with himself, and grinning from ear to ear, Nick said, 'That's how you do it; now it's your turn.'

For the next fifteen minutes the boys took turns in practicing their dribbling techniques. Nick also explained that if you go in for a tackle and lose the ball, don't lose your balance, otherwise you will be in no position to recover and chase after the ball.

Feeling a little exhausted, the boys decided to take a small rest. While they were talking, they were distracted by the sight of a blonde girl in her school uniform walking across the green.

'She looks nice,' leered Keith. 'Do you know her?'

'No,' replied Nick, 'haven't seen her around here before.'

As they watched her walk across the road to the foot path, a blue and white Ford Anglia pulled up beside her. The passenger side window was wound down and the driver leant over to speak to the girl.

'Do you think he's trying to chat her up?' asked Don.

'Well, he's not having much luck. Look, she's walking off,' replied Nick.

As the girl started to walk away, the driver of the car got out and grabbed her. With one hand gripping her arm, he opened the passenger door with the other and tried to force her into the car. The boys looked on in shock.

Nick was the first to react, screaming, 'He's trying to kidnap her! Come on and bring the ball.'

The boys ran to the road; the car was about twenty yards away. The man had managed to force the girl into the car and was driving towards the boys. Nick grabbed the ball from Don and kicked it with all his strength towards the car. It hit the windscreen with such force it made the driver lose control of the car, and the boys stood, mouths open, as the car mounted the kerb and hit a lamp-post.

'Let's go and rescue the girl,' said Nick, running towards the car.

They quickly ran to the passenger side of the car. Nick opened the door and screamed to the girl, 'Quickly. Get out. You're safe now.'

The girl hesitated and gave Nick a confused look. By this time the driver of the car had got out and started screaming at Nick.

'What the hell do you think you are doing?'

The girl hadn't moved by the time Keith and Don arrived.

'We saw you try and kidnap this girl,' barked Keith. 'You're in a lot of trouble now, matey.'

'Kidnap? You stupid boys. This is my daughter and she should have been home an hour ago,' said the man, who was about forty dressed in a drab suit and had more than a passing resemblance to the girl.

'Oops,' said Nick.

'And look at the state of my car.'

Nick looked at the front of the car and said, 'doesn't look too bad; just a small dent in the bumper.'

'And what are you going to do about it?' he screamed.

Nick looked at Keith, then Don. They looked back and both gave a small nod.

'Run,' said Nick, as the three boys ran as fast as they could towards the lane. As soon as they reached the lane, they headed for a small hiding place which they knew. Once inside and completely out of sight, Keith spoke: 'That went well…I don't think.'

'Easy mistake,' replied Nick, slightly blushing.

Keith shook his head. 'You're obsessed. Kidnapping, murders, conspiracies, that's all you see now.'

'That's a bit tough,' said Don. 'It did look a bit odd and blonde girls are going missing. It's best to be safe than sorry. That's what I say.'

The boys were quiet for a moment before Keith, said 'Well at least she can tell all her mates that she was rescued by three knights in shining armour.'

'More like three nutters in muddy football boots,' smirked Don.

The three boys all burst out laughing. Then they left their hiding place and walked home for their tea.

'Actually, she wasn't a bad looker was she?' commented Keith.

Wednesday 11 March 1964

It was a cold miserable afternoon when Nick and Keith made their way to the changing rooms for their favourite lesson of the week – games.

'What do you think we'll do this afternoon?' asked Keith. 'It's drizzling a bit so we might have to stay in the gym.'

'I hope not,' replied Nick. 'With the cup final coming up soon I want as much practice as possible.'

The boys made their way to their usual spot in the changing room and started to change into the sports kit. The rest of the class were already there, having decided it was warmer there than in the playground.

'Have you heard?' a voice whispered to Nick. It was Gordon Booth, a tall, lanky lad with long hair who wasn't a bad goalkeeper, 'Mr Freeman's been suspended.'

'You're joking,' gasped Nick. 'Why?'

'No idea. No one's seen him since last week.'

'So who's taking games?'

'Not sure, but rumour has it they've employed a temporary sports master.'

'I hope he likes football.'

Nick's question was quickly answered when the door to the sports office opened and a giant of a man appeared. He stood at least six foot four inches; with blonde hair, broad shoulders and slim at the hips. Any good looks that he might have had were spoilt by his cauliflower ears and twisted nose. He was carrying two rugby balls.

'Quiet, please,' he bellowed. 'My name is Mr Large and I'll be your sports master for the near future. Are there any questions?'

'When will Mr Freeman be back?' asked Keith.

'Oh, I don't think you'll be seeing him for a long time', replied Mr Large with a smirk on his face. 'I think our Mr Freeman will soon be looking for a new job. Now, if there are no more questions, let us make our way to the playing field.'

'Excuse me, sir,' interrupted Nick 'but I think your balls are the wrong shape.'

Mr Large turned and looked at Nick and said in a raised voice 'what's wrong with my balls?'

The class burst out laughing as Mr Large's face turned crimson.

'They are rugby balls, sir. We normally play football, and footballs are round.'

'Sorry, I see what you mean,' he replied. 'Well, let me tell you, there will be no more football at this school while I'm sports master.'

The class gasped.

'But sir,' said Nick, 'what about the Benevolent Cup final? We need to practice and we much prefer football to rugby.'

'Well, Sonny Jim, you are going to be disappointed. The Headmaster has given me a free hand, so my decision goes.'

There were groans from the rest of the class.

'I'll have to take this up with the Governors,' said Nick, trying to sound a bit authoritarian.

Mr Large wasn't impressed, and asked, 'What's your name, boy?'

'Nick Allen.'

Mr Large laughed. 'So you are the famous Nick Allen. I've heard all about you ….the people's champion; protector of the good; enemy of the bad.'

'That's a bit strong,' protested Keith.

'And you must be his trusty sidekick, Keith Nevin.'

'I didn't come to school to get insulted,' groaned Keith.

'Where do you normally go?' asked Mr Large, laughing at his own joke. 'Now let's get out there and play a proper game. Remember, rugby is a game for gentlemen; football is a game for the lower classes.'

Although Nick quite enjoyed a game of rugby, his heart wasn't in it. He could catch the ball, pass reasonably well and enjoyed making rugby tackles, but his mind was elsewhere. After the lesson as he walked to the bike shed with Keith, he said 'it's no good. I've got to go and see the Headmaster and find out about Mr Freeman.'

'Are you sure; it's really none of our business,' replied Keith.

'We need to find out what's going on. Mr Freeman is a good teacher; I can't see him doing anything wrong. And besides, if he doesn't come back soon, there'll be no more football.'

'I see your point; let's do it.'

Nick and Keith made their way to the Headmaster's office where they met the school secretary, Mrs Kelley, an efficient but stern woman in her mid-fifties with permed white hair.

'And what can I do for you?' she asked looking up from her desk.

'We need to speak to the Headmaster,' replied Nick.

'It's very urgent,' added Keith.

'I'm sure it is,' said Mrs Kelley looking down her nose, 'I'll see if he's free.'

She rose from her desk, knocked and entered the Headmaster's office. She returned within the minute.

'He's free now,' she said, 'but don't be long, he's a very busy man.'

'Thank you,' said Nick sarcastically. 'You're so kind.'

They entered the Headmaster's office. He was seated behind a very tidy desk; he ushered the boys to sit down. Mr Mills was in his late fifties, a tall, distinguished looking man with a good crop of grey hair and a neatly trimmed moustache. 'Now lads, what can I do for you?' he asked.

Nick felt very nervous. He took a deep breath and said, 'Can you tell us why Mr Freeman has been suspended?'

'Straight to the point, I like that' said Mr Mills, 'but no, I can't tell you.'

'That's not fair,' said Keith.

'Life isn't fair, and the sooner you realise it, the better,' replied Mr Mills, as he opened a draw in his desk, took out his pipe and started to fill it.

'I can understand that, but you could at least tell us where he lives so we can visit him; it is very important,' asked Nick.

A very serious look came over Mr Mill's face as he lent forward on his desk and said in a very loud voice, 'under NO circumstances must you ever try to find or attempt to contact Mr Freeman. Is that clear?'

Both boys sat there, mouths open and nodded. They left the office and walked in silence to the bike shed.

'What do we do now?' asked Keith.

'We must find out where Mr Freeman lives,' replied Nick.

'We could look him up in the phone book.'

'Not sure that would work; I think all teachers are ex-directory. Stops unruly kids pestering them; anyway, there must be loads of Freemans in the phone book and I don't even know what his first name is.'

'Why don't you phone your friend from MI5? I'm sure he could find his address. After all, he owes you a favour?'

Nick, a short time earlier had befriended an MI5 agent called Arthur Martin when the school caretaker had been recently murdered.

'What other choice do we have? Come on there's a phone box at the end of the road'. The boys quickly cycled the 200 yards to the phone box, jumped off their bicycles and rushed into the booth.

'Hope he's there' said Nick as he put the pennies into the box.

It answered after three rings. Nick pressed button A. A woman answered.

'Can I speak to Arthur Martin, please?' asked Nick.

'Hold on. I'll see if he's available,' she replied.

Nick heard a couple of clicks before a familiar voice said, 'Arthur Martin. How can I help you?'

Feeling very relieved, Nick gasped, 'Thank god you're there, its Nick, Nick Allen.'

'Hello Nick, good to hear from you. I take it by your first remark; this is not a social call?'

Nick gave a nervous laugh. 'I can see why you're head of intelligence; no flies on you. But you are right - I have, or we have, a big problem at the school and I wonder if you could help.'

'Go on, I will if I can.'

'Well, our sports master Mr Freeman has been suspended and the

Headmaster won't tell us why; and when I asked him for his address he got quite angry. He told us that we mustn't try to contact him. But we must help him, and the new sports master is vile, and mean, and he won't let us play football.'

Arthur could tell that Nick was getting quite agitated and said in a soothing voice, 'Okay, Nick, calm down; I can tell that you are upset, so what do you want me to do?'

'We need to talk to him, but we don't know his address, so could you please find out where he lives?'

'That should be okay, I'll phone you back. Are you at home?'

'No we're in a phone box, but Mum will be in getting my tea ready, so leave a message with her.'

'Okay, I'll do that, but listen, Nick: please be very careful. It's normal practice for someone who's been suspended not to have contact with their work colleagues or students where teachers are involved. It could impede the investigation. So, if I get you the address make sure no one finds out that you are visiting him. Is that clear?'

'Understand.'

'Okay, I'll see what I can do.'

'Thank you,' replied Nick as he heard the line disconnect.

'There's a message for you' said Mrs Allen when Nick and Keith walked in the kitchen.

'I've written it down. Ah, here it is,' passing Nick a piece of paper with an address on it.

'Thank you,' said Nick. 'Dalton Street. He lives in Dalton Street.'

'That's not far is it,' replied Keith grinning.

'We'll visit him this evening,' said Nick. 'As soon as it gets dark; Mum, can Keith stay for his tea?'

'Of course he can. We've got Shepherd's Pie, so there is plenty to go round.'

Turning to Keith, Nick said 'Mum makes the best Shepherd's Pie in the world.'

Mrs Allen blushed and said, 'Don't be silly.'

Nick laughed, 'That's because she uses minced lamb and not minced beef like most people do.'

'I'm looking forward to it,' laughed Keith. 'Can I phone my Mum to tell her I'll be late home?'

Dalton Street is located off Catherine Street and consists mainly of terraced Victorian cottages. Nick and Keith stood outside number 15, nervously looking at the windows with all the curtains drawn.

'Are you ready?' asked Nick taking a deep breath.

'It's now or never,' replied Keith biting the inside of his lip.

Nick rang the doorbell and waited. He rang again and was just about to suggest to Keith that they should try again tomorrow, when the door opened. Standing there was a tall plain looking woman in her mid-thirties. She had a stern face, no make-up, thick glasses and her light brown hair pulled back in a pony-tail. They both could tell that she had been crying.

'What do you want?' she snapped.

'We would like to see Mr Freeman. It's urgent,' said Nick in a confident voice.

'I don't think that's possible,' replied the woman.'

'Who is it, darling?' said a voice from inside the cottage. Nick recognised it as belonging to Mr Freeman.

'Just a couple of snotty nosed school kids. Don't worry; I'll soon get rid of them.'

'Charming,' said Keith.

Nick shouted, 'It's me Mr Freeman, Nick Allen! We want to help you.'

'Just cause more trouble' retorted the woman.

Mr Freeman shouted, 'Quickly let them in before anyone sees them.'

Nick and Keith quickly entered the cottage, each giving the woman a little nudge as they walked passed her. From the front door they entered the lounge, a neat room with three comfortable arm chairs, a television on a stand and two floor-to-ceiling bookcases, either side of an open fire place, jam packed with books. There was also a small sideboard on which stood a record player. Nick noticed the album cover next to it, *Joan Baez in Concert*. Walking through the lounge they came to the dining room where Mr Freeman was sitting. He beckoned them to sit with him at the table. The woman followed and stood, arms folded, looking at them.

Mr Freeman smiled and said, 'It's good to see you boys. Please excuse my wife; this whole episode has shaken her up quite badly.'

Nick turned to Mrs Freeman and said, 'we didn't mean to upset you, we just want to help.'

'And how can two schoolboys help my husband?' she asked, as she picked up packet of Consulate cigarettes, taking one out and lighting it. As she blew the smoke into the room Nick thought, she's not cool as a mountain stream.

Mr Freeman smiled again and said, 'don't underestimate these two, they can be quite resourceful. If anybody can help us, it's these two; Nick has friends in very high places.'

Nick blushed, 'that's how we found out where you live. We only heard you had been suspended this afternoon.'

'Hear that, darling? I told you they were good. Now be a good girl and make some tea.'

Mrs Freeman said, 'yes dear,' turned, and went through to the kitchen.

Mr Freeman looked at Nick and smiled. Nick could tell that he was worried. He seemed to have aged ten years; his face was gaunt and there were signs of grey in his hair.

'Can you tell us what happened?' asked Nick.

'Okay. It happened last Friday at about seven o'clock. I'd just finished my tea when there was a knock at the door. It was the Headmaster. I was a bit surprised; he's never called at my house before. I asked him in, but he refused. He just told me that there had been a serious accusation made against me and that I had been suspended. I asked him what sort of accusation and he said that I had acted improperly towards one of my pupils. He gave me a large envelope and said it was all detailed in there. He told me not to contact any other member of staff or students, and to contact my union representative.'

Nick could tell Mr Freeman was getting upset, but at that point Mrs Freeman came in with the tea. 'Shall I pour?' she asked.

'Thank you, darling,' he replied.

The tea was poured and they all took a sip.

'Go on,' encouraged Nick.

It was clear that Mr Freeman was struggling at this point; he took another sip of tea. Mrs Freeman walked over to comfort him. She looked at Nick and said, 'look at him; you're just making matters worse.'

Keith, who was just taking it all in, then said, 'I know this is hard, but if he's innocent he's got nothing to worry about.'

'If he's innocent?' screamed Mrs Freeman, 'If he's innocent? Of course he's innocent. My husband wouldn't do anything like that. It's disgusting.'

Nick stood up and said, 'let's all calm down. Keith was just stating the facts. Remember, this is England, the truth will prevail. Come on now,' Nick encouraged. 'After all, we invented the legal system; it's the best in the world. Remember what Noam Chomsky[11] said: "the first step is to penetrate the clouds of deceit and distortion and learn the truth about the world, then to organize and act to change it. That's never been impossible and never been easy."'

Keith, Mr and Mrs Freeman all put their cups down and stared at Nick with their mouths open.

Nick composed himself and said, 'sorry about that; got a bit carried away.' He sat down. 'Now tell us what you can and who the students involved are.'

Mr Freeman collected himself and continued his story. 'It happened last Thursday. As you know class Upper 4A have their games period last lesson. I was in my office finishing off some paperwork. I thought all the class had changed and gone home, but I noticed there was one set of clothes left. I looked in the communal showers and found Tom Clarke lying on the floor. I bent down to attend to him. He seemed unconscious. He then opened his eyes and started moaning. Then a voice from behind me said, 'what's going on here?' I looked round to see Bob Newland standing there. At that point, Tom stood up and said, 'I'm okay,' then walked into the changing room, dried himself, got dressed and left with Bob.'

'I think I know who Tom is,' said Nick. 'Isn't he that small ginger haired lad with a face full of freckles - bit of a nerd?'

'That's the one and Bob is about six foot tall and captains the school rugby 15.'

'That's right. Wouldn't like to cross him,' replied Nick. He thought for a while then said, 'don't you think they make a strange couple? You wouldn't think they had much in common.'

'It sounds like a set up to me,' intervened Keith.

'So what's their version of events?' asked Nick.

'Apparently, I asked Tom to stay behind on some pretext and when all the other students had left, I told him to take off his clothes and go back in the shower. I then made him lie down and I started abusing him.'

Mrs Freeman started crying and fled into the kitchen.

'That's bollocks!' exclaimed Keith, slamming his fist onto the table.

Mr Freeman dropped his chin onto his chest. Nick got up and followed Mrs Freeman into the kitchen. She was sitting on a high-stool, head in hands. Nick put his arm around her shoulder. She didn't pull away. Instead she turned to him, flung her arms around him, buried her head in his chest and sobbed her heart out. He then put his arms around her and squeezed her gently thinking, what a cruel world this is sometimes. After a couple of minutes she seemed to compose herself, she eased away from him, looked up, smiled, and said, 'I'm sorry.'

Nick smiled back and said, 'Don't worry, I'll clear Mr Freeman's name if it's the last thing I ever do.'

As she looked up at him, Nick thought that if she wore some modern clothes, had a fashionable hair-style, and put some make-up on, she could be quite attractive.

'Go back in the room,' she said, 'I'll just make myself respectable.'

Nick walked back to the dining room and found Keith and Mr Freeman in deep conversation.

'Why would they do something like that; what's there to gain?' asked Nick.

Mr Freeman just shook his head.

'Okay,' said Nick. 'I think we've heard enough. Just leave it to us.'

Yeh,' agreed Keith. 'We'll do our best.'

'No,' replied Nick. 'Only wimps do their best. We'll succeed.'

'Oh,' said Mr Freeman. 'I forgot to tell you. I spent most of Saturday at the police station.'

Nick shook his head and said, 'it doesn't get any better.'

Nick and Keith rose from the table and made their way to the front door.

'We'll call you as soon as we hear something,' said Nick.

'You better not call here again in case someone sees you. I'll give you our phone number. It's safer to phone,' replied Mr Freeman.

'And I'll give you mine, if you hear anything.'

They exchanged phone numbers, said their goodbyes and left. Nick noticed Mrs Freeman in the background; she smiled and gave him a little wave.

When they were outside Keith asked, 'what do you make of that?'

'Something is seriously wrong; this is going to take some serious thinking.'

'I agree. So what happened in the kitchen?'

'Nothing much; I just cuddled Mrs Freeman and she cuddled me back.'

'That's nice; how did it feel?'

'Strange, but nice; actually, I think I felt a little twinge.'

'Too much information.'

Thursday 12th March 1964

'You know, this is my favourite pudding - chocolate sponge with chocolate sauce. Wonder if they do seconds?' said Keith as he scoped another spoonful of pudding.

It was lunchtime and Keith and Nick were sitting in the school canteen.

'Can't you think of anything but your stomach? How are we going to help Mr Freeman? That's what you should be thinking about,' replied Nick.

'I think better on a full stomach.'

'I'm glad about that,' said Nick shaking his head. 'I think first we should have a chat with our friend Tom Clarke. We'll have a wander around the playground; see if we can find him.'

'No need,' said Keith taking another spoonful of pudding. 'He's over there.'

Nick looked over and saw Tom Clarke leave his table and make his way to the door. Nick stood up, grabbed Keith by the arm and said, 'Come on. Let's follow him.'

'Let me finish my pudding first. He's not going anywhere.'

Nick sat down and waited for Keith to finish his chocolate pudding.

After Keith had managed to talk the school cook into giving him a second helping, Nick and Keith eventually found Tom sitting on a bench by the side of the playground, reading a book. They wandered over to him and sat down on either side.

'Hello Tom,' said Nick. 'I think we need to have a little chat.'

'Oh,' he said, without looking up from his book. 'I wondered how long it would take for you two to find me.'

'Why would you say that?' asked Keith.

'They said you would come. Anyway, I've got nothing to say to you.'

At that point Bob Newland appeared. 'Are you okay, mate?' he asked Tom.

'Yes, I'm fine. These two are just leaving.'

Nick looked up at Bob. He towered over them and had a menacing look on his face.

'As long as they are not annoying you then,' he said, staring at Nick.

Nick and Keith stood up and walked away. They found another bench and sat down.

'What do we do now?' asked Keith. 'We're not going to be able to get close to him with that great ape hanging around. We could have tortured him a bit, and made him confess.'

'You're right, but the direct approach is out; I didn't think it would be easy,' replied Nick. 'What we need is information about Tom Clarke. What are his interests? We need to find his weakness, and then perhaps we could blackmail him or something.'

They sat there in silence for a few minutes then Nick's concentration was broken when a tennis ball hit him on the head.

'What the ....' said Nick as he looked up and saw Danny Fooks running towards him. Danny, the stocky captain of the football team, with a mass of uncontrollable curly hair said, 'Sorry, Nick.'

Nick had an idea. 'Have you got a moment, Danny?' he asked.

'Yes, no problem,' he replied picking up the tennis ball and throwing it back to his mates. 'How can I help you?'

'What can tell us about Tom Clarke, he's in you class, isn't he?'

'Is this about Mr Freeman?'

Nick didn't reply.

'If there is anything I can do to help him, just ask. You can trust me.'

'I know I can, Danny, but we don't want to involve too many people. It could all back fire.'

'I understand, so just tell me what I can do?'

'For the moment, can you just tell us what you know about Tom?'

'Not much, really: a bit of a wimp, keeps himself to himself, not many friends, very studious.'

'What's his connection with Bob Newland?'

'I don't know. Up to a few days ago I didn't think Bob knew Tom existed; now they are inseparable.'

'That's strange, but does he have any interests outside school. What are his passions?'

Danny laughed, 'that I do know – rabbits.'

'Rabbits?' said Nick and Keith together.

'Yes, strange isn't it? But our friend Tom loves rabbits. He shows them at fairs. Won a few prizes I hear. Has a fine pair of French Lops, whatever they are.'

Nick smiled. 'Danny, I think you've cracked it. Thanks a lot.'

Danny smiled. 'I'm glad to help. Anything else you want to know, just ask.'

'Just one more thing - where does he live?'

Nick and Keith decided to visit Sally's café on St Peter's Street for a milkshake before cycling home. *Boys Cry* by Eden Kane was blasting out from the juke box. They had also arranged to meet Don there.

'Okay,' said Keith. 'You've had time to think, what are we going to do?'

'I've given this a lot of thought but I will need your help,' replied Nick. 'If this plan is to succeed, it must be carefully planned and meticulously executed.'

'Go on,' said Keith.

'We kidnap his rabbits.'

'Kidnap his rabbits? How is that going to help?'

'Let me finish. First, we kidnap his rabbits. Then, we send him a ransom note demanding he tells the truth, and then we release the rabbits.'

'First thing, where are we going to keep the rabbits?'

'Good question. That's where I need your help. I can't keep them. He's bound to inform the police and the first person they are going suspect is me. So can either of you think of somewhere we can hide them?'

The boys thought for a moment before Don said, 'I like rabbit; my Mum does a great braised rabbit. You need to cook it slowly, about four to five hours, so the meat starts falling of the bone. Delicious.'

Nick and Keith stared in disbelief.

'Sorry,' said Don. 'Got carried away.'

'Thank you,' gasped Nick. 'Now back to the problem. Where are we going to hide the rabbits?'

'No problem,' said Don. 'My uncle, on my Mum's side, has a small-holding in Wheathampstead. I'm sure he will look after them for a few days.'

'Excellent, but how do we get them there? We can't cycle there and we might get seen on a bus.'

'I shouldn't say this, but my uncle is a bit of rogue. You know, a rough diamond. I'll have a word with him and explain what's going on, and he's got a van.'

'It's all falling into place,' said Nick excitedly. 'Now listen. This is the plan. Don, your job is to contact your uncle, talk him round and arrange for him to rendezvous with us at eight o'clock on Monday evening. Keith, we need two strong cardboard boxes and some strong sellotape. Also put some straw in the bottom of the boxes and make some air holes. I'll buy some rabbit food. We'll meet at my place at 7.45 pm. Wear dark clothing.'

Saturday 14 March 1964

Nick was really excited as he prepared himself for his first ever dance. His parents had given him permission to go as long as he was home by 10:30 pm Mrs Allen had bought Nick a new shirt especially for the occasion. It was white with a round collar and two buttons on the side, as worn by Dr Kildare and the Dave Clark Five. Nick thought he looked the business as he finished grooming himself in front of the mirror. The new shirt looked excellent with his blue suit.

'What do you think, Mum?' asked Nick, as he paraded around the living room.

'I think you look very handsome.' replied Mrs Allen. 'What time is Keith coming?'

'He should be here any minute; shame Don couldn't come. His parents said he was too young.'

At that point there was a knock on the back. Mr Allen answered it and escorted Keith through to the living room.

'My, my,' said Mrs Allen when Keith walked in wearing a brand new dark blue velvet jacket over a white shirt and blue kitted tie and black trousers. 'Don't we make a pretty pair?'

Mandeville School was about two miles away, so the two boys put on their cycle clips, not wanting to get oil on their trousers. Fifteen minutes later they were securing their bicycles in the bike shed. The dance was being held in the main hall and the King Bees were in full swing playing a range of Rock and Rhythm & Blues covers. Nick looked around. There was a large crowd of teenagers, many of which Nick recognised either from school or from the youth club. Many of the girls were dancing in a circle round their handbags, whilst the boys just looked on. Nick noticed that a few girls were wearing plain white t-shirts decorated with coloured iron-on tape. They had USA on the back and their names on the front. One girl, whose name was Pat, was attracting a lot of attention as the boys were taking the word literally and patting her bosom.

Nick and Keith were thoroughly enjoying themselves, talking to their friends or just listening and watching the band. They performed a lot of Rolling Stones numbers and the old classics like *Poison Ivy* and *Love Potion Number 9*. As the evening progressed, Keith started to look a little worried.

'Are you going to ask a girl to dance?' he asked Nick.

'I want to, but I'm a bit nervous. What's happens if she says no, and if she says yes she'll soon realize that I've never danced with a girl before; I'm bound to tread on her feet.'

'Good point, but we've got to try. We can't spend all night just watching the band.'

'I know. Tell you what, when the next slow one comes on we'll watch and see what the other blokes do.'

'Good idea.'

They stood on the edge of the dance floor and waited for the next slow song. They didn't have to wait long. Two songs later the group played their version of *You'll Never Walk Alone*. Nick and Keith stared in awe as the other boys just walked up to the nearest pretty girl, mumbled a few words and within seconds were in close embrace and shuffling around the floor.

'Looks easy,' said Nick. 'Can't see what we're afraid off.'

'Absolutely,' agreed Keith. 'Let's have a wonder around and see what talent's on offer.'

The boys started to walk around the edge of the dance floor looking for a suitable partner for their first dance. They had reached the back of the hall when Nick noticed a blonde girl talking to three lads.

'Keith, isn't that Jane's sister......Veronica? You remember, we met her in Kings when I bought my Mum that purse.'

'Cor, yeh, as if I could forget her,' replied Keith. 'Who's she talking to?'

'The large bloke is Bob Newland. You know him, the one who's supposed to have seen Mr Freeman groping Tom Clarke.'

'Of course; didn't recognise him out of school uniform, but I definitely don't know the other two. Saying that, the ginger one looks a bit familiar.'

'Oh, I recognise him alright. Just look at that ugly grin. I've never spoken to him but that's Barry Prince, Alan Prince's older brother. I think we should stay well away from him. He's trouble.'

'Who's the other bloke? He looks foreign. Looks like an Arab. Not many, if any, of them in St Albans.'

The boys retreated back to the other side of the dance floor. Something inside told Nick that something was wrong. He didn't like the way those lads were acting towards Veronica. I'll keep an eye on her, he thought. Nick looked at his watch. It was ten past ten.

'If we don't do this soon, Keith, we'll miss the boat and I don't want to be late home.'

'You're right,' replied Keith. 'Next slow one; we grab the first available girl.'

'As long as she's not too ugly.'

'Goes without saying.'

It happened quicker than they hoped. The next song was *A Taste of Honey*, a personal favourite of Nick's. A good omen, he thought. Keith went to the right, Nick to the left. All of a sudden Nick saw a girl walking in his direction. Her name, Margaret Russell; he knew her from the youth club; they had spoken a few times. She was a year older than Nick and absolutely gorgeous. Margaret was a couple of inches shorter than Nick, with brown, shoulder length wavy hair, and hazel eyes. She was wearing a plain white t-shirt and denim jeans. He took a deep breath and approached her.

Nervously he said, 'Would you like to dance?'

She looked at him, smiled and said, 'Okay'.

She put her arms around his neck and he wrapped his arms around her waist. They started to move slowly with the music, shuffling around in a circle. Nick thought he was in heaven; never before had he been this close to a girl. The smell of her hair spray was intoxicating. Although the song only lasted two and a half minutes, it seemed an eternity. Half way through he realised that he had an erection and a big one at that. They were pressed together pretty close, I wonder if she's noticed he thought. Oh well too bad if she has. The song ended. She let go, looked at him, smiled again and said, 'thank you.' Then she walked away back to her friends. Nick just stood there, totally dazed.

'How did it go?' asked Keith, snapping Nick out of his trance.

'I thought I'd died and gone to heaven. Did you have any luck?'

'Yeh, no problem. Got a dance,' replied Keith with not too much enthusiasm.

Nick chuckled. 'Go on, tell me.'

'Well, she was okay. Not as pretty as yours, but got to start somewhere.'

'And?'

'She never stopped talking. I never thought someone could say so much in such a short space of time; gave me her whole bloody life story.'

'Didn't make a date then?'

'Not this time. So what did yours say?'

'Not a single word. It was wonderful.'

'Lucky you; come on, let's go. We've got ten minutes to get home.'

After saying goodbye to a few friends, they made their way to the bike shed and retrieved their bicycles. When they arrived at the school gate, Nick stopped and said,

'Isn't that Veronica getting into that flash car?'

'I think so,' replied Keith. 'You don't see those very often.'

'What is it?' asked Nick.

'It looks like a Mercedes-Benz, SL 230, and it looks nice in silver.'

Nick watched as Veronica, escorted by Barry Prince, climbed in the back. Bob Newland sat in the front passenger seat whist the driver was the foreign looking man. Nick made a mental note of the registration number.

Monday 16th March 1964

It was 7.50 pm when Nick came downstairs after finishing his homework and entered the living room. Again, he was dressed all in black, but this time without the balaclava, which was hidden in his pocket.

'Going out, dear?' asked Mrs Allen.

Before Nick could answer there was a knock on the back door.

'I'll go,' said Mrs Allen, as she made her way to the kitchen.

Mr Allen looked at Nick with a suspicious frown, and then looked round as they heard Mrs Allen burst out laughing.

'Not again,' she howled as Keith entered the back door dressed all in black and wearing his balaclava.

She escorted Keith into the living room and said, 'guess who's here?'

'I told you not to wear the balaclava,' hissed Nick.

'Sorry,' replied Keith.

'So,' said Mr Allen as he took a Manikin cigar out of its packet and lit it. 'Night manoeuvres again is it?'

'Something like that,' shrugged Nick.

'Not doing a bit of bird watching are you?' asked Mr Allen with a smirk on his face.

'Why would you say that?'

'Well, if you were, I wouldn't mind tagging along.'

Nick understood what his father was getting at and blushed. 'No, definitely no bird watching tonight,' he replied.

'That's a shame,' muttered Mr Allen attempting to blow a smoke ring.

'Well, we'd best be off. Got a busy evening,' said Nick, pushing Keith towards the door.

Once outside they ran to the road, where Don was waiting with his uncle, Peter Smith, who was sitting in an old yellow Ford van. Don opened the back doors and Nick and Keith made themselves comfortable in the back. Don sat next to Peter in the passenger seat.

'Where are we going?' asked Peter, who was about 30 years old, tall, well built, with a mop of blonde hair, and a weathered complexion.

'Gurney Court Road. I'll show you which house when we get there.'

Gurney Court Road comprises a mixture of large detached and semi-detached houses in a very middle class section of St Albans. Peter drove slowly along the road until Nick instructed him to turn right into Harptree Lane, which ran between Gurney Court Road and Charmouth Road. From Harptree Lane there was access to the rear of the gardens of both roads. Peter parked the van at the end of the alley. The boys got out of the van.

'Peter,' said Nick, 'you wait here and keep a look out. Sound your horn if anyone comes.'

'Okay,' replied Peter.

'This way,' said Nick as Keith and Don followed each carrying a large cardboard box.

'Which garden is it?' asked Don.

'It's the third one along. I came and had a look yesterday. They counted three houses and were faced with an ordinary garden picket gate with no lock. Nick motioned them to get on their knees as he opened the gate and crawled in. The rabbit hutch was situated by the fence to the right. It was a dark evening, the moon had yet to reach its first quarter, and there were no lights on at the back of the house but the hutch was just visible from the lights emanating from the next door neighbour's windows.

'I'll grab the rabbits from the hutch and put them in the box and you close the lid and take them back to the van. Got it?' instructed Nick.

'Got it,' replied Keith and Don simultaneously.

Nick opened the door of the hutch and reached inside. He felt the rabbit fur, felt his way under the rabbit and tried to lift it.

'Bloody hell,' he gasped.

'What's the matter?' asked Keith.

'It's bloody enormous,' replied Nick. 'It weighs a ton.'

'Grab it by the ears and pull it out,' suggested Don.

'Christ almighty,' said Nick.

'What is it now?' asked Keith, trying to look inside the hutch.

'The ears - they must be over a foot long.'

'Move over,' said Keith. 'Let me do it.'

Nick moved away and Keith lent forward and managed to lift the first rabbit out and drop it into the cardboard box. Then after a bit of a struggle, he finally coaxed the second rabbit to the door and pushed it into the other box.

'Well done, Keith. Now get these boxes into the van and don't forget to sellotape the lids down. We don't want them escaping.'

'What are you going to do?' asked Don.

'I won't be a minute; just one other little job to do.'

As Keith and Don struggled to carry their heavy boxes back to the van, Nick took out a sheet of foolscap paper and placed it inside the hutch. On the paper were written the words:

TELL THE TRUTH OR THE BUNNIES GET IT

With the rabbits safely in their boxes in the back of the van, and Nick and Keith crouched beside them, Peter drove away.

'Everything go okay?' he asked.

'Bit of a struggle,' said Keith. 'Those rabbits are enormous.'

'What sort are they?'

'No idea, but I've never seen rabbits that big before.'

Peter stopped the van, leant round and said, 'let's have a look.'

Keith carefully peeled off the sellotape and eased the lid open so that Peter could see inside.

'Well I never,' he gasped. 'That's a French Lop. They can weigh up to ten pounds. And look at those ears – magnificent. Someone is going to be bloody annoyed when they find out they've gone missing.'

'That's what we hope,' said Nick, who hadn't said a word since the kidnapping. 'He gets them back as soon as Mr Freeman is re-instated back at school.'

'Right,' said Peter, 'now don't you worry. I'll drop you off home, and then I'll take the rabbits back to my place. They'll be as safe as houses; just let us know when they have to be returned.'

Nick returned home at 8.45 pm His parents were in the living room watching television.

'You're home early, dear,' said Mrs Allen.

'Yes, bit tired. Thought I might have an early night,' replied Nick.

'Mission go alright son?' asked Mr Allen.

'It was interesting; kept us on the hop.'

Wednesday 18 March 1964

Nick was tired when he returned home from school Wednesday evening. Mr Freeman was still suspended and the temporary sports master, Mr Large, had put them through an intensive training programme – for rugby. Nick was now getting worried: the Cup Final was only nine days away and the team had received no training for a week. He'd just finished watching *Coronation Street*, a little indulgence that he hadn't mentioned to Keith or Don. In the episode that he had just watched Laurie tells Len to tell Joyce there's a job for her at the club. Martha withdraws her savings for her fare to London. Ted didn't think she'd take him up on the offer. Ken tells Val he's got a new job as Head of English at Granston Technical College. Jerry worries as more furniture arrives at No.13. Ena pretends Ted has proposed to her to put Martha off but as far as Martha's concerned, she's going to London.

'That was good,' said Mrs Allen as the credits started to roll. 'Anyone fancy a cup of tea?'

'That'll be nice,' said Mr Allen.

'Can I have a hot chocolate please, Mum?' asked Nick.

Just as Mrs Allen left the living room there was a knock on the front door.

'I'll get it,' shouted Mrs Allen.

Nick heard the front door open and his Mum saying, 'Oh, well you better come in.'

'Who is it, dear?' enquired Mr Allen.

'It's the police,' replied a worried Mrs Allen.

Richard Allen, Nick's younger brother, who was lying in front of the fire reading *The Beano*, said, 'Not the fuzz again.'

Nick recognised PC Adams whose younger brother attended the same school, but he was accompanied by a young looking plain clothes policeman, whom Nick had not met before.

'Evening all,' said PC Adams. 'This is Detective Constable Higgins, and he is investigating the disappearance of two valuable French Lop rabbits.'

Richard jumped up and said, 'I don't know who nicked them but Mum's rabbit stew tonight was delicious.'

Mrs Allen blushed and gave Richard a clip round the ear. 'Don't be silly. Go up to your room. Take no notice of him. Actually, we had shepherd's pie.'

'Made with real shepherds!' screamed Richard as he ran out of the room.

'Right then,' said DC Higgins nervously. 'Nick Allen; where were you on Monday evening between the hours of seven and midnight?'

'I was here for most of the evening, popped out for a walk with my friend Keith at about eight o'clock and returned about quarter to nine.'

'That's a very precise statement,' said DC Higgins.

'It only happened two nights ago. I'm only fourteen, and senile dementia hasn't set in yet.'

'No need to be lippy with me, lad,' said DC Higgins, who was clearly not very experienced at interrogation.

'What is this actually all about?' asked Mr Allen, trying to calm the situation.

'Some time on Monday evening between the times stated two very valuable French Lop rabbits were stolen from a garden in Gurney Court Road. The owner, a Mr Tom Clarke, suggested that your son, Nick, might have some information relating to the crime.'

'How do you know they were stolen? They might have escaped?' enquired Mr Allen.

DC Higgins smiled. 'Rabbits might be intelligent but I don't think they can write; a ransom note was left.'

'I see,' said Mr Allen, 'but I can vouch for Nick that he was only out for the times he stated. I think it would be very difficult for him to get to Gurney Court Road, kidnap two rabbits and get back here in forty-five minutes; and if my memory serves me correctly, French Lop are quite big rabbits?'

'Maybe,' replied DC Higgins, 'but I would like to search the house and garden.'

'Do you have a search warrant?' asked Nick.

'Why would I need a search warrant? Do you have something to hide?' sniggered DC Higgins.

'No,' replied Nick casually. 'I've just always wanted to say that.'

'Will you be lifting up the floorboards in here?' asked Mr Allen.

'I hope it won't come to that,' replied DC Higgins.

'Would be difficult; they're solid floors,' laughed Nick.

Mr Allen smiled at Nick and gave him a high-five.

DC Higgins and PC Adams conducted a thorough search of the house and gardens but found no trace of any rabbits. When they had left Mrs Allen continued to make the hot drinks.

When they were all settled, Mr Allen sipped his tea and said, 'where are the rabbits, Nick?'

Nick took a big sip of his hot chocolate and then said, 'They're safe.'

Thursday 19 March 1964

Nick had arranged to meet Keith and Don at Sally's coffee bar after school on Thursday to discuss their next move.

'Any news?' asked Don as he sipped his strawberry milkshake.

'Afraid not; Mr Freeman is still suspended and Tom Clarke still isn't talking,' replied Nick.

'I've been watching him,' said Keith. 'He looks really miserable, but I can't get near him because that Bob Newland is always hanging around.'

'It's a total mess,' sighed Nick 'and the final is a week tomorrow.'

They sat there in silence, deep in thought. Keith had a banana milkshake whilst Nick had chosen a chocolate one.

Suddenly Keith said, 'There is not much more we can do at the moment and we need something to cheer us up.'

'What do you suggest?' asked Nick.

'I know. Let's go and see that girlfriend of yours in Kings. She's good for a laugh.'

Nick smiled. 'You know she's not my girlfriend, but it's a good idea. Let's go.'

The boys finished their drinks, said goodbye to the attractive waitress whose miniskirt Keith had been trying to look up every time she bent down, mounted their bicycles and cycled the short distance to Kings. The boys parked their bikes outside and entered the shop. It didn't take them long to notice the very solemn atmosphere in the shop. Jane was in her usual position behind the counter, and for once she didn't seem overjoyed to see them.

'Not a good time for visitors?' remarked Nick.

'Afraid not,' replied Jane.

'Is there anything we can help you with? We're feeling pretty down as well.'

Jane forced a smile. 'You are very kind, but unless you can find my sister there's nothing you can do.'

'What do you mean?' asked Keith.

'We haven't seen Ronnie since Saturday. She went to a dance but didn't come home.'

Nick looked at Keith then said, 'We saw her on Saturday. She left the same time as us.'

'That's right,' said Keith. 'She left in a Silver Mercedes 300SE.'

'You must tell the police right away!' gasped Jane.

At that moment Don, who was standing by the door keeping an eye on the bikes, said, 'Thought you might like to know that a Silver Mercedes has just pulled up outside.'

Nick and Keith rushed to the door just in time to see the foreign gentleman climb into the passenger seat. Barry Prince was driving. As the car pulled away, Nick shouted, 'let's follow them'. The car turned left into Catherine Street. The boys mounted their bicycles and furiously pedalled after it. The car continued along Catherine Street into Folly Lane, which is situated on a steep hill. The hill helped the boys to keep reasonably close to the car. As luck would have it the car pulled into the petrol station at the bottom of Folly Lane. The boys watched as Barry Prince filled the car with petrol.

'What do we do now?' asked Keith. 'Whichever way he goes, it's a main road. We'll never keep up.'

The boys pondered as they watched Barry finish filling the tank, replace the petrol cap and enter the kiosk to pay. Then, for some reason the foreign gentleman got out of the car and joined Barry in the kiosk.

Sensing the opportunity, Nick rushed up to the rear of the car opened the boot and jumped in closing the boot behind him. Soon after, Barry and the foreign gentleman climbed into the car and drove off. As Nick tried to make himself comfortable in the boot of the Mercedes he thought what the hell am I doing? He tried to visualise which way they were going without much success, but after about ten minutes he sensed that they had left the main road. He could not hear any other traffic and assumed they were driving slowly down a country lane. The car stopped. He listened; he heard the car doors open. A conversation started between Barry and the foreign gentleman which Nick could not hear clearly. Then the foreign gentleman said, 'Barry, get my shopping out of the boot.'

Nick heard the click of the boot and as the rays of light stormed into his eyes he heard Barry say: 'well, what have we here?'

Trying to get his eyes accustomed to the light, he felt Barry grab him by the collar and drag him out of the boot.

'What are we going to do with him?' asked Barry.

'Put him in the cellar with the girls. I might be able to find a buyer for him. Some of my clients have peculiar tastes.'

Nick looked around as he was forced into a large country house which he didn't recognise. Once inside, he was ushered through a grand hall with expensive looking paintings hanging on the walls. At the end of the hall Barry opened a door which led to a cellar and pushed Nick through. Nick stumbled but managed to keep his footing as he descended the stairs. When he reached the bottom, he found another door. It was locked. Barry had followed him. He pulled out a key from his pocket, unlocked the door and pushed Nick through.

'Enjoy yourself,' he laughed, as Nick heard the door being relocked.

Nick gasped as he looked around at the sight that faced him. Four blonde girls were huddled together on the edge of one of two single beds. All girls were dressed as if going out for the evening, but had not changed clothes for a week. Their hair was unkempt; mascara had run down their cheeks, a sure sign that they had been crying. Big holes appeared in their tights. The cellar appeared reasonably clean with bare brick walls. Apart from the two single beds, there was an old brown two-seater settee and one matching arm chair. In the centre of the room a wooden dining table was surrounded by four wooden dining chairs. The table was bare except for a fruit bowl filled with apples, oranges and grapes. The room smelt musty with a tang of urine. Nick noticed a large bucket in the corner covered by a dirty cloth. Nick looked at the girls. All seemed very similar; late teens, good figures, pretty, and all were blondes. Nick looked closely at one of the girls.

'Veronica, is that you?'

The girl to the right of the group stood up and said, 'I know you.'

'It's Nick Allen, I'm a friend of your sister.'

'I remember now. You came into her shop a few weeks ago.'

'That's right.'

'What are you doing here?'

'I've come to rescue you.'

All the girls laughed and one said, 'Well, you're not doing a very good job.'

Nick felt insulted. 'At least I've found you, which is more than the police have done.'

Veronica walked over to him and gave him a cuddle. 'There, there, Nick. We appreciate what you are trying to do but there is no way out of here. Don't you think we haven't tried?'

'I promised your sister that I would rescue you and that's what I intend to do. Now, first of all, tell me why you are here and how many of the enemy there are?'

Veronica went back to the other girls and sat on the bed. Nick pulled up a chair, sat down and listened.

'First, let me introduced my friends. This is Linda; this is Denise and this is Pauline.'

Nick smiled and said 'Hi.'

'Each of us met Barry at a dance or disco. He offered to take us home, but instead we ended up here.'

'I was coming home from the Market Hall and it started raining, and they offered me a lift,' said Denise.

'I was at the Cavendish Hall. There was a new band called the Cortinas,' said Linda. 'My friend had got off with some bloke so I had to make my own way home and they offered me a lift.'

'I met Barry at the Jazz Club and he asked me if I wanted to go to a party. Some party that turned out to be,' said Pauline.

'But why?' asked Nick. 'There have been no ransom demands as far as I am aware.'

'We think from what we have heard, they are going to ship us off to some Arab country and sell us as sex-slaves.'

'Wow. In that case we have to get out as soon as possible. How many are there?'

Linda, who was the smallest of the four, stood up and said, 'There are four of them – or, at least we have only seen four. Do you really think we can escape?'

Pauline who had been shaking her head ever since Nick had arrived, said, 'this is silly. What can a kid like you do against those four?'

It was Denise's turn to speak, 'Let the kid finish. Anything is worth a try. I don't know about you but I don't fancy being shagged rotten by some greasy Arab in some remote harem. I mean you get all sand in your bits.

I remember once having a fumble on Margate beach. It wasn't that good; had to go back to the guest house to have a bath.'

Nick was blushing.

'Thank you for that,' said Veronica. 'I'm sure Nick doesn't want to hear about your sordid love life.'

Denise laughed. 'I'm sorry. I expect young Nick's cherry is still intact.'

'For god's sake; I'm only fourteen,' gasped Nick.

'So you don't have a girlfriend then?' asked Denise.

'Sorry. I thought we were supposed to be planning our escape, not talk about my love life.'

'Or lack of it,' quipped Pauline.

'Don't listen to them,' interrupted Veronica. 'They are getting a little frustrated being stuck down here without male company.'

'You get us out of here, Nick, and I'll take the boy out of you.' said Denise.

Nick was trying desperately to compose himself. 'Thanks for the offer but let's us get out of here first. So, you say there are four of them. We have Barry, and the foreign gentleman, who else?'

Veronica replied, 'There's a big bloke called Bob and a little creep called Igor.'

'Igor?' enquired Nick.

'That's what we call him. He's really creepy. He's an Arab as well, with rotten teeth and bad skin. Has a bit of a limp. We call him Igor because he reminds us of one of those foreign servants in a Hammer Horror film.'

Nick got up and paced around the room. There was no natural light, just a single light bulb hanging down from the ceiling. 'How often do they come down here?' he asked.

'Just at meal times, Barry opens the door and Igor carries a tray in. He puts it on the table. Once a day, usually at breakfast, he removes the bucket. It's so embarrassing, and he always sniggers.'

'What time is your next meal?'

'Usually around six.'

'Okay, that gives us about an hour. I want out of here because I don't trust you lot to keep your hands off me during the night.'

'You spoil everything,' laughed Pauline.

'First, we need some weapons.' Nick looked around, picked up a dining chair and grabbed one of the legs. The chairs were old and the joints had dried out. Nick easily pulled the leg off.

'I think you could do some damage with that,' said Nick, tossing the leg to Pauline.

The other three girls quickly reached for the other legs and pulled the chair apart.

'This is what we'll do,' said Nick, now getting a buzz of excitement. 'As soon as Igor walks in with the dinner you attack him with your chair legs and I'll deal with Barry.'

The group all of a sudden looked towards the door as they heard the stairs creak.

'They're early,' said Linda.

'Okay,' said Nick, 'spread out and hide those chair legs behind you.'

The girls formed a circle and Nick stood behind the door. They heard the key turn the lock. The door opened and Igor walked in carrying a tray. He went to place the tray on the table and said, 'I bet you are hungry after your exertions with your new playmate.'

As the tray touched the table Linda took a swipe at Igor and caught him flush on the side of the head. He fell to his knees as the other three girls joined in and rained blows to the fallen figure. As this was happening Barry burst in but tripped over Nick's outstretched leg.

'Get him!' screamed Nick, and the girls turned to face Barry.

Before the girls could start their assault on Barry, he had jumped to his feet and pulled out a flick-knife.

'Leave him to me,' said Nick, facing Barry. 'When I've disarmed him, you can have your revenge.'

'I'm going to enjoy this,' said Barry, tossing the knife from hand to hand.

Nick motioned the girls to stand behind him; he noticed they were well up for a fight, each of them banging their chair leg into their other hand. Nick frantically looked around for a weapon and grabbed a large Jaffa orange from the fruit bowl.

Barry laughed, 'what are you going to do with that - offer me a segment?'

Nick didn't reply. He just kept tossing the orange up and down. When he had a clear view he let the orange drop and then volleyed it straight at Barry. The orange hit Barry on the jaw, the impact causing him to drop the knife and clutch his face.

'Go for it girls!' shouted Nick.

Nick almost felt sorry for Barry and he turned away as the girls battered him beyond recognition.

'I think he's had enough. Let's get out of here,' said Nick, ushering the girls out of the cellar and up the stairs.

As the last girl left the cellar, Nick looked round at the two bodies lying on the floor covered in blood and groaning. He saw the flick knife on the floor, picked it up and put it in his pocket. He climbed the stairs entered the hall and was immediately faced with Bob Newland and the foreign gentleman. The girls showed no fear; they had tasted blood and were looking for their next victims. The rhythmic banging of the chair legs into the hands was accompanied by a low moaning. Nick looked at the four girls. Their eyes were bulging and their teeth were bared; they looked almost demonic.

'I didn't sign up for this,' said Bob, as he turned and made a dash to the door.

'Come back here!' screamed the foreign gentleman. 'I'm paying you to protect my investment.'

'Stuff your investment,' shouted Bob as he opened the door and disappeared. Just as he stepped outside, two police cars appeared. Three policemen jumped out of the first car and chased Bob as he fled towards the woods.

Nick looked at the foreign gentleman, and then looked at the four girls who were baying for blood. He thought the police will be here any second, but what the heck.

'Get him!' he commanded, as the girls rushed towards him screaming like Banshees. The police entered the hall and dragged the girls away but not before they had each struck a couple of good blows.

When the girls were finally subdued and the foreign gentleman had been taken away Nick stepped outside and saw Keith and Don standing there. Both were sweating profusely.

'Alright?' asked Nick.

'Fine,' said Keith and Don together, breathing very heavily.

'What kept you?' asked Nick with a sly grin on his face.

'Up yours,' replied Keith and all three boys burst out laughing.

Friday 27 March 1964

Nick sat on the bench in the home changing room of St Albans City F.C. and thought about the previous seven days. Keith had explained that he and Don had frantically cycled after him in the Mercedes–Benz.

Due to heavy traffic, they had managed to keep the car in view. They just managed to spot the car turning into the Childwickbury Estate[12]. They had just arrived in time to see Nick being dragged into the house. Keith had then cycled back out of the estate and phoned the police from the petrol station on the Harpenden Road. The police had visited Nick on Monday evening; this time DC Higgins was accompanied by a senior officer called Detective Inspector James, whom both Nick and his father found very amicable. He explained that the foreign gentleman was called Hamdam Al-Hamasin and was trying to impress his uncle, Abdullah Al-Hamasin, who was well known as a white slave trader. His idea was to kidnap young blonde girls and sell them to his uncle who in turn would sell them to wealthy Arab Sheiks. As it happens, Abdullah Al-Hamasin didn't take his nephew seriously and wasn't even in the country. Hamdam Al-Hamasin had met Barry Prince at university and they become friends. Hamdam recruited Barry with the promise of a great deal of money. Barry then recruited Bob Newland who was a neighbour of the Princes. By coincidence, Barry had also persuaded Bob to frame Mr Freeman, as a favour for his brother, Alan, to get revenge over Nick and stop Sandridge Grammar School playing in the Cup Final. Once the word got round that Bob had been arrested, Tom Clarke made a full confession to the police and mysteriously his rabbits re-appeared the next day. Nick had asked what would happen to Tom. DI James informed Nick that no action would be taken against Tom, but his parents had taken him out of Sandridge Grammar and moved him to another school.

Nick's thoughts were interrupted as Mr Freeman entered the changing rooms.

'Right lads,' he said. 'This is it. I've picked the team for this afternoon. In goal Simon Francis, right back Pete Thomas, left back Andrew Hardy, right half Barry Dudley, centre half Roger Prime, left half Danny Fooks, outside right Mick Parsons, inside right Nick Allen, centre forward Keith Nevin, inside left John Wright and outside left Andy Graham; any questions?'

No one replied, as every player had known what the team was going to be days ago.

'Now, before you get changed I have a surprise for you. The Headmaster has allowed me to buy some proper football kit. He thinks it will reflect badly on the school if we wore our usual rugby shirts.' He opened a big brand new sports bag and produced a set of pure white football shirts with the school badge proudly stitched onto the chest. These were followed by dark blue shorts and white socks.'

He looked at Nick, and said 'I thought you might appreciate the colours.'

Nick beamed from ear to ear and said, 'They are just perfect.'

As they were changing Nick noticed that Mr Freeman and the captain Danny Fooks were in deep conversation and kept glancing Nick's way.

At five minutes to three, a bell sounded in the changing room. It was time to enter the field of play. The players all stood up and formed an orderly line behind Danny Fooks.

'Before you go, lads, I have a small announcement,' said Mr Freeman. 'Because of all that has happened, and Danny agrees, I think we should make Nick captain for the day.'

Spontaneously all the team clapped their hands and started cheering. Nick was overcome with emotion as he walked to the front of the line. Danny handed him a ball and said, 'well done, mate. We wouldn't be here if it wasn't for you.'

Mr Freeman stuck out his hand and said, 'Thanks for everything.'

Nick was struggling to see as his eyes filled up with tears.

'Go on, son,' said Mr Freeman. 'Lead us to victory.'

Nick puffed out his chest as he led the team down the tunnel into the bright sunshine that was beaming down on Clarence Park. They were greeted by a loud cheer of about three hundred supporters. Nick looked around and spotted some very familiar faces in the stand. Standing together and cheering furiously were Mr and Mrs Allen, his young brother Richard, Don Patrick, Mrs Freeman, Jane and her sister Veronica. Also there were Linda, Denise, Pauline and, surprisingly Arthur Martin and Peter Wright. He had never felt as proud as he did that day.

Did they win the cup????

Of course they did.

PART 5

THE MONDAY CLUB

Prologue
Aylesbury Assizes, Buckinghamshire.

'Call, Nicholas Allen.' The voice echoed down the corridor to where Nick Allen was sitting.

Nick stood up and was led into the courtroom by the court usher. As he made his way to the witness stand, he could feel the stare of at least one hundred pairs of eyes focused on him. He was physically shaking and beads of perspiration were trickling from his brow. He looked round to observe his surroundings – the judge, defence lawyers, prosecution lawyers, jury, court officials and the public gallery. It was the public gallery that made him nervous. Looking down on him was the roughest, toughest, meanest looking bunch of men and women he had ever seen. Is that Ronnie and Reggie Kray he thought, and I'm sure that's Charlie Richardson.

Standing in the dock was Ronald 'Buster' Edwards. After taking the oath, the defence lawyer began his questioning.

'Please state you name.'

'Nicholas Stanley Allen,' replied Nick, in a hardly audible voice.

'Speak up boy,' shouted Mr Justice Edmund Davis, the presiding judge.

'Nicholas Stanley Allen,' bellowed Nick.

'Lying bastard,' screamed a voice from the public gallery.

I'm sure that's my name, thought Nick.

'It wasn't me,' yelled Buster from the dock.

'He's lying,' screeched a woman now standing in front of him.

Nick was confused, I haven't said anything yet, he thought.

'We'll get you,' bawled Ronnie Kray.

'You can't hide from us,' shouted Reggie Kray.

Nick looked around; the entire public gallery was now standing, waving their fists, shouting abuse. The Judge, who seemed oblivious to the commotion, started to fill his pipe and the defence lawyer was pouring a cup of tea from a thermos flask. The foreman of the jury was dealing cards from a pack he had removed from his pocket.

'Have you got clean underwear on?' said Nick's mother, who was suddenly standing next to him.

'What did you say, Mum?' replied Nick, as his mother removed a handkerchief from her handbag, spat on it and started to wash Nick's face.

'Stop it!' yelled Nick, as he felt someone prodding him in the back.

Sunday 29 March 1964

'Wake up, you're dreaming again,' it was Nick's younger brother Richard.

'Sorry bro,' said Nick, rubbing his eyes and gasping for breath. 'Bad dream.'

'Not again, look at you, you're covered in sweat, I'm gonna call Mum.'

At that point Nick's Mum, a pretty petite woman in her late thirties, appeared.

'What's all the noise?'

'Sorry Mum, bad dream. I'll be alright in a minute. I'll make a cup of tea; do you want one?'

'It's a bit early and I like a lie-in on Easter Sunday, but you get one. Richard, get back to bed.'

'How many times do I have to tell you – call me Dick.'

Nick made his way downstairs, still breathing heavily, to the kitchen and put the kettle on. He found the teapot and put in three teaspoonfuls of tea. 'Don't forget one for the pot,' he said to himself. Nick wasn't feeling too good this morning. Apart from a restless night's sleep, Nick had toothache. Nick's Mum had made an appointment for him on Tuesday and he wasn't looking forward to it. Let's put the radio on thought Nick, not expecting to find any pop music. Radio Luxembourg, the only station that played decent music, had closed down until this evening. He twiddled with the tuning knob hoping to find something other than classical music, religious programmes or the boring news. Then something wonderful happened – he came across a station, where normally there was just hissing, playing the Beatles *Can't Buy Me Love*, which had just reached number one in the charts. He stood there transfixed; they played the song through to the end and then, after a short introduction, they played *Walk Like a Man* by the Four Seasons. Nick had discovered Radio Caroline – a new commercial radio station that had started transmitting pop music from a ship in the North Sea.

Feeling a little better, he put two cups of tea on a tray along with a small plate of custard creams. I know thought Nick, and he unlocked the kitchen door - It's Easter Sunday. He ventured into the garden, picked a daffodil, returned to the kitchen found a small vase and placed the on the tea tray.

'Ah, that's nice,' said Nick's Mum as he walked in her bedroom carrying the tray. Nick's dad was still fast asleep.

Nick returned to the kitchen and poured himself a bowl of Kellogg's Rice Krispies. He sat at the kitchen table – engrossed in Radio Caroline. The music seemed to relax Nick, which was good as he had a lot of things on his mind. Two days ago, Nick had scored the winning goal in a thrilling football match. His school, Sandridge Grammar School, had defeated Batchwood Boys School 3-2 in the final of the Benevolent Cup. Exciting as it was, that meant no more school football until next September. Also, his Mum had decided that it was about time he got himself a job to help finance all his new hobbies. Going out to dances, going to the cinema, buying records are not really hobbies – that's just part of growing up, he thought. Deep down he knew she was right – half-a-crown pocket money doesn't even buy one 7 inch record. Nick's Mum maybe small in stature but she had a big heart and personality to match. So she had secured him his first job, as a paperboy, working for Heading and Watts newsagent in Catherine Street. He was to start next Friday. The present paperboy had just left school and was starting his first proper job on Monday. But, before he left the paper shop, he would give Nick two days training.

Although Nick was dreading getting up at six o'clock every morning, he knew it was the right thing to do and the twelve shilling and sixpence a week would come in very handy. Especially as he now had a girlfriend, - well, sort of. Actually, he had arranged to take a girl to see *Zulu*, which was being shown at the Gaumont that week. They had made a date for

Friday; her name – Carol Savage. He had met her at a friend's birthday party last night. Barry Page, who lived a few doors away, was celebrating his 14th birthday. His parents had decided that it would be a good idea to hire a disco and hold the party at the Waverley Club, a working man's club in Waverley Road. It was a pleasant evening, but the youngsters were outnumbered by the adults. At the end of the evening, the dance floor was packed with the 'oldies', including his parents. About nine o'clock there was a break for food. Nick put a couple of sandwiches and three sausage rolls on a paper plate and ventured outside to eat them. He was deep in thought when he was approached by Carol.

'Hello,' she said. 'Are you Nick Allen?'

'Yes,' coughed Nick, as he struggled to swallow a mouthful of sausage roll.

'I heard you scored a winning football goal yesterday.'

After a few more coughs, he managed to clear his throat with a mouthful of lemonade. He looked at the girl, he recognised her, but didn't know her name. She was slim, small breasted, why did he always look there first he thought. He composed himself and looked into her face. She was reasonably pretty, with shoulder length auburn hair and a pretty smile. But it was her freckles, for some reason, that made him attracted to her. They had hit it off straight away, he found her easy to talk to and she seemed interested in what he had to say. He felt comfortable in her company and found it easy to ask her out.

Monday 30 March 1964

'Dad,' said Nick.

'Yes,' replied Mr Allen.

'Tell me about girls.'

Nick and his dad were sitting alone in the living room watching the six o'clock news. Mrs Allen was in the kitchen cooking tea and Richard was out having his tea with a friend.

'What's brought this on?'

'Well, you know that girl I was talking to at Barry's party. I've sort of asked her out.'

'What do you mean – sort of?'

'Sorry, I'm taking her to the cinema on Friday.'

'That's nice. So what do you want to know?'

'Anything – I've never taken a girl out. I don't want to embarrass myself.'

'Okay son, listen carefully – you may have noticed that girls are different to us. But remember they are still human. Girls like to talk about themselves – so you need to be a good listener. Don't overdo the jokes, just one perhaps, and then let her continue talking about herself. Don't be vulgar – excitable bouts of wind-breaking will not impress her. Keep playing sport – doesn't matter what. A ruddy complexion is more attractive than a corpse-like pallor of a bookworm. Also, if you see a girl in need of help – unable to lift something, for example, do not taunt her. Ask her if she needs help. Do it with a smile and a cheerful disposition. Finally, make sure you are well scrubbed – you know, hair washed, finger nails clean and so on.'

'It's a lot to take in, but, thanks Dad. I'm sure it will help.'

'Any time, son.'

At that point Mrs Allen walked in, 'tea's ready, what are you talking about?'

'Nothing much,' replied Nick.

Tuesday 31 March 1964

Mr Kenyon, Nick's dentist, practiced from his residence in London Road. Mrs Allen insisted that she accompanied Nick, to his appointment, Tuesday morning. Nick had an immense fear of dentists and dragged his feet all the way for the thirty minute walk. With the aid of a small mirror and his torch, he had, as best he could, examined the troublesome tooth. It was definitely bad – his worst fear. It would have to be extracted. Someone told him that they put you to sleep and you feel nothing. Someone else he injection really hurt. Either way, he wished he was going somewhere else.

They arrived at number twenty-five, London Road, and Nick, reluctantly opened the wrought iron gate and made his way down the concrete path to the front door. A brass plate gleamed at him stating that Mr Kenyon was a dental practitioner and had lots of letters after his name. Big deal, thought Nick. The receptionist, a sour faced woman with a turned-up nose told Nick, that Mr Kenyon was ready for him.

'Now be a brave soldier,' said Mrs Allen, practically pushing Nick into the examination room.

Nick walked over to the dentist's chair, sat down and tried to make himself comfortable. The room was just like a nice sitting room in a posh house but without a three-piece-suite. The bay window looked out on the front garden and he could hear the noise of the traffic flowing up and down London Road.

'What seems to be the trouble?' asked Mr Kenyon, a tall thin man in his mid-fifties. His grey hair was cut 'short back and sides' style, and he had a military look about him. He didn't seem all that friendly.

'Toothache,' replied Nick, in an "I feel sorry for myself" voice.

'Are you brushing your teeth twice a day?'

'Of course.'

'Eating too many sweets, I expect. Now, open wide.'

Nick closed his eyes, opened his mouth wide and gripped the arm rests as firmly as he could. He held his breath, as he felt Mr Kenyon prod, poke and scrape around in his mouth.

'Aaaah,' screamed Nick.

'Think we've found the problem,' commented Mr Kenyon. 'That bottom tooth is full of decay; have to come out.'

'Good,' said Nick. 'Can I go now?'

'We might as well take it out now,' replied Mr Kenyon. 'I'm free till twelve.'

Nick stumped back in the chair as Mr Kenyon called in the receptionist.

'Mrs Baxter will assist me if that's okay?' asked Mr Kenyon.

'Do I have a choice?' asked Nick sarcastically.

'Not really,' replied Mr Kenyon, as he wheeled over a trolley carrying two gas bottles.

'Now Nick, there is nothing to worry about. I'll put this mask over your face, you take a few deep breaths and you'll be asleep in no time.'

It took a few minutes for Mr Kenyon to set up his equipment, checking the gas flow, making sure his implements were all neatly arranged.

'Right then,' he said. 'Let's get started; open wide.'

He put a block of leather into Nick's mouth and said, 'bite on this.'

Nick hated anything in his mouth and he started to retch. He just managed to calm himself when a black rubber mask was placed over his face. Nick was not claustrophobic but he started to panic.

'Calm down Nick, just breathe deeply.' Mr Kenyon's voice had a sinister tone to it.

Nick opened his eyes. 'Thought I wouldn't find yer?' said Buster, looking down at Nick. 'You grassed me up and no-one likes a grass.'

Nick tried to speak, but nothing came out. 'I don't think Carol will find you attractive after I've finished with yer,' said Buster, waving a pair of rusty pliers in front of him.

Nick closed his eyes again and tried to scream. He could feel the pliers gripping his tooth and the pressure on his jaw. He felt he was being pushed deeper and deeper into the chair. There was a sickening noise, like a bone being crushed and then the taste of blood in his mouth. Tears were trickling down his cheeks and his hands felt clammy as he released his grip from the arm rests.

'Wake up, Nick,' said a familiar voice. 'There, that wasn't too bad was it? Now if you would just like to take a rinse.'

Nick gradually sat up in the chair, gave his head a quick shake before reaching over and taking a swig of the pink liquid that was waiting at the side of the chair for him. When he felt that his mouth was reasonably refreshed he sat back up, breathing deeply and exploring his mouth with his tongue till he felt the gap between two of his lower back teeth.

'I should rest a while in the waiting room before you go home,' said Mr Kenyon. 'And make another appointment for six months' time.'

Nick almost fell out of the chair, feebly said 'thanks', and made his way to the waiting room. Mrs Allen stood up as soon as she saw Nick. 'Everything okay?' she asked.

'Do I look okay?' he replied still breathing heavily. 'That was bloody awful. He's a sadist.'

The next patient, a ten-year old girl started crying. Her mother gave Nick a spiteful look. 'He should be reported for child abuse,' said Nick as he stumbled his way to the seat next to Mrs Allen.

Mrs Allen, clearly embarrassed said, 'It must be the gas, they say some people react funny to it.'

The door to the examination room opened and Mrs Baxter stuck her head out and said 'Denise Freeman, you're next.'

Denise screamed and grabbed her mother. Nick looked up and said 'that's my girl,' before passing out.

Friday 3 April 1964

Nick was just finishing his breakfast, a boiled egg and bread soldiers, when his mother asked, 'have you seen the Herts Ad, this morning?'

Stupid question thought Nick I've seen hundreds of them. Which was a bit of an exaggeration, but he had seen plenty. Nick had reluctantly started his paper round this morning. He had set his alarm clock for 6:15 am and managed to get out of bed, have a wash, get dressed, and make a cup of tea, then cycle to the paper shop by 7:00 am. The sun rose at 6:30 am and the sky was clear, but there was still a chill in the air. He introduced himself to the owner of the paper shop, a round-faced, jovial man in his fifties called Ron Hart. Ron introduced Nick to Colin Deaver who was to show Nick the round. Colin, who was fifteen, was wearing drain-pipe trousers, winkle-picker shoes, and a leather jacket. Colin had decided to leave school at Easter and become an apprentice with the Easter Electricity Board. When asked why he wasn't going to stay on and take his 'O' levels he explained that his dad had said that people like us don't do 'O' levels. Just find a job that will give you an apprenticeship and you will be okay.

The round that Nick was to take on was called St Michaels. It started at New England Street and finished at the entrance to the Gorhambury estate on Blue House Hill. It consisted of about thirty deliveries. Nick found Colin good company and was an enthusiastic teacher. He showed him the best way to put the papers into the bag and how to fold the papers before pushing them through the letter boxes. He advised not to push them all the way through; just in case you made a mistake and needed to retrieve them. He also showed Nick which houses had dogs. The nastiest dog lived at 3 Branch Road, opposite the dairy. He advised him to rattle the gate and wait. If the dog didn't show, then it was safe to enter. Otherwise, just wait until the old lady came out to collect the paper. He also added that she was a miserable ol' cow. Colin also stated that the round was heavier on Fridays because most customers like to have the Herts Ad, delivered. Nick had realised that after Colin had suggested that he carried the bag, just to get used to it. When the last delivery had been made Nick said goodbye to Colin and cycled down Blue House Hill, looking forward to his breakfast. Nick had to admit to himself that he actually quite enjoyed delivering the papers.

'I haven't actually had time to read the Herts Ad, Mum; I've been too busy delivering. Why? Is there something interesting in it?'

'Only a very nice picture of you,' she replied, smiling from ear to ear.

'Let's see,' said Nick, leaping out of his seat and looking over his mother's shoulder.

She was right, beneath the headlines Sandridge Grammar Win Benevolent Cup and a detailed match report there were two photographs. To the left, a team photo of Sandridge Grammar with the Cup and to the right a close up photo of the muddy faced Nick Allen, with a beaming smile holding the Benevolent Cup.

'We must get a copy of that,' said Mrs Allen. 'I'll phone the Herts Ad, this morning.'

Nick smiled to himself, not bad he thought. I hope Carol sees it, she'll be well impressed.

Nick had arranged to meet his friends, Keith Nevin and Don Patrick. Keith who was a good two inches taller than Nick and had dark brown hair and a slight oriental look due to his mother being Vietnamese. Don was a year younger than Nick and Keith, a good looking boy with jet black hair, neatly cut Boston style. They had decided to take a walk around Batchwood Golf Course, treat themselves to an ice cream, and have a game of putting.

'What time are you meeting Carol?' asked Keith, as Nick was about to attempt to putt a six-footer.

'About three o'clock, the film starts at three-thirty,' replied Nick, as the ball stopped six inches short of the hole.

'Are you nervous?' asked Don.

'Bricking it,' laughed Nick.

'I can understand that,' replied Keith, showing a rare glimpse of sensitivity.

'After all the things we've been through over the last few months, girls still frighten the life out of me.'

'You'll be alright mate.' said Don. 'My uncle Fred always said "treat them mean, keep them keen".'

'Is that the same uncle Fred who's divorced and who's second wife has just left him?'

'That's the one; but he's just been unlucky. Always seems to pick a wrong 'un.'

'Wasn't his first wife a vicar's daughter and his second one deputy head of an infant school?'

'That's what I mean, you can just never tell.'

'What are you going to wear?' asked Keith, who was now winning by three holes.

'That's another problem, I just don't know. If I wear my suit I'll look overdressed. If I wear my jeans, she'll think I'm scruffy and I can't afford anything new till I get my paper round money.'

'I know; wear your suit with that nice polar neck jumper you Mum bought you recently. That will look really cool,' said Keith.

'Good idea, thanks mate.'

They finished the game, Keith won easily. As they walked home the boys discussed all the aspects of this afternoon's big date.

Nick thought, well, that wasn't too bad, as he opened the kitchen door after walking Carol home. Mrs Allen was in the kitchen finishing the washing up.

'How did it go?' she asked.

'Very well, actually, Mum,' replied Nick, sitting down at the table. 'Very well indeed…. put the kettle on, Mum, I could murder a cuppa.'

It had gone well, they enjoyed the film and Nick managed to get his first snog during the Pathe News. Afterwards Nick had taken Carol to the Wimpy Bar for a meal. He laughed to himself as he remembered pulling out the chair for Carol to sit on and she sat on the chair opposite. Then, how embarrassed he felt when she asked him if he always put sugar on his fries when he mistook the sugar shaker for a salt-cellar.

Monday 13 April 1964

Nick was in a thoughtful mood as he cycled to school on the first day of the summer term. It was a beautiful day, a bright blue sky and the sun was shining. He was reflecting how his life had changed over the previous week. Heeding his mother's advice about having a girlfriend – have a girlfriend but don't ignore your other friends - he had managed to see Carol quite a lot during the last week. Smiling to himself, he (not for the first time) recalled the events of last Wednesday afternoon. His father was at work and his mother had taken his younger brother, Richard, to town to buy him a new pair of shoes. On the pretext of listening to his new LP *With the Beatles* that his parents had bought him for Easter, Nick had invited Carol round to his house. Nick was prepared; as soon as the house was empty, he ran himself a bath, slightly overdid it with his Mum's talcum powder, put on a clean pair of jeans and a brand new T-shirt. He also poured some lemonade into a large jug, with loads of ice, a sliced lemon and a sprig of mint.

Carol arrived on time and he escorted her into the living room. She was wearing a black mini-skirt and a thin white V-necked jumper. They sat on the sofa and listened to the first two tracks of the album. Nick had decided that the third track *All My Loving* would be his signal. After the first line, he casually put his arm round her shoulder and turned to kiss her. She did not pull away. While they kissed, Nick thought he was becoming quite a good kisser. He had learnt how to use his tongue to gently caress the inside of her mouth – she seemed to like that. The only problem was that whenever he kissed her he got an erection, the feeling he enjoyed except it became uncomfortable if it was pointing down and he had to discreetly adjust himself.

Now for the big moment – he placed he hand on her breast and squeezed. It felt good - even though they were quite small and she had a bra on. After about a minute she whispered in his ear, 'I can't feel much.'

Taking the hint straight away his hand darted under her jumper and straight for her bra catch. As much as he tried, he could not undo it. She pulled away, smiled and said, 'Oh, let me do it.' She stood up, pulled her jumper over her head, put both hands behind her back and unhooked her bra. It took less than five seconds. Nick's jaw dropped – she was naked from the waist up. He just stared at her small, pert, lily white breasts. He fell in love with those very light pink, rose bud nipples. She sat back down and said, 'Well? Do you like them?'

Nick just leant over and kissed them. She held his head as he immersed himself in the ecstasy of her breasts. When he emerged he looked at her and said, 'They are beautiful.'

She smiled and lent forward and kissed him passionately, whilst his hands continued caressing her breasts. After a while he thought to himself let's try the next stage. Subtlety he moved his hand away from her breast, moving it down her body over her flat belly onto her thigh and down to her knee. Then slowly he reversed the motion, rising slowly to the hem of her mini skirt, which had risen quite high. He was just about to explore beneath the skirt when her hand pulled his away. She looked at him, smiled and said, 'Not yet – when we are a bit older.'

Nick wasn't too upset, after all it was the furthest he had every gone before and he wasn't quite sure what to do if he actually got inside her knickers. They should come with a manual he thought. There must be books about what to do; then he remembered someone telling about a book call *Arabian Nights*. Apparently it tells you all sorts of things about girls and it was written by Elizabeth Taylor's husband Richard Burton – so it must be good. Don't suppose it will be in the school library.

He arrived at school in good time, greeted his friend Keith who was waiting by the school gates. After parking and securing their bicycles, they made their way to their form room for registration. From there they made their way to the school hall for Assembly. The teachers took their usual seats at the back of the stage whilst the Headmaster, Mr Mills, gave his usual address. After the morning prayers, hymn singing and lesson reading, Mr Mills welcomed the school back after the Easter holiday and then read out the school notices. Just as he finished Mr Freeman, the sports master, walked to the front of the stage carrying the Benevolent Cup. Mr Mills took the Cup and with a smile that could rival the Cheshire cat's, raised it above his head.

'I'm sure that there is no need to tell you what I'm holding, On Good Friday, our magnificent Under-15 football team won a titanic match against Batchwood Boys School. I would like the captain of the football team, Danny Fooks, to come up on the stage to receive the cup.'

There was a rapturous applause as Danny make his way to the front of the hall, climbed onto the stage and received the cup from Mr Mills. Nick was clapping so hard his hands were aching as he joined the chant of 'Danee, Danee'. As Danny lifted the cup above his head, the cheers got even louder. After about two minutes the noise eventually abated; Mr Mills spoke again.

'Thank you, thank you. Now, as I am a man of my word, I have spoken to Mr Freeman and from next year there will be a school football team for every year and hopefully we can build on the success of this season.'

There was an outburst of clapping and cheering.

'Thank you,' he shouted, 'but before you go back to your studies I have one more presentation to make.'

The school suddenly went extremely quiet.

'Our success in the Benevolent Cup was built on team work and every member of that team has my whole-hearted thanks. But, sometimes you have to recognise one person's individual efforts. I think that without the contribution this particular student made, we might not have been so successful. So, it is my great pleasure to award 'school colours' to - Nick Allen.'

The school erupted. Nick managed to make his way to the end of his row before a group of his team mates grabbed him and chair-lifted him to the stage. Nick received his school colours, mumbled a few words of thanks and shook every member of staff's hand.

Tuesday 14 April 1964

Geography was not one of Nick's favourite subjects and after a long day he just wanted to go home. He was seeing Carol tonight and he couldn't wait. He liked to know where the various countries were and the name of their capitals. He was also fascinated by maps, but all the other stuff just bored him. Also the geography teacher, Mr Duncan, was not the most inspirational teacher. Nick reckoned he was about forty, spoke with a very posh accent. He always wore a tweed jacket with leather patches on the elbows. Not a bad looking bloke thought Nick, but it would help if he smiled once in a while. In today's lesson, Mr Duncan was discussing the erosion of the coastline. He was about five minutes into his opening address when Walter Roberts, a first-year student, walked into the classroom.

'Sorry to interrupt your lesson, sir, but the Headmaster wants to see Nick Allen straight away,' he said, in a confident manner.

Nick didn't move, waiting for Mr Duncan's instruction. Mr Duncan looked at Nick with spiteful glare. 'Okay,' he said 'off you go, Allen, and come straight back.'

Nick made his way to the Headmaster's office and was told to go straight in by his secretary, Mrs Kelley. Mr Mills was sitting behind his desk smoking his pipe; he had a worried look on his face.

'Sit down, Nick,' said Mr Mills.

Nick made himself comfortable, then said, 'are you alright sir, you look worried.'

'Disaster, Nick,' replied Mr Mills, 'Disaster.'

The Headmaster started to empty the dottle from his pipe by taping it on his ashtray. He opened the draw in his desk, pulled out a packet of Dunhill Standard Mixture and started to refill his pipe.

After about a minute, with his pipe now truly alight, he said, 'someone has stolen the Benevolent Cup.'

Nick gasped, 'that's awful; who would do such a thing? Have you called the police?'

'They have just left.'

'What did they say?'

'They are looking into it; they'll be in touch.'

Nick's mind was in turmoil and then he said, 'I appreciate you telling me, sir, but why have you asked to see me?'

'Desperation, I suppose. Look, Nick, you have a knack for certain things and I was just wondering if you could sniff around a bit. You never know, you might stumble on something the police have missed.'

'Of course; we can but try.'

'I knew I could rely on you.'

'Well,' said Nick, biting his bottom lip. 'Can you tell me when you last saw the cup and what was going on Monday night?'

'Certainly; we had a staff meeting that ended at about six o'clock. I came back to my office, finished off some paperwork, and then left about 6.15 pm. I walked past the trophy cabinet.' He chuckled, 'I stood there admiring it, I am so proud of you lot; and then I went home.'

'Did you see anyone suspicious hanging around?'

'No; as far as I am aware, all the staff had gone home.'

'So who locks up?'

'The caretaker; there were no evening classes last night. Normally, the badminton club would use the gym, but they cancelled last week. I think they were having their AGM down the pub.'

'Was the trophy cabinet locked?' asked Nick, who was now enjoying himself. Questions just kept flooding into his head.

'Yes.'

'And where is the key kept?'

'In my office, there's a hook on the wall.'

'Was your office locked?'

'No.'

'Why not?'

'So the cleaners can get in.'

'What time are they in?'

'They start about five o'clock; I don't know what time they finish.'

'Do you know the cleaning supervisor's name?'

'No, the caretaker takes care of that.'

'I'll have to talk to the caretaker; and do I have your permission to interview all the staff?'

'Of course,' he opened the draw and took out a sheet of paper. 'Here is a list of all the staff that attended the meeting.'

'Thank you, Headmaster,' Nick stood up to leave. 'I think that's all for now, I'll keep you informed of any developments.'

Mr Mills smiled. 'Am I a suspect, Nick?'

Nick nodded his head. 'I'm afraid I can't rule anyone out at this stage of my investigation.'

Nick ran back to his class, and took his seat next to Keith.

'What did the Headmaster want?' whispered Keith.

Nick lent towards him, 'someone has stolen the Benevolent Cup.'

'You must be joking, who would do such a thing?'

'I don't know, but the Headmaster wants…..'

'Nick Allen,' bellowed Mr Duncan.

Nick looked up, he knew what was coming.

'You may be the Headmaster's little blue-eyed boy, but you are not mine. I think you are an arrogant, jumped up, little know-all.

He was walking down the aisle towards Nick. He was carrying his cane.

'Whatever it was that the Headmaster thought so important that he called you out in MY lesson, can wait until after school. Now put your hand out.'

Don't show any fear and pretend it didn't hurt, thought Nick as the cane stung the palm of his hand.

'Now class, copy the notes on the board into your note books. Read them thoroughly, there will be a test next lesson.'

Nick's hand was stinging and he was finding it difficult to hold a pen. He pretended to write down the notes; he would borrow Keith's book and copy them up tonight at home when his hand was better. Nick found it was difficult to concentrate, his mind was elsewhere. Who would want to steal the Benevolent Cup and why? How much was as it worth? Was it an act of revenge against the school or even against him? Could it have been Alan Prince? No, he's still hobbling about on crutches. But he could have got someone else to steal it. His thoughts were interrupted by the school bell.

Nick and Keith cycled slowly home together as Nick was finding it difficult to cycle with one hand.

'So tell me,' asked Keith. 'What did the Headmaster want?'

'I told you,' snapped Nick, instantly regretting his tone. 'Sorry, I just don't feel that good.'

'That's okay; he certainly gave you a good wallop. Still think on the bright side – Carol will be kissing it better later.'

'Oh; I forgot she was coming round tonight. She's helping me babysit my little brother.'

Keith sighed, 'you've been looking forward to it all day, hoping to get to second base.'

Nick smiled, 'I don't think this hand will be doing much wandering tonight, it hurts like hell. I was hoping to see you so that we can discuss how we are going to find the Benevolent Cup.'

Keith gave Nick a confused look, 'what do you mean WE are going to find the Cup?'

'Oh, didn't I say – the Headmaster asked me to find it. He thinks I have a better chance than the police.'

Keith slammed on his brakes and dismounted. Nick followed suit. 'Let's walk and discuss this, before you have an accident. You're wobbling all over the place. Look, there's a sweet shop over there; I'll treat you to a frozen Jubbly. That will refresh you and sooth your hand.'

'Thanks mate,' replied Nick.

As they walked home pushing their bikes and sucking on their frozen Jubblys, Nick told Keith all that the Headmaster had told him. After a period of silence, Keith said, 'and you want me to help with this investigation?'

'Of course – we're a team. We're the three musketeers.'

'There are two of us,' stated Keith.

'Well, Don can help as well … … when, or if, the investigation leads us outside the school.'

'Okay,' said Keith reluctantly. 'Where do we start?'

'Right then, Porthos, this is what I suggest ….,'

'Isn't he the fat one?' interrupted Keith.

'Does it matter?'

'No; suppose not.'

'Good, now let me continue. First, we need to interview all the staff that attended the staff meeting. Excluding the Headmaster, that leaves twenty one, I suggest we take ten each. We need to do it as soon as possible, so it's still fresh in their minds.'

'What about Mr Duncan?'

'We'll leave him till last; do him together, safety in numbers.'

'What do I ask?'

'Did they leave the meeting and go straight home or did they hang around. If so, did they see anything suspicious? Treat each one as a potential suspect; make sure that have a legitimate alibi.'

'Excellent, we'll start tomorrow.'

Mr Allen had an important darts match that evening and he had asked Mrs Allen along to support him. By 9:00 pm Richard was safely tucked up in bed leaving Nick and Carol alone. Nick had borrowed the Gerry & the Pacemakers LP, *How Do You Like It*, from Keith and this was playing on the radiogram.

'Now,' said Carol, 'let me have a look at your poor little hand.'

Nick showed it to her, the red mark across the palm clearly visible.

'There, there,' she sighed. 'Let me kiss it better.'

She very gently kissed his hand, then his wrist, working up his arm to his neck. When she started nibbling his ear he went all cold and things stated to stir in the trouser region. It was pointing down. Hoping she wouldn't notice, he slid his hand in his trousers to make the adjustment.

She stopped kissing his neck and looked down. 'Can't you control that thing?' she giggled. 'You're always fiddling with it.'

'I'm sorry it bothers you,' snapped Nick, fully aware that he had turned a deep shade of crimson. 'It's your fault anyway; it's got a mind of its own. That's the effect you have on me….. I think I love you.'

Carol stood up and said 'I'll put the kettle on and make a cup of tea, let him settle down. With that she made her way to the kitchen. He was back to normal when Carol returned with the tea tray and a packet of custard creams. They sat in silence drinking their tea, dunking custard creams and listening to the music. Nick was quite taken by Gerry's version of *Summertime*, written by someone called Gershwin; never heard of him, thought Nick. At 9:30 pm Carol said she had better be going, put on her coat, kissed Nick on the cheek and said goodbye.

'Call you tomorrow,' mumbled Nick, as he waved Carol goodbye.

Wednesday 15 April 1964

'I'm not actually looking forward to this,' admitted Nick as he boarded the coach, which was waiting for Class upper 3A outside the school gates. 'I think it's a bit early in the year to go swimming, especially in an outside pool.'

'Absolutely,' agreed Keith. 'And where the hell are we going, that we need a coach?'

'Okay lads, settle down,' shouted Miss James, the new English teacher. 'I'm sure you are all looking forward to a nice afternoon swimming. This is going to be a regular occurrence until the school can afford to build a pool of its own. Are there any questions?'

Keith stuck his hand up straight away, 'where are we going?'

'Kimpton,' she replied.

All the boys looked at each other, shaking their heads and muttering 'Kimpton? I didn't know there was a swimming pool at Kimpton. Why aren't we going to Cottonmill?'

It took about twenty minutes to reach the pool, set on a hill to the west of the village. Nick and Keith took their time changing, before emerging and taking in the scene before them. It wasn't a very big pool, about 30 yards by 10 yards and the rest of the class were reluctantly hovering at the side, shivering.

'In you get, boys,' encouraged Miss James, who Nick noticed was well wrapped up. She turned to Nick and Keith, 'ah, there you are, boys. It will feel warmer once you're in.'

'If you say so, Miss,' replied Nick. Nick and Keith jumped in.

'There, not that cold, is it?'

'It's bloody freezing,' shrieked Keith.

Ignoring his remark, Miss James, asked 'can you both swim?'

'Yes, Miss,' replied the boys, both looking at Miss James and violently shivering.

'Have you got your 25 yard swimming certificate?'

'Yes, Miss.'

'Would you like to get your 100 yard certificate?'

'Yes, Miss.'

'Well then, get practicing. Swim up and down for as long as you can. Can you swim in the deep end?'

'Yes, Miss.'

'That's good, when you can do four lengths without putting your feet down, tell me and then I'll watch you. Okay?'

'Yes Miss.'

For the next thirty minutes Nick and Keith swam up and down the pool till their limbs started to ache.'

'I've had enough of this,' gasped Nick.

'Me too,' replied Keith. 'Let's call it a day.'

As the boys emerged from the pool, Miss James approached them. 'Are you okay, boys?'

'Exhausted, Miss; I think we're ready to do our 100 yards, will next week be okay?'

'That will be perfect, you've done really well. Now go and get changed and warm up.'

After changing back into their school uniform, the boys walked down the hill towards where the coach was waiting. But first they stopped at the small shop to buy a cup of hot chocolate. As they slipped the hot beverage, allowing it to thaw their frozen bodies, Miss James approached them. 'How are you feeling now, boys?' she asked.

'Well, Miss,' replied Nick, trying not to laugh 'I'm okay now, but for a split second whilst I was changing I thought I'd turned into a girl.'

Miss James blushed and said, 'well, hurry up and finish you drinks; the coach is waiting.'

She quickly turned to the other boys and shouted, 'no time to buy a drink, please get to the coach.'

Nick and Keith looked at each other and burst out laughing.

Thursday 16 April 1964

'Have you seen the papers, Nick?' asked Mrs Allen, the moment Nick walked into the kitchen after completing his paper round.

'Yes, Mum. I've just delivered thirty,' replied Nick.

'I know that, but did you read the headlines? Those train robbers got thirty years. I know they did wrong, but thirty years, it's a bit steep.'

'Yes, Mum, I saw that. I think the government must have had a little word. They're making an example of them, trying to impress the voters.'

'Could be, but now they are banged up inside, perhaps you will stop having those nightmares.'

'I hope so, but Buster Edwards is still at large and it's him who is the focus of my bad dreams.'

'I'm sure that he's left the country by now; anyway, I'm think he's got more things to worry about than you.'

'I hope so, Mum, I really do.'

It was break time, Thursday afternoon. Nick and Keith had interviewed all ten of the teachers they each had on their list. They were sitting on a bench at the edge of the playground, discussing their results.

'It's like: they all have the same alibi. Every teacher I spoke to said they attended the staff meeting, it ended at six o'clock, and then they went home. No one saw anything out of the ordinary,' said Nick, despondently.

'Mine's exactly the same; all left at six and went home for their tea,' replied Keith. 'What do we do now?'

'Well, we've still got Mr Duncan to see. We'll see him straight after school; expect he'll say the same.'

Last lesson on Thursday was maths, which was one of Nick's favourite subjects. Today's topic was statistics, a subject that Nick found particularly easy. He was hoping for something a little more challenging to take his mind off their forthcoming interview with Mr Duncan. Mr Asher, the maths teacher, was in an exceptionally good mood and kept cracking jokes. 'Mathematicians that refuse to use the Mode and Median averages are just Mean.' The class groaned.

'Did you hear about the constipated mathematician? Worked it out with a slide rule.' More groans.

Nick wondered if all teachers were taught to crack corny jokes; is joke telling part of the curriculum at teacher training college? What was that joke Mr Ashley told in the physics lesson? He thought hard and then it came to him: 'where do you get mercury from? - Hg Wells.' Nick was just finishing shading in his pie chart when the school bell sounded. He looked at Keith and nodded. Keith nodded back. They packed their bags and grabbed their coats, hoping to catch Mr Duncan before he left his classroom.

They were in luck. Mr Duncan had kept a student behind and the boys could hear the screams as the cane connected with the poor student's backside. Nick and Keith recognised the boy, a second year student called Martin Cooper, as he left the classroom with tears streaming down his cheeks. The boys nervously walked into the classroom; Mr Duncan looked surprised to see them.

'Well, if it isn't Jewel and Warris[13],' said Mr Duncan, laughing at his own joke. 'What can I do for you two?

'We're investigating the disappearance of the Benevolent Cup and we would like to ask you a few questions,' replied Nick.

Mr Duncan shook his head, 'you just can't help yourself, can you? Have to stick your nose in. Does the Headmaster know what you are doing?'

'His idea,' replied Keith.

Nick just smiled.

'Right then,' moaned Mr Duncan. 'Better get on with it, I do have more important things to do, you know.'

'More important than the honour of the school,' scowled Keith.

'So, why the two of you? Good cop, bad cop?'

Nick was now sitting on the edge of Mr Duncan's desk, feeling surprisingly calm. 'Safety in numbers,' he commented. 'Now, in your own words tell us what you did after the staff meeting on Monday.'

'The meeting ended about six and I went straight home.'

'Did you see anything suspicious?'

'No.'

'Did you see anyone hanging around outside, in the car park, for example?'

'No; I always walk home, so I never went to the car park.'

Keith walked to the front of the desk, leant down, looked Mr Duncan straight in the eyes and said,' are you sure you didn't double back when you thought the school was empty.'

'No, I didn't.' He stood up. 'I'm getting bored with this.'

'Sit down, Mr Duncan,' responded Nick in a calm reassuring manner. 'We won't keep you much longer, but I'm sure you realise the importance of this matter and if you are innocent you have nothing to fear.'

Mr Duncan sat down, bemused by Nick's confident approach.

'I'm sorry,' he said. 'If I knew anything, I would certainly tell you.'

Nick was now struggling to think of what to say next. After a short pause he said, 'who do you think would have taken the cup?'

'Who have you talked to so far?'

'Everyone who was at the meeting.'

'Who else do you plan to ask?'

'We just have the caretaker and the cleaning supervisor.'

'Well, good luck,' and with that he walked stood up and walked out.

'So what do we do now?' asked Keith.

'Let's hang around till the cleaners turn up and then have a word with the supervisor,' replied Nick.

Nick and Keith decided to take a walk around the playing field to kill time.

'Bloody Spurs lost last night, can you believe it; 2-0, away to Sheffield

Wednesday. Bang goes our chance of winning the league, at this rate we'll be lucky to get runners-up,' moaned Nick.

'Yeh, what a bummer,' replied Keith. 'Who have they got Saturday?'

'Home to Bolton, then two away games - Burnley and Leicester; can't see them winning all three.'

'So how's it going with Carol, got past first base yet?'

'As if I'm going to tell you, anyway why are you so interested in my love life? Shouldn't you be finding yourself a girlfriend?'

'Who say's I haven't got a girlfriend,' replied Keith with an enormous grin on his face.

'Good show, who is she, anyone I know?'

'You may do, she lives down your road – Moira Harris?'

'I know who she is, never spoken to her, Catholic girl, not a bad looker.'

'That's the one; perhaps we can go out on a foursome sometime.'

'I'd like that; what are you doing tomorrow? The Zombies are playing at Faulkner Hall; I'm taking Carol, why don't you join us?

'That would be great, how much is it to get in?'

'Three and six, can you afford it?'

'Just about; our first foursome, we're growing up quite fast, aren't we?'

'I know,' laughed Nick. 'Next thing you know we'll be shaving. Come on, let's get back and see if the cleaning supervisor is in yet.'

Nick and Keith walked back to the main building and found the cleaners already doing the business. Enquiries led them to the supervisor, a brassy forty-year old with bleach blond hair and thick make-up. She was wearing light blue slacks which showed off her large backside to perfection and a turquoise blue halter-neck jumper that showcased her massive bosom. She introduced herself as Mrs Seabrook. Nick explained the reason they were there and they went and sat down in the reception area, outside the Headmaster's office.

'Now, what can I do for you young lads?' asked Mrs Seabrook as she made herself comfortable.

Nick looked to Keith, who was supposed to conduct the interview, but he was totally transfixed by Mrs Seabrook's breasts.

'What's wrong with 'im?' asked Mrs Seabrook. 'Hasn't he seen a pair of tits before?'

Keith appeared not to hear this remark and continued staring. Nick gave him a sharp dig with his elbow.

'What?' said Keith, as though he'd just been abruptly woken-up.

'Please excuse my friend; he was bottle-fed as a child.' said Nick giving Keith a dirty look.

Turning to Keith he said, 'It's your turn to ask the questions.'

'Sorry,' replied Keith. 'Right; now Mrs Seabrook I want you to answer the following questions to the breast of your ability. When you had finished cleaning, did you notice if the D-cup was still there?'

Nick was getting a little frustrated and cut in, 'what he is trying to say is, was the Benevolent cup still in the trophy cabinet when you finished cleaning?'

'Yes,' replied Mrs Seabrook.

'That's what I said,' interrupted Keith looking confused.

Nick ignored him, 'and you say that all the teachers left about six o'clock and the Headmaster left at about quarter past.'

'Yes … …. except Mr Eames, the history teacher.'

Nick looked at Keith, and then said, 'so your saying Mr Eames was still here when you left?'

'That's right, he always stays late. Sits in his classroom marking; not that he does much marking. Has a pile of students books in front of him, but he just sits there staring into space. Don't think he can face going home, mind you, don't blame him; have you met his wife? We know who wears the trousers in that house.'

'That is interesting, thank you Mrs Seabrook. Is there anything else you think might be of help to us?'

'No, I don't think so. If that's all can I get back to my cleaning? Don't want to be late home; my Bert will be expecting his tea.' With that she stood up left.

'What do you make of that?' asked Keith.

'Oh, you're back with us, now that there are no tits to ogle.'

'Sorry about that … …..but they were lovely weren't they?'

'I didn't notice,' replied Nick trying to suppress a giggle. 'That is strange about Mr Eames though. There is something at the back of my mind, just let me think for a while. Got it! I remember; when we were celebrating after our victory at Clarence Park, Mr Eames came in the changing room to congratulate us. He was admiring the Benevolent Cup and said that it was donated to St Albans Schools Association or something by the 4th Earl of Verulam. Apparently, it was given to the family by none other than the Duke of Wellington. I think we need to keep a close eye on our Mr Eames.'

'Are you sure this is a good idea?' asked Keith as he cycled alongside Nick back towards the school; it was six o'clock.

'It won't take long, I just want to see what Mr Eames is up to,' replied Nick.

'Well it better not, and don't forget we're going to see The Zombies tonight.

'Don't worry; we'll only stay for a little while.'

'What are we going to do exactly?'

'It's obvious – we are going to spy on him.'

'But how? We can't just look through the door; we'll be seen.'

'Trust me.'

The boys cycled through the school gates and left their bicycles in the bike shed. Nick was carrying a duffle bag and led Keith round the back of the school to where Mr Eames' classroom looked out across the playing fields. They crept up to the window and sat down underneath it.

'So,' said Keith, 'how are we supposed to see what he's up to without him seeing us?'

'Easy,' replied Nick, opening his duffle bag and pulling out, what appeared to be a long wooden box.

'What's that?' asked Keith.

'A periscope; dad showed me how to make one a few months ago. You just get some wood and make a box leaving a gap at the bottom and at the top on the other side. Inside, I fixed two mirrors, each at 45 degrees. So let's see what he is up to.'

They took turns in using the periscope and had to wait twenty minutes before anything happened. It was Keith's turn when he said, 'someone has come into the room.'

'Who is it?' asked Nick.

'Bloody hell, it's Miss James, the new English teacher and blimey, she's not helping him with his marking.'

Nick grabbed the periscope from Keith and said, 'let me look.'

What he saw was Mr Eames and Miss James in a full passionate kiss; his right hand was squeezing her left buttock.

'Now we know why he stays late,' said Nick.

'What do we do now?' asked Keith.

'We need evidence,' Nick gave the periscope to Keith and put his hand in his duffle bag. He pulled out a camera, and then carefully took some photos as the couple enjoyed their passionate embrace.

'Time we left,' said Nick. 'We'll have a little word with Mr Eames on Monday.'

Nick, Keith and their dates had arranged to meet at 7.45 pm at the bus stop opposite Waverley Stores and catch the 325 bus to St Peter's Street. Both Nick and Keith were wearing blue jeans and button-down shirts with slim ties. Carol wore a black and white quartered dress with white boots. Nick didn't realise how pretty Moira was; she stood about five foot five inches tall with shoulder length light brown hair. She was wearing a blue sleeveless party dress. They both looked a picture. The gig was a sell out and the foursome only just managed to get in before they closed the doors.

During the interval, Nick said he would try and buy some Cokes from the refreshment bar; he told Keith to look after the girls. After some pushing and shoving, he managed to purchase four bottles of Coke. As he tried to make his way back to his friends, he spotted Colin Blunstone, the lead singer of The Zombies.

'Hi, Colin,' said Nick. 'Really enjoying the gig; I'm Nick, by the way.'

'Nice to meet you Nick,' replied Colin.

'I hear your doing really well in the Herts Beat Contest[14], when is the final?'

'Sunday, May 10th, will you be there?'

'I hope so.'

'Anyway, nice to meet you; must go, we're starting now.'

'Yeh, see you Colin.'

Nick made his way back to where Keith and Moira were standing.

'Where's Carol?' asked Nick, handing each of them a bottle of Coke.

'She's over there talking to some bloke,' replied Keith, pointing to where Carol was.

'Who is he?' asked Nick, feeling the first pangs of jealousy.

'Don't know,' said Keith. 'I've never seen him before.'

I recognised him,' said Moira. 'He had his picture in the *Herts Ad*, last week. He's an athlete, runs for the County; should make the National team.'

Before Nick could reply, the lights were lowered and The Zombies returned to the stage. Carol eventually rejoined them and the foursome enjoyed the rest of the evening. The Zombies started the second half with their rendition of *Roll over Beethoven*, followed by *One Fine Day* and *The Monkey Time*. Nick loved every song; he thought no more of Carol's indiscretion, and, despite the large crowd, the four managed to dance to every song.

Sunday 19 April 1964

The weatherman had predicted that Sunday would be a glorious sunny day, so Nick suggested to Keith and Don that they take their girlfriends for a picnic at Verulamium Park. As Don didn't have a girlfriend, Keith had persuaded Moira to bring her little sister Elizabeth. Mrs Allen had made some spam sandwiches and Mrs Nevin supplied six scotch eggs. Don's contribution was six Wagon Wheels and a bottle of Tizer. The girls clubbed together and purchased a selection of sweets which included Sherbet dips, black jacks, fruit salads and liquorice sticks. As they walked towards the park, Keith produced a packet of Barrett's sweet cigarettes. They all took one, pretended to smoke, and commented how sophisticated they all looked. The first attraction was the swings and all three girls ran to claim theirs. For the next ten minutes, the boys pushed the swings to see which girl could go the highest.

Once they had tired of the swings, they made their way to the lake to feed the ducks. All six carried a bag containing stale bread which they broke into small pieces. Nick started showing off by naming all the ducks. 'That one,' he said, 'is a mallard, the drake is very recognisable nearly all year round by its metallic green head, brown breast that is delineated from the head by a white neck ring, grey body and black tail. And that one is a moorhen which has a white tail and a red bill. Over there is a coot with the white head, hence the saying bald as a coot.'

Keith then cut in and trying to mimic Nick and said, 'over there, that big white thing is a swan. Now swans can be very dangerous; I hear that they can break a man's arm with their wings.'

'Do you actually know anyone who has had his arm broken by a swan?' asked Nick.

'Well, no; but that's what my Mum said, so it must be true.'

'My Mum said that as well,' commented Don.

'And mine,' added Elizabeth.

'Okay,' said Nick, 'so has mine. So let's just be careful.'

They all laughed and continued to feed the large flock of ducks that had appeared.

'I fancy an ice cream,' exclaimed Carol.

'So do I,' agreed Moira.

'Look, there's a Tominey's[15] ice cream van down there,' said Elizabeth, pointing to the brightly coloured van situated at the far edge of the lake.

There was a small queue but they didn't have to wait long before it was their turn.

'Six 99s, please,' said Nick to the man in the van.

'Hello, Nick,' replied the man. 'Nice to see you again, how's your mum?'

'Sorry Doug, miles away. She's fine, how's business?'

'When the weather's like this, I can't complain.'

Doug served them their ice creams and then said, 'I'll charge you just for five, for old time's sake.'

Nick paid Doug, and then said 'Thanks a lot, great to see you again.'

As they walked away, Don said, 'how do you know him?'

'My mum used to work for them, she made the ice lollies. Doug's a really great bloke. They have a small factory in Sandridge Road; I used to go there sometimes in the school holidays.'

As they made their way to the Roman Wall, they noticed a small crowd sitting around a hollow listening to a group of church goers singing Christian songs. They listened for a few minutes before finding a nice quiet part of the park for their picnic. As they ate the sandwiches and drank their Tizer, Nick thought that this was one of the best days of his life.

At the end of the afternoon, the boys walked the girls' home, and Elizabeth gave Don a little kiss before thanking for a lovely afternoon.

Monday 20 April 1964

The school bell rang to indicate the end of the school day; Nick and Keith were in no hurry to leave. They took their time packing their things into their duffle bags.

'How are we going to play this?' asked Keith.

'Leave the talking to me and just follow my lead,' replied Nick.

When they were sure that Mr Eames was alone they entered his classroom. Exactly as Mrs Seabrook had told them, Mr Eames was sitting at his desk, surrounded by school books and staring into space. He was definitely put out when the two boys entered the room.

'What do you want?' said a flustered Mr Eames. 'I've told you all I know, please leave me alone.'

'Are you expecting someone, Sir?' asked Nick.

'I don't know what you mean.'

'Of course not; but we're here because you lied to us. We have a witness that swears you were still here at seven o'clock on the night of the robbery.'

'And we know about your sordid little meetings with Miss James,' said Keith.

'It's a wicked thing to tell fibs,' stated Nick.

The boys watched as the blood visibly drained from Mr Eames' face.

'You can't prove that,' replied Mr Eames, now extremely shaken.

'That's not exactly true,' said Keith, who was now thoroughly enjoying himself.

'What do you mean?'

'We have photos.'

'Are you blackmailing me?'

Keith, who had now perched himself on the edge of Mr Eames' desk and inspecting his nails said, 'blackmail is such an ugly word.'

'No, we are not going to blackmail you, we just need to know the truth,' intervened Nick. 'Please tell us what you saw.'

'Life at home isn't very good at the moment; Mrs Eames is rather a difficult woman to live with and the kids are driving me crazy. And.... well....Miss James seems to like me. I don't know why; I mean, I'm fifteen years older than her. Anyway, we meet most evenings. I wait here and when she's ready she visits me. We get on really well .....'

'Okay, we don't want to know the gory details,' interrupted Nick. 'Just tell us what happened when you left.'

'It was about 7.30 pm when we left. I walked Miss James to the school gates, said goodbye and we went off in different directions.'

'Did you see anyone suspicious hanging around?'

'I don't think so, I waved to the caretaker. He was just starting to lock up and I saw the cleaning supervisor get into a car. I think it was her husband's.'

'Okay, now tell us all you know about the Benevolent Cup. You mentioned that you knew its history.'

'I first set eyes on the cup about five years ago when I was teaching at Batchwood Boys' School. The cup fascinated me so I looked up its history. Apparently The Iron Duke was a close friend of the first Earl of Verulam and he gave him the cup as a present after the Battle of Waterloo in 1815. It is a very important piece. I'm surprised it's not in a museum.'

'Do you think that could be the reason it was stolen.'

'It wouldn't surprise me.'

'I think our work is done here, Keith. We'll let Mr Eames get on with his little illicit romance; wouldn't like to stand in the way of true love.'

Mr Eames blushed as Keith slid off the edge of his table, 'but I must say you have a jolly good taste in women, Sir; I quite fancy her myself.'

As the boys walked back to the bicycle shed, Keith asked, 'what do we do now?'

'I think a visit to Gorhambury and have a little word with the latest Earl of Verulam. Hopefully, he can shed some light on who might want to steal the cup.'

Tuesday 21 April 1964

'Do you think we can just knock on the door and they'll let us in?' asked Keith as the two boys cycled up the mile long drive that led to the great house.

'Good point, but we've got to talk to the Earl one way or another. We could have phoned and made an appointment, but he might be sympathetic and see us right away.'

'I hope so; I could have seen Moira tonight.'

'Sorry about that; anyway, how's is going with Moira.'

'She's lovely.'

'And are her tits as big as Mrs Seabrook's.'

'I'm too much of a gentleman to answer that question.'

Before Nick had chance to reply they had reached Gorhambury House[16]. They dismounted and stood in wonder as they cast they eyes over the magnificent white building.

'Where's the front door?' asked Keith.

'No idea; I didn't realise it was this big. We'll leave our bikes here and have a wander round. There must be a tradesman's entrance somewhere.'

Nervously they approached the big house and started to circle it. At the side, they found a door that had a bell.

'We'll try this one,' said Nick, and then pushed the bell-button.

They waited for about thirty seconds and just as Nick was about to press it again the door opened.

'Can I help you,' said the tall, bald-headed man standing in front of them. From his attire, Nick guessed he must be the butler.

'Sorry to disturb you, but I was wondering if we could have a quick word with the Earl. It's most important.'

The butler looked down his nose, sneered, and then said, 'the Earl is a very busy man, but I'll inform him of your request. Stay there. With that he closed the door. The boys stood there looking at each other for a full five minutes, before the door opened again.

'The Earl will see you now, follow me,' said the butler as he beckoned them in.

He led the boys through the kitchen along the hall until they reached the study.

'The Earl is in there,' said the butler as he opened the door.

The study was a magnificent room with floor to ceiling bookcases. Most shelves were full of books whilst other contained framed photographs.

Standing beside his desk was John Grimston, the 6th Earl of Verulam. Nick guessed would be about early to mid-fifties; he was tall, bald with white hair around the ears which definitely needed a trim. He had pleasant face and a friendly smile; Nick instantly liked him.

'Now lads, what can I do for you? I am expecting visitors so I can spend fifteen minutes with you,' asked the Earl in a pleasant tone.

'Well, sir, my name is Nick Allen and this is my friend Keith Nevin, and we are investigating the disappearance of the Benevolent Cup, which was won by our under-fifteen football team, on Good Friday. Our intelligence tells us that the cup was donated by the 4th Earl of Verulam and it was originally presented to the family by the Duke of Wellington after the Battle of Waterloo. So we were wondering if you could think of anyone who would want to steal it.'

The Earl laughed, 'so am I a suspect?'

Keith, who had been quiet so far and curiously looking around the room suddenly said, 'can you tell us where you were between the hours of six and eight on the evening of Monday 11th of April.'

'Keith,' said Nick, rather annoyed. 'The Earl is not a suspect.'

'No,' said the Earl smiling. 'Everybody is a suspect until they can prove otherwise. Now let me think…..are yes, I had a quiet night in with my family. I'm sure the staff can vouch for me.'

'Thank you, Sir', said Nick, a little embarrassed.

'But,' the Earl continued. 'Your intelligence is flawed. The story about the Iron Duke is not true. My father was a great story-teller and one evening at a dinner party after a few too many brandies, he made up the story. As I'm sure you are aware, some people are very gullible and so the story stuck. The cup has no real historical value.'

'Do you think, Sir' asked Nick 'that someone, today, actuality thinks it's true and stole the cup?'

'Anything is possible, but I doubt it. From what you have told me, I think it was an opportunist theft.'

Keith, who had been busy looking at the photographs, suddenly picked one up and said, 'excuse me, Sir, but who is this man in this photo.'

The Earl took the photo and said, 'ah yes, that would be Charles Duncan, my wife's youngest brother. He's what one would call the archetype black sheep of the family. Haven't seen or heard from him for years; could be out of the country for all we know.'

'Well, you'll be pleased to know he's alive and well and teaching us geography.'

The Earl was visibly shaken for a moment, but quickly pulled himself together when there was a knock on the door and the butler entered.

'Sorry to disturb you, Sir, but your guests have arrived,' said the butler.

'Thank you, James,' replied the Earl. 'Well lads, I'm very sorry but I'm afraid I must ask you to leave, but it has been an absolute pleasure to meet you. And I hope you find your thief.'

At that point a tall, thin gentleman in his mid-forties with sharp features walked in.

'Ah, Victor, my good fellow, let me introduce you to my two new friends. This is Nick and this is Keith and they are trying to track down a valuable family heirloom that has been stolen. Boys this is Victor Goodhew, your Member of Parliament.

'A pleasure to meet you, Sir,' said Nick and Keith, as they each in turn shook hands with Victor.

'I say,' said Victor, in a very posh accent. 'Didn't I see your photo in the local rag? John, you didn't tell me your friends were celebrities.'

Everyone laughed, as Nick turned a very dark shade of crimson. The Earl rang a bell and James the butler returned.

'James, would you be so kind, as to show these lads out,' said the Earl.

'Certainly, sir.'

Nick and Keith said their goodbyes and James escorted back through the kitchen to the door.

As Nick and Keith made their way to where they had left their bikes, they noticed more guests arriving at the house.

'Must be having a party,' said Keith.

'Could be,' replied Nick. 'And some of those faces look familiar.'

Nick and Keith retrieved their bicycles and started pedalling down the drive towards home.

'So,' asked Keith, 'do you think Mr Graham stole the Cup?'

'Well, at this point in time, he must be our prime suspect. I put it to you Keith that Mr Graham holds a grudge against his sister's family and wants revenge. He's believes the story of the Iron Duke and the Benevolent Cup, so he steals it.'

'But why, what's he going to do?'

'I don't know, but I expect it is something dastardly and he does have sadistic tendencies.'

'I agree, but what do we do next?'

'Well tomorrow, we have another little chat with Mr Eames and find out all he knows about Charles Duncan.'

Wednesday 22nd April 1964

As luck would have it, Nick and Keith both had history with Mr Eames, last lesson in the morning before dinner. After a not very interesting lesson on Anglo-Saxon Britain, Nick took their time packing away their books allowing all their classmates to leave. When the class was empty, they approached Mr Eames.

'Oh no, what do you want?' moaned Mr Eames nervously.

'Just a few more questions,' replied Keith. 'Tell us all you know about Mr Graham.'

'You know I'm not allowed to divulge that information.'

'I see,' said Keith, turning to Nick. 'I must say Nick, those photographs you took were exceptionally clear, what film did you use?'

'Okay, okay, what do you want to know?'

'Everything, friends, family, background, and hobbies.'

'Actually, I don't know much; he's a very secretive man. But I know he's not married, no idea about his family, doesn't mix with his colleagues. Not sure where he lives, but it can't be far away as he walks to work every day. The one thing I do know is that he is a very good bridge player. Plays every week, Thursdays I think.'

'Okay, thanks for your help,' said Nick and then beckoned Keith to leave.

Nick was deep in thought as he ate his school dinner, shepherd's pie.

'What are thinking?' asked Keith.

'Well, this shepherd's pie is not as good as my mum makes,' replied Nick.

'No, about Mr Graham,'

'Ah that; well, I think we should follow him home tonight and find out where he lives. Then tomorrow night, we hang about outside his house; hopefully, he will go out to play bridge. If he does, we break into his house and retrieve the cup.'

Nick and Keith waited at the school gates until Mr Graham appeared and they watched him turn right. Keith then cycled ahead and stopped by the telephone box at the T-junction. Nick then pushed his bike following Mr Graham at a discrete distance. At the T-junction, Mr Graham turned right; Keith watched then waited until Nick joined him. This time Nick cycled passed Mr Graham and then waited at the traffic lights whilst Keith walked behind. At the traffic lights Mr Graham turned right and continued walking towards the village of Sandridge. Nick had a feeling that Mr Graham lived in this road, so they both followed him at a safe distance. They didn't have to wait too long before Mr Graham turned in to a large detached house. As soon as he was out of view, the boys mounted their bicycles, pedalled frantically and were just in time to see him disappear through his front door.

'Excellent,' said Nick. 'Now we know where his lives and it's pretty secluded.'

I'm still not sure about breaking in,' replied Keith nervously. 'What if we get caught? I don't fancy going to Borstal.'

'In that case we must make sure that we don't get caught.'

'But if we find the cup and give it back, he'll know we took it.'

'True, but he isn't going to admit that it was taken from his house, because that's admitting that he stole it.'

'When you put it like that.'

'Are you sure this is a good idea?' asked Keith, as the three boys hid behind a bush on the opposite side of the road to Mr Graham's house. 'And do we need to involve Don as well?'

'Don't worry about me,' said Don. 'I'm all for a bit of breaking and entering.'

'I told you,' encouraged Nick. 'Don can keep a look out, while you and I search the place.'

'I have a funny feeling about this,' said a worried Keith. 'If he comes back and catches us, there will be hell to pay and you know how sadistic he is.'

'What day is it?' asked Nick.

'Thursday,' replied Keith.

'Yes, I know that, but it is also St George's Day. Remember, he who slain the dragon. It's an omen, good will overcome evil.'

'Nick, get into the real world. If we get caught, we've had it.'

Nick was now getting a little annoyed, 'well, if you don't want to be here, then bugger off. I'll do it on my own.'

Before Keith could reply, Don said, 'he's leaving.'

Nick and Keith turned and watched as a blue Austin A40 pulled out of the drive; Mr Graham was driving.

Nick turned to Keith and asked, 'are you in?'

Keith thought for a while, before saying, 'let's do it.'

The boys casually walked across the road, looking both ways to make sure nobody was watching as they approached the house.

'We need to find an open window,' said Nick.

'Try the garage door,' said Don. 'I didn't see him lock it.'

Nick tried the up-and-over garage door and Don was right; it lifted straight up. The garage was relatively empty apart from a few shelves with car parts on. At the far end of the garage was a door.

'Let's try that door, it must lead inside the house,' said Nick, his pulse now racing. It was open. 'Not very security conscious is our Mr Graham. Keith, shut the garage door.'

The door led to the kitchen.

'We need to check each room and every cupboard very carefully. The cup is quite big so if it's hidden it should be easy to find. Don, go upstairs and find a good place to keep a look out; shout if anyone comes.'

There were five rooms downstairs: a kitchen, utility room, family room, dining room, and a living room. Nick and Keith conducted a thorough search which revealed nothing. They ventured to the first floor, which consisted of three bedrooms and two bathrooms. One bedroom had been converted to a study. There was still no trace of the Benevolent Cup. Whilst Nick was searching Mr Graham's study, he came across a file, labelled The Monday Club. After studying it for a while he called Keith, 'look at this.'

The file contained a list of names and individual sheets with a photo attached and personal information. Nick recognized some of the names and faces. It was the first two names that caused Nick some concern – Victor Goodhew and John Grimston.

'What does it mean?' asked Keith.

'I'm not sure, but I recognize some of these faces. Look, he was at Gorhambury that night we were, and so was he.'

'Who are they?

'This one is Paul Bristol, apparently he's the chairman, and this one is Ronald Bell, QC, Member of Parliament for South Buckinghamshire. Look, Keith, I want to study this file for a while, you search this room. Something doesn't smell right.'

Thirty seconds later Keith said 'Oh dear, I knew this was a bad idea.'

Nick turned to see Keith staring into an open draw. Inside the draw lying on its own was a gun.

'What is it?' asked Nick.

'It looks like a Smith and Wesson 38 service revolver.'

As they stood transfixed looking at the gun, Don shouted, 'he's back.'

'Quick,' screamed Nick. 'Put the gun back in the draw,' as he replaced the file back on the desk. 'Under the bed.'

All three boys rushed into the main bedroom and scampered underneath the large double bed. It was very dusty and Don sneezed just as the front door opened. Paralyzed with fear, the boys listened as they heard footsteps climb the stairs. They held they breathe and Don held his nose, suppressing another sneeze, but their luck was in. Mr Graham did not enter the bedroom. Although they couldn't see out of the bedroom, they guessed that he went to collect something from his study. After a brief period of silence the sound of the footsteps told the boys that Mr Graham was now climbing down the stairs. They heard the front door slam and the roar of the Austin's engine told them they were safe.

'That was close,' said Don, before letting out a rather load sneeze. 'I think he needs to hire a cleaner.'

'Let's just check the second floor, and then we're out of here,' said Nick. 'You two do it; I want to check something out.'

A quick sweep of the two bedrooms on the second floor revealed nothing, so the boys left by the same means they entered. Retrieving their hidden bicycles the three boys cycled up the hill towards St Albans. They reached their destination Sally's café, left their bicycles against the shop front and made their way inside. *Tell Me When* by the Applejacks was playing on the Juke Box as the boys' ordered three milk shakes and found themselves an empty table.

'That was close,' said Keith, in between taking large slurps of his drink.

'I thought it was fun,' remarked Don, who seemed to enjoy these little bouts of danger.

'But what have we learnt?' asked Nick. 'It doesn't look like Mr Graham stole the cup, and what's this fascination with the Monday Club, and why does he have a gun?'

'All good questions,' replied Keith. 'What exactly is the Monday Club?'

'From what I could make out, it's a political club made up of prominent Conservatives. It must be important, that's what he came back for.'

'Is Mr Graham a Conservative?'

'I wouldn't think so, but it's the one thing we need to find out.'

'And you are just going to ask him,' said Keith sarcastically.

Nick ignored that comment. 'And we need to find out more about the Monday Club.'

Viva Las Vegas by Elvis Presley was now blaring out of the Juke box. 'Not sure whether I like Elvis,' commented Don. 'Definitely prefer British groups – Beatles, Stones.

Both Nick and Keith glared at him, but he didn't notice. He had his eyes closed and was singing along with Elvis. Nick thought how funny it was that someone who didn't like Elvis knew all the words.

Nick suddenly said, 'I've got a great idea, we'll ask that new kid. What's his name … …. Neil Hamilton? I've heard he's into politics; rumour has it that he's a member of the Young Conservatives. First, we'll ask him about the Monday Club, and then we'll get him to ask Mr Graham who he is going to vote for in the forthcoming General Election.'

'And you think he will do that? Most of the kids in our class are shit-scared of Mr Graham.'

'I'm sure we can persuade young Neil to co-operate.'

Friday 24 April 1964

As luck would have it, Class Upper 3A's second geography lesson of the week was straight after morning break, which gave Nick and Keith time to have a quiet word with Neil Hamilton. Neil had joined Sandridge Grammar School at the beginning of the summer term. Formally a student at Ammanford Grammar School in Carmarthenshire, he moved to St Albans with his family following his father decision to take up a position in London. Although Neil didn't mix with the same crowd as Nick, he seemed a rather pleasant chap. Nick and Keith approached him as he sat on a bench by the tennis courts eating a packet of cheese and onion crisps.

'Hello, Neil,' said Nick, as he sat down next to Neil. Following their normal interrogation procedure, Keith sat on the other side of him.

Neil looked suspiciously at the two lads. He had heard that these two only ever talked to you if they wanted something and it usually led to trouble.

'Can I help you?' asked Neil, feeling very nervous.

'Information,' said Nick, pinching one of Neil crisps. 'Not sure about these, I prefer potato crisps with lots of salt but, you never know, flavoured crisps might catch on.'

'What sort of information?'

'Well, we've heard through the grapevine, that you're into politics. And we were wondering if you knew anything about the Monday Club?'

Neil instantly relaxed and asked: 'what do you want to know?'

Keith, who so far had said nothing, whispered menacingly in Neil's ear, 'everything.'

Ignoring the threat, Neil began 'The Conservative Monday Club is a group of members and supporters of the Conservative Party and Conservative Associations. The club was formed to promote traditional conservative values and is dedicated to the monarchy and the sovereignty of a British Parliament under the Crown. It also maintains that Great Britain remains an independent country. It also has strong views on law and order, immigration and citizenship, and the economy amongst others.'

'Interesting,' replied Nick. 'So other party's may have different ideas.'

'Definitely, you could say that the Monday Club is the far right in politics; so, far left factions would oppose everything they stand for.'

'Would you think Mr Graham swings to the left?'

'I don't know for sure, but I think he may have left wing tendencies.'

'Well, Neil. You have been very helpful,' said Nick, as he began to rise, then sat down again. 'One more thing – will you ask Mr Graham who he is voting for in the next General Election?'

Nick watched as the blood drained from Neil's face: 'you must be joking, he'll slaughter me.'

'Not if you ask him nicely; come on, you want to be a politician. It will be good practice.'

'What's in it for me?'

'What do you mean?'

'I'm not doing it for nothing.'

'Okay, I'll give a shilling.'

'Two shillings.'

'One and six.'

'Okay, one and six, but I want it now.'

'Sixpence now, and the rest if we're satisfied.'

'And if you not satisfied?'

'We give you a smack.'

'Deal.'

They shook hands and Nick gave Neil a sixpence.'

'Wait till about ten minutes before the class ends, then casually ask him.'

Mr Graham's lesson wasn't too boring; they were looking at the world's largest cities and locating them on maps in their atlases. With ten minutes remaining Neil looked at Nick. Nick nodded.

'Excuse me, sir,' said Neil, raising his hand to attract Mr Graham's attention.

'What is it, boy,' replied Mr Graham.

'I was just wondering, as we are near the end of the lesson, could I ask you a question not related to geography?'

'That depends,' said Mr Graham, looking at his collection of bamboo canes, 'on what the question is.'

'Can you tell the class which party you will be voting for in the forthcoming General Election?'

'Mr Hamilton, you know I can't answer that. It's against the rules – a teacher should never show his political bias.'

'I totally understand and applaud you honesty, sir, but we can't vote until we're twenty-one, so you are not really going to influence us, are you? Anyway, I still think we should have some idea about politics and what each party stands for. And, anyway, you've always come across as a chap who knows his mind, not like some of the other teachers; they just follow the pack. I think you're a man of conviction, know the difference between right and wrong, and stand up for what he believes in.'

Boy, he's good thought Nick. Mr Graham was certainly enjoying the compliments. 'When you put it like that,' he replied.

'I'm sure the class would love to hear your views, sir, and I can assure you that whatever you say will stay within these four walls.'

Mr Graham was a little taken back. He looked round the class and every boy was waiting in anticipation. Never before had he had such a captive audience. 'Well, if you are sure.' He spent the next ten minutes explaining to the class all the benefits of socialism and why Harold Wilson will make a great Prime Minister. He was just about to start criticizing the Conservative Party when the school bell sounded, indicating the end of the lesson. Mr Graham was surprised when the class actually started clapping.

'Thank you very much, sir,' said Neil, as he packed his books away, then left the classroom. He waited outside for Nick and Keith.

'You were brilliant,' gasped Nick as he walked out of the classroom to where Neil was standing.

Neil was beaming from ear to ear. 'I really enjoyed that; mind you, he was talking a load of bollocks.'

Nick smiled as he noticed Neil's hand was sticking out. He fished a shilling from his pocket, 'worth every penny.'

'Thank you,' replied Neil.

'I've just had a thought,' said Nick, 'If and when you become a Member of Parliament, that could become a nice little earner.'

'What do you mean?'

'Charging people to ask questions for them, you could call it "cash for questions",' laughed Nick.

'You know, that's not a bad idea,' said Neil as he pocketed the shilling and walked away whistling.

'So what have we learned?' asked Keith as the boys went in search of their next lesson.

'We know that Mr Graham is no fan of the Monday Club.'

As Nick and Keith cycled home, Keith asked Nick, 'what are you up to tonight?'

'Haven't made any plans; Carol's washing her hair tonight,' he replied.

'Moira's not available either, so you fancy going out somewhere? We could ask Don to come; haven't seen much of him since I started seeing Moira.'

'Sounds good; have you got anything in mind?'

'Funny you should ask; how about going to the Alma Road Youth Club? They always have a group playing on Friday nights.'

'Isn't it a bit rough? Doesn't the gang from Dellfields hang out there?'

'God, you can be such a snob at times, Nick. Yes they do go there, but they're alright – once you get to know them. Might be good to expand our circle of friends, you never know when you might need them. Last time I was there I spoke to Digger Barnes; he's a pussy cat really.'

Nick gasped, 'you spoke to Digger Barnes. He sends shivers down my spine just looking at him. Have you seen that scar on his face? It must be six inches long.'

'Yeh, I've seen it, but they say the other bloke came off worse.'

'Okay, I'll come. You call for Don and I'll meet you at your place a half seven.'

Nick always looked forward to his tea on Friday's. His Mum, being a little bit of a traditionalist, always cooked fish and chips. A nice bit of cod, bought from Warwicks, the fishmonger on Catherine Street, and homemade chips. After his tea Nick just had time to scan the Herts Advertiser before getting changed for his night out. An article on page four caught his eye; after reading it a couple of times he put the paper back in the rack and made a quick phone call.

The three lads decided to walk to the youth club and Nick thought how nice it was to be out with Don and Keith again. He loved being with Carol and enjoyed being alone with her, but he had to admit that a night out with the boys was something he could never give up.

As they walked, Nick and Keith filled Don in on the details of their investigations. They told him that they still hadn't recovered the Benevolent Cup and that Mr Graham is just a poor deluded socialist. Nick also commented that he couldn't understand how Spurs managed to lose 7-2 to Burnley on Tuesday and hoped they would do better in the last game of the season away at Leicester. Keith said that he didn't like the new number one – *World Without Love* by Peter and Gordon. Nick argued that it was a lovely song and he hoped to buy it tomorrow. By the time they reached the youth club, the boys were in such a good mood that surely nothing could spoil their evening. It was then that Nick spotted Mr Graham walking on the other side of the road. The St Albans branch of the Labour party had their headquarters in a white building directly opposite the youth club. The boys watched as Mr Graham entered the building.

'I know what you are thinking Nick; don't do it,' said Keith.

'I'm sure he's up to something; I'm not going to be happy until I find out what it is. If I'm not back in thirty minutes, call the police,' replied Nick.

Nick crossed the road and entered the white building, which was the St Albans Labour club. As he entered the hall he was approached by a plain looking man in his early fifties who introduced himself as John Higginbottom, membership secretary.

'Right, lad,' he said, in a Yorkshire accent. 'How can I help you?'

Slightly flustered, Nick replied 'ah, hello. I was just passing and ….well….we're doing a project at school on the forthcoming general election and I was wondering….do you have any leaflets on what the Labour Party stands for? My parents always vote Labour. I think that's because we live on a council estate. But I would really like to know what they are actually voting for.'

Mr Higginbottom looked suspiciously at Nick then said, 'okay, come to my office and let's see what we've got.'

He led Nick through to a large office; it was full of filing cabinets and the walls were covered in posters.

'Take a seat, lad,' said Mr Higginbottom. 'Out candidate for the forthcoming election will be Mr Bruce Douglas-Mann; he's thirty six and a top man.'

For the next fifteen minutes Nick listened to Mr Higginbottom ramble on about politics and what a great candidate Mr Bruce Douglas-Mann will make. Although losing the will to live, Nick kept smiling and adding comments like…..that's good,…absolutely, and I couldn't agree more. Armed with a stack of pamphlets Nick stood up and said, 'Mr Higginbottom. You're been so kind and helpful, but I must be on my way. Thanks very much, I'll see myself out. Thanks again.'

'No problem, lad; any time.'

Nick, quickly left the office and walked towards the front door and opened it. Glancing round to see if the coast was clear, he turned round, allowed the door to slam and ran up the stairs to the first floor. At the top of the stairs there was a small chest of draws. He opened the top draw and stuffed in his pamphlets. He could hear voices coming from a room at the other end of the landing. The door was slightly ajar and he recognized the voice as belonging to his teacher, Mr Graham. Nick managed to look through the gap in the door, seated around a rectangular table were six men; Mr Graham was the only one standing, his back towards Nick.

'Gentlemen, let us congratulate ourselves on the success of Operation Bowtie. John Profumo, the Secretary of State for War, has resigned and the government is in turmoil. Harold Macmillan has resigned as Prime Minister and that idiot, Sir Alex Douglas-Home, has taken his place. Hopefully the electorate will take a dim view of this scandal, but we must not be complacent. I think we need one more humiliation and then we can end the thirteen-year Tory rule.'

'What do you have in mind?' asked another voice.

'Operation Red Monday. I have devised a cunning plan to discredit the Monday Club. As you know the Monday Club is made up of some of the most right-wing Tory politicians. If we can expose them as just a perverted sex club, instead of a distinguished political organization, it will shatter the government.'

'How do you intend to do that?' another voice asked.

'The Monday Club regularly meets at my brother-in-law's residence – Gorhambury. We have installed a mole into the household staff; she regularly reports to me on the comings and goings of the Monday Club.'

'Do we know her?' asked the first voice.

'I prefer that we keep her identity a secret, but for the time being we shall call her Sylvia R. She recently found out that in two weeks' time the Monday Club will be holding their Annual General Meeting at Gorhambury. My sister will be away for that weekend and they are bringing in outside caterers. The head of the catering firm is an acquaintance of mine and sympathizes with our cause. I shall be providing the waitresses. The plan is to drug the wine with a little something that – shall we say – will release their inhibitions. The waitresses will encourage their advances, so by the end of the evening it should turn into a full blown orgy. When the 'party' is in full swing I, along with a few dodgy free-lance reporters and photographers, will make our entrance.'

Nick was so transfixed listening, that he failed to hear the foot steps behind him. Only when his sixth-sense kicked in did he turn to see who was approaching him. But it was too late; Mr Higginbottom pushed him through the door and Nick fell to the floor.

'He was listening at the door,' said Mr Higginbottom.

Mr Graham was the first to his feet. 'Grab him!' he shouted.

The two men nearest to Nick rushed over and grabbed him, taking an arm each and pulling him to his feet. Mr Graham slowly walked towards Nick, his face full of fury.

'Well, look who's come to join us,' he sneered.

'Who is he?' asked the first voice.

'Gentlemen, let me introduced you to St Albans' most irritating student – Nick Allen.' With that Mr Graham slapped Nick round the face with a backhander.

'What are we going to do with him?' asked the second voice. 'We can't let him go, he's heard everything.'

'Don't worry about him, he won't say a word. I think our young friend here will have a nasty accident very soon. Now, tie him up and let's get on with our business.'

Someone found an old tea cloth, rolled it up as used it as a gag. Nick could taste stale beer. His hands and feet were quickly bound and then he was dumped unceremoniously in the corner of the room. Nick tried to make himself comfortable, his face was stinging and he was pretty certain that he had a small cut on his cheek from Mr Graham's signet ring. Nick wasn't taking much notice of what was being said at the meeting; he was too busy trying to think of an escape plan. He wondered if Keith took him seriously about calling the police. How long had he been there, it was difficult to tell: fifteen, twenty minutes? Nick looked at the window, it was dark, the sun set just after eight o'clock. His head was swimming, the gag was tight and he was having trouble breathing through his nose. The ropes around his wrists were hurting and his bum had gone to sleep. How long was this meeting going on for? He was suddenly alerted to loud voices in the distance. Suddenly the meeting went very quiet as the sound of heavy footsteps running up the stairs. The door suddenly burst open and in walked Digger Barnes, dressed as usual, black tee-shirt, blue jeans, studded leather jacket and green hob-nailed boots. He was followed by a large group of his mates. Digger quickly surveyed the room; spotted Nick tied up in the corner, and then shouted 'he's in here.' Keith pushed his way through the crowd, rushed over to Nick and pulled off the gag.

'Who did this to you, Nick?' asked Digger.

'He did,' replied Nick, nodding towards Mr Graham.

'Okay lads, let them have it, but leave that creep to me.'

What happened next could only be described as complete carnage. Digger grabbed Mr Graham and head-butted him. This was followed by a severe kicking as he fell to the floor. The rest of Digger's mates, about twelve of them, set about beating up Mr Graham's colleagues. As Keith struggled to untie Nick, they saw Don rush in and start demolishing the room. He systematically took all the framed photos off the wall and smashed them on the floor. Next he threw all the tea cups and glasses at the wall. By the time he had turned the table over and broken all the legs on the chairs, Keith had managed to untie Nick.

'I think we'd better get Don out of here,' said Keith looking very concerned.

Nick laughed, 'it seems such a shame though, he's seems to be enjoying himself.'

All of a sudden the action stopped, when hearing a police siren, Digger shouted, 'our work is done, let's scarper.'

Digger and his mates, closely followed by Nick, Don and Keith had just reached the bottom of the stairs when the door opened and two police entered.

'Charge,' shouted Digger. The two constables were knocked to the ground by the tide of youths rushing through the door. By the time they had regained their senses, there was not a youth to be seen.

Back in the Youth Club a good crowd has assembled to see a group called Terry and the Tramps make their debut performance. The assault team quickly mingled with the crowd, Digger ushered Nick away to the table-tennis room.

'Are you okay, Nick?' asked Digger.

'Not too bad, thanks; but why did you rescue me?' inquired Nick.

'Well, I can't let Stan Allen's lad get into trouble, can I?'

'You know my dad?'

'Of course I do; he's one of the finest dart players in the county. I'm good, but I've never beaten him yet. He's very proud of you, you know. And I saw you score the winning goal down the park. So when your friend Keith told me that you might be in a spot of bother, we had to help.'

'Well, it is much appreciated.'

'Don't mention it; anyway, haven't had so much fun for ages.'

Aren't you worried about the police?'

'Been here all evening; got loads of witnesses.'

'And for the last half hour you have been thrashing me at table-tennis.'

'Exactly; I like you, young Nick Allen.'

'And I like you Mr Digger Barnes.'

The pair shook hands and made their way back to the main hall just in time to hear Terry murder Buddy Holly's, *Peggy Sue*.

Saturday 25 April 1964

It was 8:30 am when Nick opened the back door to his house after finishing his paper round. Mr Allen was sitting at the kitchen table eating his fried breakfast and Mrs Allen was standing by the cooker watching the contents of her frying pan. Nick sat in the chair opposite his father.

'Egg and bacon okay, Nick?' said Mrs Allen.

'That's fine Mum, thanks,' replied Nick.

Nick noticed that his father was staring at the small cut on his right cheek and the bruising around his eye.

'Dare I ask how that happened?'

'If you want,' replied Nick, shrugging his shoulders.

'Nick, what happened to your eye?'

'Well Dad, I'll tell you two versions. One is the truth, the other a lie; you can choose.'

'Go on,' said Mr Allen raising his eyebrows.

'Well, the first version goes like this – I stumbled on a conspiracy to overthrow the government, than I was kidnapped, beaten up by my mad geography teacher, then rescued by Digger Barnes and his mates. The second version – I walked into a door.'

Mr Allen sat there shaking his head mumbling, 'unbelievable.'

Mrs Allen had now finished cooking Nick's breakfast and plated up. As she placed the plate in front of Nick she noticed his eye.

'What have you done to your eye, Nick?' she asked.

'Walked into a door, Mum,' he replied.

'You're getting very clumsy lately. Let me put a cold compress on it.' With that she found a clean flannel, rinsed it under the cold tap, squeezed out the excess water and put it on Nick's eye.

'Hold it there for a while, that'll bring the bruise out. What will Carol say when she sees it?'

As normally happens on Saturdays, Nick, Keith and Don visited St Albans market. Nick wanted to buy Carol a nice present. He decided on a chromium plated identity bracelet with her name engraved on it. There was a man on the market who had a good selection and Nick chose one that he thought was quite dainty. After their usual visit to the Record Room, they decide to call in at Christopher's for some refreshment; as normal they each ordered a milkshake.

'That was some night last night,' said Keith.

'It certainly was and that group was rubbish,' replied Nick.

'Very funny; you know what I mean.'

'I'm surprised the police didn't come after us,' commented Don.

'So am I,' agreed Nick. 'But thinking about it, if they collared me, they knew I would tell them what I heard and they certainly wouldn't want that.'

Keith laughed, 'and Mr Graham was definitely not in any state to say anything.'

'He certainly took a beating; don't suppose we'll see him a school for a few days.'

'Bet you a shilling he doesn't come back,'

'No chance; I think that's the last we've seen of him.'

'Anyway,' interrupted Don. 'We still haven't found the Benevolent Cup.'

'Oh, didn't I tell you – it's been recovered.'

'When?' cried Keith and Don in unison.

'Last night; the police phoned me this morning.'

'Why did they phone you, Nick? What haven't you told us?' asked Keith.

'I tipped them off. It was obvious really when you think about it; but yesterday when I was reading the Herts Ad, I noticed an article about a chap called Albert Seabrook who had been sent to prison for six months for house breaking. Well Mrs Seabrook, our cleaner, told us that she had to get home to get her husband Bert's tea, and Mr Eames saw Mrs Seabrook's husband in a car outside the school. Anyway they searched their house and that's where they found the cup.'

'Oh dear,' sighed Don. 'That wasn't much of an adventure.'

Nick and Keith laughed, 'You're just annoyed that you didn't get the chance to smash up someone else's home.'

'Yes, I did get a little carried away, but I do love the sound of breaking glass.'

Nick walked slowly to the bus stop; he was in no hurry. It was a warm night, the sun would be setting soon and he was at peace with the world. He had arranged to meet Carol at 7:30 pm; he was taking her to a dance at the St Albans College of Further Education, and they had arranged to meet Keith and Moira there. He had plenty of time; never keep a lady waiting he thought. He felt like a proper grow-up – escorting a beautiful lady to dance. Nick arrived at the bus stop five minutes early – the bus was due at 7:40 pm. He waited. He checked his watch that showed 7:35 pm, she's a bit late he thought. He could see the bus coming in the distance – don't worry we can catch the next one. The bus arrived; Nick let the other people waiting board the bus. He waited. Thirty minutes. She'll be here soon, he thought. More people arrived at the bus stop, it was getting quite crowded. Every time a person joined the queue, he moved back. The 8:10 pm us arrived and departed, Nick was still waiting there. A small girl about ten years old, with similar coloured hair to Carol rode past on her bicycle. She stopped about ten yards away, turned round and cycled towards Nick. She stopped, gave Nick a funny look, and then said, 'Are you Nick Allen?'

'Might be, who wants to know?' he replied.

'Are you waiting for Carol?' asked the girl.

Nick didn't rely.

'She's not coming. She doesn't want to go out with you anymore.' She gave Nick a quick smile, and then cycled away.

Nick had suffered a lot of pain during the last year, but the pain he felt in the pit of his stomach was like nothing he had felt before. His head was spinning and he wanted to vomit as he fought back the tears. A blackbird settled on the metal railing next to him. Nick had always liked blackbirds; he thought they were uncomplicated, just black with a bright orange beak. This one looked at him as though he was sharing his pain. Nick left the bus stop and walked home, his head in a total daze. When he opened the back door to his home, he heard his mother shout, 'is that you Nick, are you alright?'

He ran upstairs, entered his bedroom and flung himself on his bed and burst out crying. A few second later Mrs Allen walked in and sat down beside him.

'Whatever's the matter, dear?' she asked.

Nick sat up and sunk his head in her lap. 'She's chucked me and it really hurts.'

Mrs Allen cuddled her son, as she fought to hide her tears as she tried to soothe away her son's pain.

Aftermath

Mr Graham never returned to Sandridge Grammar School; he took early retirement due to ill health and left the area.

A General Election was held on 15th October 1964; the Labour Party won with a majority of 4 seats.

Nick eventually got over the loss of Carol; he vowed never to get involved with another girl again – well, we've all said that, haven't' we?

PART 6

THE BEAT GOES ON

Prologue
Stradtroda Hospital, Germany

Thursday 2 April 1942

My darling Polly

I hope this letter finds you well and I'm sorry that I haven't written earlier, but as you may have guessed I have been captured by the bloody Germans. I don't know how long I will be kept here before I am moved to a Prisoner-of-War camp, but I'm in a pretty rough state so it could be quite a while.

It happened last July; I was flying in my A.W.38 Whitley when I was shot down over Eindhoven in Holland. We all managed to parachute out; there were five of us. Unfortunately Ken Staughton died but the rest of us landed safely. Soon after landing the Germans were on us. Archie Taylor and I got separated from the other two and we hid in an irrigation ditch. We held out there for a while but were pinned down by a German sniper, who managed to hit me in the side. Archie then decided to make a dash for it. I told him I didn't think I could make it and he said 'never mind, you'll be alright' and with that he was gone. I stayed there for a while until I was found by a dog. When the Germans came, I surrendered but they still shot me in both legs. I was helped by a kind German orderly who cut me out of my flying suit, put me on a stretcher, and I was taken to a hospital, run by nuns, in Krefeld. The nuns were really horrible and treated the patients very badly. My right leg went gangrenous and I was transferred to Res Laz Hospital in Dusseldorf. After two operations on my legs, I was moved to Dulag Luft Hospital at Hohemark. This was up in the mountains, where there was lots of snow; it was very beautiful. I was put in solitary confinement and interrogated regularly. I told them nothing. Yesterday I was transferred here. I still need a couple more operations before (hopefully) I can walk properly again.

I hope you are keeping well and it's the thought of seeing you again that keeps me going.

All my love,
Charlie

xxx

Sunday 7 June 1964

Nick Allen was in a reflective mood as he sat, all alone in his living room. It was a beautiful sunny afternoon and his parents had taken his younger brother, Richard, swimming at the Cottonmill swimming pool. Unfortunately, Nick wasn't allowed to go, due to the fact that he was recovering from a bout of German measles. He still had a rash on his face and body but, according to his mother, it should clear up any day now and thankfully the itching had stopped. As the infection was contagious, he hadn't had many visitors. He hadn't seen much of his two best friends, Keith Nevin and Don Patrick. Keith was away for the weekend with his parents. Don hadn't had German measles, so his parents wouldn't allow him to visit. Thinking back, he realised that he hadn't really seen much of Keith for the last month. Keith had a girlfriend called Moira Harris, who he was seeing quite a lot of and since Nick was unattached, they couldn't go out on foursomes. Carol, Nick's last and only girlfriend, so far had chucked him seven weeks ago (not that he was counting) and he was still trying to come to terms with the rejection. He had banned his family from mentioning her name, but was reminded of her every time his mother gave him two poached eggs for breakfast. He had heard through the grapevine that she was now dating a boy called Roger Connolly, who ran for the county and was due to have trials for the national team. I can do better than her, he said to himself; I mean, I've got a date with Christine Keeler when I'm eighteen, if she's out of prison. But, he had to admit to himself that he missed touching Carol's pert little breasts.

He made himself a cup of tea and put on his new LP, which he had recently purchased. It took him a few weeks to save the £1/12/3 to buy the new Rolling Stones LP. He hardly heard first track *Route 66,* as his mind wondered back over the last couple of months. Spurs had finished fourth in Division One; they had won their last game 1-0 at home to Leicester, and John White scored the only goal. Nick thought that John White was a great player. His favourite pop star, Cilla Black had reached Number 1 for one week with *You're My World.* There was only seven weeks to go before the end of the school year and his parents had booked the family a week's holiday at Dovercourt, a Warner's holiday camp near Harwich in Essex. They said that Nick needed a break after all the scrapes he had been in over the last year. He was brought back to reality when he noticed side one had finished. He turned the LP over and listened to one of his favourite tracks *I'm a King Bee.* The next track was entitled *Carol,* which always brought a lump to his throat. He was just about to skip that track when he heard a knock on the front door. He got out of his seat, opened the door, and was surprised to see Keith's girlfriend Moira standing there.

'Hello,' she said, 'I was just passing and I thought I'd pop in to see how you are. Can I come in?'

'Erm, I'm not sure, I think I'm still contagious ....'

'Don't worry about that,' she interrupted. 'I've had German measles, so I'm immune.'

'Well, in that case, please come in, I could do with some company.'

Nick escorted Moira into the living room.

'Would you like a cup of tea?' he asked.

'Thank you,' she replied.

'Okay, well make yourself comfortable, I won't be long.'

Nick made his way to the kitchen and put the kettle on. He thought how nice Moira looked; she was wearing a pretty, light blue mini dress. She had nice legs and her breasts looked a little bigger than Carol's. She was also very pretty. Although they had been out a few times as a foursome, he had never really spoken to her in a one to one situation. When the kettle had boiled, he poured the water into the teapot then left to brew whist he searched the larder for some biscuits. He was in luck, he found two Wagon Wheels.

As he poured the tea, he shouted out, 'how many sugars?

'Two please,' was the reply.

Nick felt a little uncomfortable as they sat there drinking their tea and eating their Wagon Wheels.

'I like this album,' said Moira. 'It has some good songs on it. I especially like *Tell Me*.'

'It's one of my favourites too,' replied Nick. 'So, how's it going with Keith? Must be six weeks now.'

'Yeh, it's okay. He's a nice lad.'

Nick laughed.

'What's funny?' asked Moira, with a big smile on her face.

'Nothing.'

'Oh, come on, what's funny?'

'You've been going out with him for six weeks and the best you can say is that he's nice.'

Moira laughed. 'What do you want me to say? That I'm madly in love with him and my world would fall apart if he wasn't mine.'

'No, of course not; but I thought something in the middle.'

'Keith is a nice guy and I enjoy his company, but I'm not in love with him and I don't plan to marry him.'

'I think fourteen is a bit young to start thinking of marriage.'

'You know what I mean. Anyway, I was sorry that you and Carol broke up.'

'Just one of those things, still three weeks, that's a record for me.'

'How can that be a record, it was your first girlfriend?'

They both burst out laughing.

'Anyway,' Moira continued. 'She wasn't right for you. She only went out with you because you scored that winning goal. Now she's going out with that running chap. If you ask me she's turning into a right groupie. You deserve someone better.'

For the next hour they talked, laughed and took the Micky out of each other. It was when Moira looked at her watch and said 'my, look at the time. Mum will wonder where I've got to.' She stood up, 'thank you for the tea and biscuit and I'm glad you're on the mend.'

They walked into the hall and Nick opened the front door. Moira turned and gave Nick a kiss on the cheek. As she pulled away, their eyes met and a strange feeling came over him. Then she said goodbye, turned and walked away. Nick closed the door behind and stood momentarily very still.

Tuesday 9 June 1964

By Tuesday Nick was thoroughly bored, his rash had disappeared and for once he was really looking forward to going back to school. His Mum had said it was okay for him to go out and mix again with his friends. So after his tea, he phoned Keith and Don to see if they were free. As it happened both of them were at loose ends and were delighted to hear from him and they arranged to meet at Nick's house at 6.30 pm. Keith suggested that they play cricket on the green. He had found an old cricket bat in the attic and was dying to give it a go. Unfortunately, neither boy had a proper cricket ball, but Nick said he had decent tennis ball, which would suffice.

Nick's younger brother Richard asked if he could play, so the teams were selected; the Allen's would be playing the rest or Australia v England. Keith won the toss and elected to be England. Keith would be Geoff Boycott and Don, Fred Trueman. Australia was represented by Bob Simpson aka Nick and Richard, who considered himself a decent wicketkeeper, would be Wally Grant. They used a sapling tree for a wicket; Nick stuck a twig in the protective metal mesh for the bails. Twenty two yards were paced out and indicated by Richard's jumper. The Rules were agreed, single wicket, if the ball went on the road – 4 runs and no LBW. The rest would be made up as they went along. Keith would bat first, Don would field, Richard behind the wicket and Nick would bowl. The game flowed along quite nicely; Richard was thoroughly enjoying himself diving every time the ball came to him. Keith batted solidly until being caught and bowled for 35. Don was next into bat and had reached 10 when a middle-aged man approached them. The boys were just about to make a dash for it, thinking he was a council ranger. There was a notice on the green that clearly indicated that no ball games were allowed.

Reading their minds the man said, 'Don't go, lads, I just want a quick word.'

The boys thought that he looked friendly enough, so waited to hear what he had to say.

'Hope I didn't frighten you,' he said. 'It's just that I've been watching you and I just wondered if you fancied playing for a proper team.'

'Go on, we might be interested,' replied Nick.

'I'm starting up an under-15 team; I've got about ten boys interested so far and we're having a practice or trial if you like next Saturday; interested?'

Nick looked at Keith, then Don. Each gave a subtle nod.

'I'm up for it' shouted Richard. 'You won't find a better wicketkeeper.'

'I've been watching you, young lad, and you show a lot of promise, but I think you need to wait a year or two.'

'Shit!' said Richard.

'Okay, we'll give it a go. Where is this practice happening?' said Nick.

'Next Saturday, Verulamium Park, one o'clock, upper pitch.'

'We'll see you there. By the way I'm Nick, that's Keith, and he's Don. And you are?'

'Sorry, I should have introduced myself, I'm Archie. Archie Taylor.'

The boys in turn shook hands with Archie and watched as he made his way to his blue Ford Zephyr 4.

'What do you think?' asked Keith.

'He seems a nice bloke, could be quite good. I've never played in a proper match have you?' replied Nick.

Both Keith and Don shook they heads.

'Hopefully it should keep us out of trouble.'

Saturday 13 June 1964

Nick was feeling rather excited and looking forward to the cricket practice. Keith and Don were expected at 12:30 pm and they would venture down to the lake together. When his dad asked him what he was going to wear, he had to confess that he hadn't really thought about it. His dad told him that if you want to impress, you must look the part and to look the part he needed to wear white. Nick admitted that he didn't have any cricket whites and he couldn't afford to buy any. Luckily his dad had an old pair tucked away and he could use those. His Mum, who was a dab-hand with the needle, said that she would alter them, so they wouldn't fall down. His Mum also said that he could wear one of his white schools shirts as he needed new ones for the next school year. So, along with his white plimsolls, Nick looked the complete cricketer.

At exactly 12:30 pm Keith and Don knocked on the door. Keith was sporting a brand new pair of cricket whites and a white t-shirt. Don was wearing his white football shorts and a short sleeved white cotton shirt.

'All set?' asked Nick.

'Raring to go,' replied Keith, playing an imaginary cover drive with his old bat.

'See you brought your bat.'

'Of course, it feels like an extension to my arm.'

Nick loved Verulamium Park and never needed an excuse to visit. As he walked towards the cricket pitches, he turned to admire the magnificent cathedral rising majestically up out of a sea of green trees. When the boys arrived at the upper pitch, there were about a dozen lads eagerly anticipating the practice. The stumps were in position, one boy had claimed the wicketkeeper's pads and the others were throwing balls at each other. Archie spotted them immediately and called them over.

'Hi, lads, I'm so glad you could make it, looks like we have a good turnout. Let me introduce you to our captain.'

He called over another boy.

'This is Victor Farmer; sorry I've forgotten your names.'

Nick replied 'I'm Nick, this is Keith, and this is Don; pleased to meet you.'

'Likewise,' said Victor, as he shook each boy by the hand.

Nick guessed that Victor was maybe a year older than him, slim, athletic looking and immaculately dressed for the occasion. It was clear this boy knew his cricket.

'So tell me lads, what are you, bowlers, batsmen or all-rounders?'

Keith was first to answer, 'I'm an opening bat, Nick fancies himself as a spin bowler and Don is the all-rounder.'

Since when could I spin a ball thought Nick?

For the next two hours each boy had a turn at batting and bowling, whilst Victor often stopped the play to help each boy improve their technique. He showed Nick how to leg spin, showing him how to hold the ball with two fingers up and two down, with the split between the second and third fingers, which are spread across the seam. He explained that the spin on the ball is roughly 30 degrees so that the ball both spins sideways and dips with the overspin. He showed Keith how to play a forward defensive shot and tried to explain that it is not necessary to try and hit every ball out of the ground. Keith's guess that Don would be a good all-rounder proved correct as he did extremely well with both bat and ball. At the end of the session, the boys said their farewells to Archie and Victor and thanked them for their kindness and support. Archie said he would ring them during the week with details of a match next Saturday.

The boys were feeling pretty pleased with themselves as they said goodbye to Archie, Victor and the rest of the team.

'I think that went really well; this old bat certainly knows where the boundary is,' said Keith, still playing defensive shots and deft little dabs to fine leg.

'I didn't realise you were such an accomplished batsman,' replied Nick.

'My dad taught me, he used to play Minor Counties cricket before the war, but hasn't played since. I still prefer football, but cricket just comes naturally to me.'

'Well, I think we all did jolly well', interrupted Don. 'Do you think we'll make the team next week?'

'I hope so,' replied Nick. 'There are a few useful players there but I think we could hold our own.'

'What do you think of the captain, Victor what's-his-name?' enquired Keith.

'Doesn't smile much,' commented Don.

'I like him,' said Nick. 'He's knows his cricket, gave me a lot of useful tips about my bowling. But I know what you mean. Actually, I did see him smile once, you know, when Don collided with that other player trying to catch the ball. He's got quite a nice smile.'

Don grimaced: 'I can't believe that, he was much nearer to the ball than me and he shouted "yours". I could have caught it, but he just stood in my way; unbelievable.'

As the boys neared the lake, still taking about their cricket practice they noticed a group of lads, in a circle throwing something to each other. As the approached, they could clearly see that in the circle was a young schoolgirl desperately trying to retrieve her school satchel. There were five boys; all dressed similar in skin tight jeans, black or white T-shirts and black leather jackets. Nick estimated that they were, maybe a year or two older than him. The girl, clearly distressed was about eleven years old, wearing a school uniform of black skirt, black jacket with school logo and a cream blouse. The boys were laughing and mocking the girl as she frantically chased her satchel as it was thrown repeatedly over her head.

Keith sensed what Nick was thinking and said, 'Don't get involved; Nick, and we don't want any more trouble.'

Nick turned and looked at Keith and said, spitefully, 'we can't just let them do that; look at the poor thing, she's in tears. Come on, back me up, we've handled worse than this. Remember what Mr Campion used to say: "bullies are always cowards". Anyway, they might just give her the bag back, if we ask nicely.'

Off went Nick towards the group, leaving Keith and Don slowly following behind. 'Okay, lads, you've had you fun; I think you should give the little girl her bag back and let her be on her way.'

The boy nearest to Nick turned to face him, snarled and said, 'What do we have here then?' Come to rescue your girlfriend?'

He turned to the rest of the group, as on cue they started laughing.

'Five greasy Rockers against one little schoolgirl; hardly a fair contest,' mocked Nick.

The boy raced towards Nick and pushed him on the shoulders. Nick was taken a little by surprise, stumbled and fell on his backside. The boy turned again to receive a chorus of laughter. Nick sat there for a second, and then got to his knees. The boy hovered over him. Nick brought his right leg forward and just before he got to his feet, he grabbed the boy round his thighs; in one swift movement he stood up and dropped him over his body. A perfect Back Body Drop; Kent Walton[17] would have been proud of me thought Nick, those hours watching Saturday afternoon wrestling have not been wasted. The boy was clearly winded and Don ran towards him and stood on his chest, not allowing him to move. Keith rushed to Nick's side, brandishing his cricket bat and shouting, 'anyone else fancy their chances?'

The remaining boys, clearly not interested in any more aggro, walked away mumbling things like 'just having a bit of fun,' 'no harm meant,' 'bloody psychos.' When the boys were a safe distance away, Don removed his foot off the remaining boy and said, 'go on, clear off before I get really angry.' The boy didn't need to be told twice as he scampered away after his mates. Nick smiled and looked towards Keith and Don and said, 'told you, no bother.' In their excitement they had temporality forgotten the little girl, but were quickly reminded when she rushed over to Nick and gave him a great big hug.

'My hero,' she gasped.

Nick gently prised her away and blushing he said, 'anytime.'

'You were like Robin Hood and his Merry Men rescuing the Lady Marion from the evil Sheriff of Nottingham, or St George rescuing the damsel in distress from the dragon, or Robert Taylor as Ivanhoe or… … ….'

'Yes, yes, we get the idea. Now tell us your name and what are you doing here.'

'Okay,' she said in a positive manner, 'sit down and I'll tell you my story.'

The boys did as they were told and sat down in a small circle ready to listen to the little girl. Nick looked at her and thought how pretty she looked. She had a slight Mediterranean complexion and olive green eyes. Her long shoulder length hair was a rich brown with gentle waves, and a smile that would break many hearts in the years to come.

She began; her slightly high pitched voice, more than confident for a girl of her age, 'my name is Caroline Cohen, I'm eleven years old and I attend the Manchester Grammar School for Girls. I'm on a school trip, visiting various Roman sites. I was on my way to see the Roman Theatre when I needed to go to the toilet. I have a weak bladder, but you do not need to know that. I told my teacher and said that I would catch them up. Unfortunately, I was intercepted by that group of Neanderthals, and, well, you know the rest.'

'So, where have you been so far?' asked Nick.

'Well, we have seen the Cathedral, the Roman Wall and the Hypocaust. Next, as I mentioned is the Roman Theatre and then we finish at the Museum.'

'Sounds really good, but as much as we like sitting here talking to you, I think we had better get you back to you teacher.'

'Okay,' she said, brushing the grass off her shirt, picking up her satchel and grabbing Nick's hand. 'Do you know where the Roman Theatre is?'

'Of course,' replied Nick. 'And along with my faithful companions we shall deliver you safely to your teacher.'

Caroline looked at up at Nick and gave him a big smile. Nick smiled back and thought, Oh God. Caroline held Nick's hand very tightly as they made their way to the exit by St Michael's Church.

'Did you know that St Alban was the first British Christian martyr? On his way to the execution, he had to cross a river, and finding the bridge full of people, he made the waters part and crossed over on dry land. And the executioner was so impressed with Alban's faith that he also converted to Christianity on the spot, and refused to kill him. Another executioner was quickly found; whose eyes dropped out of his head when he did the deed. After Alban was executed, they executed the first executioner who become the second British Christian martyr,' said the confident Caroline.

'That is interesting,' replied Nick.

'And,' Caroline continued, 'did you know that after Thomas Beckett was murdered in 1170, he was made a saint by Pope Alexander III and his shrine became the most famous in Europe? Of course, this had an effect on the town of St Albans because the pilgrims stopped coming here and started going to Canterbury instead. So the new Abbot of St Albans, Simon, borrowed lots of money and made St Alban's shrine more impressive. When Simon died the money had not been paid back and all the moneylenders came in person to dun the new Abbot. One of them was a Jew called Aaron of Lincoln.'

They had reached Blue House Hill and were waiting to cross the road to the entrance of the Roman Theatre when Keith said, 'I think that's your teacher over there.'

They all looked across the road to where a smart looking woman in her mid-forties was waving frantically. When the road was clear, the three boys escorted Caroline across the road towards her teacher.

'I believe she's one of yours?' asked Keith.

'Oh, Caroline, I was getting so worried. We thought you had been abducted.'

'Don't worry your pretty little head,' said Keith, taking the lead. 'There was a minor problem but my friends and I took charge and brought the young girl safely back to you.'

Nick, for a moment wondered what had got into Keith, then he realized. The teacher was wearing a neat pleated shirt and a very tight roll neck jumper which showed off her impressive bosom. She had a hard, but pretty face, and her prematurely grey hair made her look older than she really was. Visibly relieved the teacher said, 'Thank you, boys, you are so very kind. Now say thank you, Caroline and go and catch up with the other girls.'

'Yes, Miss,' she replied, and reached up and gave Nick a big kiss on the cheek. With that she ran towards the theatre.

'I hope she wasn't too much of a problem.'

Keith replied, 'No problem at all and it's been a pleasure meeting you.' He offered his hand and she gently shook it. 'Oh, and by the way, my name's Keith.'

As the three boys walked down Blue House Hill, Nick said to Keith, 'what's all this "oh, my name's Keith"?'

'I don't know what you mean.'

'You fancied her, didn't you?'

'Course not; just being friendly.'

'I know you, Keith Nevin; she was just your type.'

'What do you mean – my type?'

'If my memory serves me right, and Don will back me up on this, when asked yesterday for three women that you fancy, you said – Jayne Mansfield, Diana Dors and Sabrina. Don, what do these women have in common?'

'They have an excess of bosom,' Don replied.

'Delicately put, Donald.'

'And our Miss Jean Brodie definitely had an excess of bosom.'

'Who's Miss Jean Brodie?' whispered Don.

'It's a book my Mum recently read about a prim and proper teacher in a Scottish girls school set in the 1930s.'

'Okay, okay, so I found her a bit attractive; nothing wrong with this is there? Anyway, it's better than fancying an eleven-year old,' retaliated Keith.

'I didn't fancy her; if anything, she fancied me.'

'She sure did,' laughed Don.

'I think you getting desperate, Nick Allen; you haven't had sniff since Carol chucked you,' snorted Keith.'

'Alright, I liked her, but not like that. She was intelligent, funny and she had lovely green eyes.'

'See, I told you,' laughed Keith. 'It's not natural fancying eleven-year olds.'

'If I could just butt in for a minute,' said Don. 'Let me get this straight – according to Keith, it's unnatural to fancy a girl three years younger than you BUT, it's alright to fancy a woman thirty years older. Oh dear, I've got a lot to learn.'

Nick and Keith burst out laughing, put their arms around Don's shoulders and Keith said, 'stick with us, kiddo, and we'll teach you all you need to know about women.'

'God help me,' replied Don, shaking his head.

As they walked back towards Nick's house, Nick said, 'you must admit that when she gets older, that Caroline will be a stunner, way out of our league.'

Keith and Don nodded in agreement.

Wednesday 17 June 1964

Nick was just helping himself to a second helping of his Mum's delicious homemade rice pudding, making sure that he didn't get any of the skin, when the phone rang. Mr Allen, who was nearest answered it, then said 'it's for you, Nick.'

'Hello, Nick Allen speaking.'

'Hi Nick, it's Archie Taylor; just to let you know that you, Don, and Keith, have been selected to play on Saturday.'

'That's great; have you phoned the others or shall I tell them?'

'That would be good if you could phone. We're playing at Sandridge Grammar School, do you know it?'

'I go there.'

'Even better; I hope you don't mind me asking, but could you get there a bit early to help me mark out the pitch and get the ground ready?'

'No problem; what time would you like us?'

'Well the game starts at two, be there for twelve; that will give us plenty of time.'

'Sounds good, by the way who are we playing?'

'Panshanger Boys Club.'

'Never heard of them ... ... and what are we called?'

'Do you know in my excitement I haven't thought of a name.' Nick heard a chuckle. 'I'll think of one by Saturday. See you then.'

Nick phoned Don and Keith and quickly arranged a practice session in half an hour.

As they were pacing out the twenty two yards, Keith said: 'any luck with a new girlfriend yet?'

'Afraid not,' replied Nick

'Listen, I've got a plan; we'll get you a date by the end of the evening.'

'And how do you reckon to do that?'

'Lots of girls live on this estate, right?'

'Right.'

'Well one or two are bound to walk past. When they do, I'll hit the ball towards them. You run after it, making sure that you get as near as you can, then ask them out.'

'Just like that?'

'Well, you might have to say something first, like how nice they look.'

'And you think it will work?'

'What's the worst that could happen?'

'Apart from me be totally humiliated?'

'Just an idea.'

'Okay, but only the decent looking ones.'

So it was arranged; Keith would bat and Nick and Don would take turns in bowling. They didn't have to wait long.

'Here's one, she looks alright. Do you know her?' asked Keith.

'I know her, she's nice. Her name is Susan Golding,' replied Nick.

'Let's do it.'

Don bowled a full toss to Keith's legs and he hit it beautifully to square leg in the direction of Susan. Nick chased after it, but not too fast, allowing the ball to go within six feet of her.

When he caught up with it, he looked at Susan, smiled and said, 'hello Susan.'

'Hello Nick,' she replied, looking down her nose.

'Can I ask you a question; I've been meaning to ask it for ages?'

'Go on.'

'Did it hurt when you fell out of heaven?'

Susan let out a big sigh before saying, 'If you want to ask me out, just ask me.'

'Sorry; would you like to go out with me one evening?' replied Nick, feeling a little more confident.'

'Piss off.'

Nick ran back to the bowlers end.

'How did you get on?' shouted Keith.

'She's a bit busy at the moment,' said Nick, feeling his face turn very red.

Five minutes later Keith noticed another girl walking towards them.

'Shall we try this one?' asked Keith. 'Do you know her?'

'Seen her about, don't know her name,' replied Nick.

The boys performed the same routine and when Nick came face to face with the girl he said, 'do you believe in love at first sight or shall I walk past again?'

The girl looked at Nick curiously the said, 'you're Nick Allen, aren't you?'

Confidence rising again, Nick replied 'so you've heard of me?'

'Certainly have, they said you were weird and they were right.'

Nick returned to his friends and said, 'she's already got a boyfriend.'

After a few more overs, the light was diminishing and the sky became overcast. Nick could feel a few spots of rain.

'Let's call it a day; I think it's going to rain.'

As the boys gathered their things Keith noticed another girl walking up the pavement.

'One more go,' he said.

'You must be joking, look she's ginger,' replied Nick.

'What's wrong with ginger girls?' asked Don.

'Nothing's wrong with ginger girls, but you can't be seen going out with one. Think of my street cred.'

'Cilla Black's ginger.'

'I know Cilla Black's ginger, that's different.'

'How is it different?'

'It just is; anyway, hers is out of a bottle.'

'I know her,' said Keith. 'Anne-Marie; she'll let you look down her knickers for a shilling.'

'Charming,' replied Nick.

'Waste of money,' said Don.

Nick and Keith both looked at Don and said, 'what do you mean, waste of money; have you had a look then?'

'Of course not, but I found a magazine in my dad's bottom draw. It had lots of totally naked women in it and there was nothing down there to see.'

'And what was this magazine called?' asked Keith, inquisitively .

'*Health and Efficiency.*'

'You can't actually see anything because they blur out that particular region; even if you look there through a magnifying glass,......not that I've tried or anything.'

It was Keith's turn to blush as Nick and Don burst out laughing.'

Saturday 20 June 1964

It was just after noon that the three boys arrived at the school gates, looking immaculate in the makeshift cricket whites. They had agreed to meet Archie on the school playing field. The boys were really excited and talked of nothing else as they cycled all the way. They parked their bicycles in the bike shed and walked through the school buildings to the playing field. Nick commented how strange it seemed without the buzz of students running around. It felt like a ghost school. As they walked towards the cricket square, Nick looked out across the playing field towards the adjacent farmer's fields full of wheat and other crops and thought how beautiful it looked. The sun was high in the sky, a slight breeze cut across the field, a perfect day for cricket. Keith was still practicing his forward defensive shots when Nick noticed something strange in the far corner of the field.

'What's that hanging from that tree in the corner?' he asked.

'Looks like an old sack,' commented Don.

They quickened their pace, and then started running towards the tree.

'I don't think that's a sack,' said Nick, now sprinting.

Then suddenly, about ten yards from the tree they stopped. It was not a sack hanging from the tree, it was Archie Taylor.

They just stood there staring, before Don said, 'Do you think he's dead?'

'Well he's not moving, but we better take a closer look.'

As they approached Archie, they could see his face was the colour of claret and his eyes, prominent in their sockets, their whites discoloured with specks of red. Nick went to feel the pulse in his wrist, but the hand was deathly cold. He pulled his hand away and sunk to his knees.

'Why is it always us?' he shouted. 'Why can't I have a normal life like other kids?'

'I don't like this,' cried Don. 'I'm scared.'

'Okay,' said Keith, taking command. 'Go and call the police, Don. Just knock on the first house that you think has a telephone.'

Don didn't need telling twice as he ran across the field like an Olympic sprinter. Keith turned back to Nick and said, 'Come on mate, pull yourself together. You're the one and only Nick Allen – the people's champion.'

Nick chuckled, 'Which pratt said that?'

'I think it was that temporary Sports Master, do you remember him, Mr Large.'

'Oh yes, I remember him; the one with the odd shape balls.'

'That's better; come on let's take a proper look at this. Why do you think he committed suicide?'

'But was it suicide? Let's stand back and observe.'

The two boys stood back a few yards and assessed the scene. The body was hanging from the main bough of the tree which was about ten feet from the ground. The rope was connected to the bough by a neat round turn with two half hitches and to Archie's neck with a perfect hangman's noose. The noose was to the left of Archie's neck. The length of rope between Archie's neck and the bough was about four feet, which left Archie's feet dangling about 12 inches from the ground.

'How did he get up the tree?' asked Keith. 'I can't see him climbing, there's nothing to get hold of.'

'And why would he do it here, of all places, and how did he get here? Did you see his car parked anywhere?' replied Nick.

'Well, to tell the truth, I wasn't looking out for his car. I was too excited about the match.'

'Fair point, but this doesn't look right. I think he was murdered.'

'How did I know you were going to say that? But for once I agree with you. Look at that tree; there are no scuff marks to indicate he climbed up there.'

Before Nick could answer his train of thought was interrupted by the sound of a police siren. A minute later two police cars came speeding across the field to where Nick and Keith where standing. First on the scene was Detective Constable Higgins, whom Nick had met before. 'Hello, hello, hello, what do we have here then?' asked DC Higgins.

Nick looked at Keith and shook his head and held back on a clever witticism.

'Did you find the body?' asked DC Higgins.

Nick looked around then at Keith and said, 'nobody else here, must have been us.'

DC Higgins gave Nick a dirty look then recognised him. 'Oh, not you again; moved along from kidnapping rabbits, have we?'

'Don't know what you mean, officer. We just came here to play cricket and we stumbled across this; just in the wrong place at the wrong time.'

'So you came all this way to play cricket, just the two of you?'

'I can vouch for them, officer,' said a voice behind him.

It was Victor Farmer; Don was with him. 'I'm the captain of this cricket team and we have a match here at two o'clock. These lads arrived early to help Mr Taylor mark the pitch out.'

'And where is this Mr Taylor?' asked DC Higgins.

'I believe that's him hanging from the tree.'

The uniformed police taped off the area, the police photographer took photographs, before the body was cut down and taken away in an ambulance. Nick, Keith and Don gave their statements before being allowed to go home.

The boys were in a solemn mood as they cycled home. As they said goodbye to Don, Keith said, 'Are we still okay for tonight? We need a distraction; it will take our minds off the suicide.'

The boys had arranged to go to a 'Mammoth Fun Fair' on the Cottonmill Estate complete with a Grand Firework Display. Keith was taking Moira; Don had agreed to accompany Moira's sister, Elizabeth. Unfortunately, Nick was still unattached.

'Looking forward to it,' said Nick. 'Come round my house at seven, and then we can call for Moira and Elizabeth on the way.'

When Nick arrived home, his mother was sitting at the kitchen table having a good old gossip with her best friend and next-door neighbour, Margaret Stuart; or affectionately known as Auntie Marge.

'You're home early dear,' said Mrs Allen, looking surprised to see Nick. 'And look at the state of your trousers; you've got mud on the knees.'

'Don't fuss Mum, I've have a bad day,' he replied as he slumped on the vacant kitchen chair. 'The game was called off.'

'Why's that love, didn't the other team turn up?'

'We found Mr Taylor; you know, I told you about him. He runs our team and he arranged the game.'

'Go on.'

'Well, we found him hanging from a tree; looks like he committed suicide.'

'Oh my poor thing,' said Mrs Allen, as she stood up and hugged Nick.

That's awful,' said Auntie Marge.' Did you call the police?'

Nick nodded, 'yes, it's all in hand.'

'What you need is a nice cup of sweet tea. The kettle just boiled, I'll make a fresh brew.'

When Nick had finished his tea and explained all that had happened he retired to the living room, turned on the TV and watched the second Test Match between England and Australia, which was being played at Lords. Nick smiled to himself as he thought – everyone on the estate will know about this by the morning. Auntie Marge is like the 'Bush Telegraph'.

As usual, Keith and Don knocked on the back door at exactly 7.00pm. Nick thought that they must wait outside until the exact time before knocking; their punctuality was just too perfect. Even though Nick didn't have a date, he had decided to dress really smart. He had recently purchased a new pair of Levi jeans and a light blue Fred Perry shirt. His Mum had treated him to a pair of brushed suede hush puppies and along with a pair of dark sun glasses; he thought he looked the business. Moira lived in the same street as Nick, about 200 yards away. They knocked on the front door and were invited in by Mrs Harris, Moira's Mum.

'Come in, dears,' said Mrs Harris with a broad Irish accent. 'The girls won't be long. Their just finishing off making themselves look gorgeous for you.'

Mrs Harris was about the same age as Nick's Mum, pretty with a fuller figure.

'So Nick, how's your Mum, haven't seen her for a while?'

'She's fine thanks, Mrs Harris,' replied Nick nervously.

'You're looking very smart tonight Nick, who's the lucky girl?'

'I don't have a date tonight, Mrs Harris.'

'Please call me Mary.'

'Yes, Mrs Harris.'

'I can't believe that; a good looking boy like you. If I wasn't married, I'd snap you up straight away.'

Nick blushed.

'Ah, look at him; he's gone all shy.'

Nick was saved from any further embarrassment by the arrival of Moira and Elizabeth. All three boys simultaneously stood up.

'Don't they look a picture,' cooed Mrs Harris. 'I must take a photo; go on, stand together in the light. That's lovely.'

When the photo was taken they all said goodbye to Mrs Harris. Unfortunately, Nick was the last to leave and was accosted by Mrs Harris. She gave him a big squeeze and a kiss on the cheek. 'Have a nice time,' she shouted before closing the front door behind them.

'Is your Mum always that full on?' asked Nick.

'Not normally; she usually doesn't pay much attention to any boys I bring home. That was out of the ordinary. I think she's taken a shine to you.'

'That's understandable,' replied Nick, having got his composure back. 'After all, she's only human.'

The 325 bus took the happy gang all the way to Cottonmill and from the bus stop it was just a short walk to the fair. The fair was situated on the edge of the estate adjacent to the old mill. Even though it was still early, the lights from the rides and stalls still shone out like the Blackpool illuminations.

'Where shall we go on first?' cried Elizabeth, the excitement getting the better of her.

'Let's look around first; we've got lots of time and the fireworks don't start till nine,' replied Moira.

After wandering around the various attractions, saying hello to the many friends and acquaintances they met, they decided the first ride would be the Octopus. Once fastened in their seats they enjoyed a fast exciting ride that not only gave a see-saw motion, as the arm rises and falls, but a wildly spinning sensation as the car rotated quickly.

'Wow, I enjoyed that,' exclaimed Don, as he clambered out of the car. 'What's next?'

'How about the Twist?' suggested Moira.

'Sounds good to me,' replied Keith.

This ride, known in the UK as the American Twist is an open-top machine with an elevated 4-arm spider frame. Revolving shafts are suspended from each arm carrying smaller spider frames, each mounted with four cars.

When that ride was over, Elizabeth announced that she would like some candy-floss. The stall was quickly located and they all battled to consume the mass of sticky pink-spun sugar. As they walked round the stalls hoping to ignore the cries of the vendors to try whatever their stall had to offer, Elizabeth said 'Come on boys, which one of you is going to win me a teddy bear?'

They reached the shooting gallery where you could win a teddy bear of various sizes, using either an air-rifle, a bow and arrow, or even six darts. The boys accepted the challenge and after spending more money than they intended, they were presented with the smallest bear on offer. Nick, who always thought he was a decent shot, was sure that the sights on the air-guns were out of true; still, Elizabeth was happy.

'What do you fancy next, Nick? It must be your choice now,' asked Keith.

'Okay,' said Nick, looking around. 'How about a nice gentle ride on the carousel?'

'Excellent.'

The ride was just about to start as they jumped on the platform and each found themselves a brightly coloured horse. As the ride started, Nick noticed the attendant walking round collecting the fares. Nick immediately recognised the greasy looking rocker with his white t-shirt and skin tight jeans.

'Hello Joey,' said the girl on the horse directly behind Nick. 'Gonna give me a free ride?'

'Come back to my caravan later and I'll give you a free ride. If you know what I mean, darling,' replied Joey.

Nick hoped that Joey wouldn't recognise him. He had the exact change and handed it to him without looking him in the face. Joey took the money and moved on without saying a word. When the ride was over Moira suggested they take a ride on the Ghost Train. Nick still had a small worry about Joey. He told them that he didn't fancy the Ghost Train and he needed a wee. He would meet them by the hot-dog stall in ten minutes. Nick walked out of the entrance to the fair and made his way to the small river that ran alongside the field housing the fair. He knew Joey was following him. He walked about 100 yards before turning and facing Joey.

'Can I help you?' asked Nick.

Joey, who was now swinging a bicycle chain, replied 'We've got some unfinished business.'

Mr Campion, Nick's late self-defence teacher, told him that if an opponent has a weapon, like a baseball bat or the like, get in close. The closer you are the more difficult it is for them to swing at you. Nick stared to approach, never taking his eyes off his opponent. As soon as he was in touching distance, he suddenly moved his head and looked over Joey's shoulder. Joey's reaction was to following Nick's glance, which gave Nick just enough time to deliver a perfect right-hook on Joey's chin. He was out cold before he hit the ground. Nick looked around, nobody saw him. He quickly bent down and removed Joey's belt and used it to tie his hands behind his back. He then dragged Joey's limp body into a bush and dumped it there. Before he went back to the fair he gave Joey a quick kick in the ribs.

By the time Nick had arrived at the hot-dog van his friends where tucking into their jumbo hot-dog with onions and lots of mustard.

'Where have you been?' asked Moira. 'We were getting worried.'

'Sorry,' Nick replied. 'Lost track of time.'

'And what have you done to your hand?'

'Nothing,' he replied, automatically giving it a rub. 'Tripped over.'

'Come on,' said Don. 'Let's go and get a good spot to watch the fireworks.'

Elizabeth and Don followed by Moira led the way to the adjacent field. Keith stayed back to walk with Nick.

'Are you okay, mate?' asked Keith. 'I saw that bloke follow you out.'

'No problem, he's sleeping it off under some bush. Didn't want the girls to see; didn't want to spoil their evening.'

'Sometimes you're so thoughtful; I'm surprised you haven't been made a saint.

The rest of the evening continued without any worry or trouble. The firework display was spectacular and was accompanied by lots of Ooo's and Aaah's.

Sunday 21 June 1964

Nick woke up at about seven o'clock Sunday morning and had the sudden urge to go to church. It was about two years ago that he went through his religious period. He attended confirmation classes and subsequently got confirmed but over the last year, his attendance on Sunday mornings had waned. He wanted to say a prayer for Archie Taylor however the added attraction was that a certain girl, named Mary Hyde, would be there. He had fancied Mary for a long time, but whenever he had plucked up the courage to ask her out, she already had a boyfriend. It was convenient that the last delivery on his paper round was actually opposite St Michael's Church.

Nick completed his paper round without incident, which meant not being attacked by any of the vicious dogs. He left his bicycle along with his delivery bag in a quiet corner of the churchyard and managed to get settled five minutes before the Family Communion at nine o'clock. The service was run-of-the-mill, the sermon uninspiring, and the only hymn Nick was familiar with was *Dear Lord and Father*, which happened to be one of his favourites. He spotted Mary just a few pews in front of him, with some new boy in tow. As he queued to take Holy Communion, he had managed to smile at Mary; she smiled back, but he would have to wait a little longer.

It was about eleven o'clock than things got interesting. Nick had finished his breakfast of egg and bacon with fried bread and was totally engrossed in the *News of the World* when there was a knock on the front door. Mr Allen answered it and was heard to say, 'come in officer, he's in the living room.'

Nick looked up and was surprised to see Detective Inspector James.

Nick had met Inspector James before during a previous adventure and had thought he was a pleasant enough chap. He must have been in his early forties, of middle height and broad shouldered. His thick brown hair and dark eyes must have made him quite desirable to some women.

'Hello Nick, nice to see you again,' said DI James.

'Nice to see you too,' replied Nick nervously. 'What can I do for you?'

'It's about the death of Archie Taylor; I just need to ask you a few questions.'

'I gave a statement to the wooden-tops yesterday.'

'I know, but things have taken a dramatic change.'

'You mean you think he was murdered, I could have told you that yesterday.'

'I'm sure you could,' replied DI James, biting his bottom lip. 'Unfortunately DC Higgins doesn't possess you great intuition.'

Nick smiled and said nothing.

'So,' said DI James taking out his notebook. 'What led you to deduce that he had been murdered?'

'Many things: first, there was no suicide note; second, why commit suicide there? Third, how did he get there? No sign of his car. Fourth how did he climb the tree? Also, although I had only known him a short while, he was enjoying life; he loved his cricket and was really looking forward to the match. Need I go on?'

'I see, that's very similar to our way of thinking.'

'Have you found anything that might help with our theory?'

'Well, I shouldn't really tell you but the preliminary post-mortem revealed some interesting facts.'

'Go on.'

'Archie had consumed a rather large amount of whisky and, according to his wife, he never touched the stuff. Also the palms of his hands were burnt. At first, we thought they were rope burns; you know where he tried to free himself? But on closer inspection they were inflicted by a blow touch.'

'So, to stop him trying to escape,' interrupted Nick.

'Exactly,'

There was a pause, both man and boy deep in thought.

'What do you know about hanging,' asked DI James.

'A little,' replied Nick. 'I researched it once, when I was bored. Basically, if my memory serves me correct, there are four main forms of hanging.

1, short drop hanging where the prisoner drops just a few inches, and their suspended body weight and physical struggling causes the noose to tighten, normally resulting in death by strangulation. 2, suspension hanging where the executee is lifted into the air; death is the same as short drop hanging. 3, standard drop hanging where the prisoner drops about 4 to 6 feet, which may or may not break their neck. And last, the long drop hanging, which has been practiced in Britain since 1874. The distance of drop has been calculated according to weight and height. How am I doing?'

'I would worry about you if you were my son.'

'Tell me about it,' said Mr Allen, shaking his head.'

Nick shrugged his shoulders. At that point Mrs Allen entered carrying a tea tray.

'Thought you might like a cuppa.'

'That's very kind,' said DI James, taking a cup.

'Help yourself to sugar; I'll just fetch the biscuits.'

After a brief interlude, Nick said: 'I would guess that Archie died of strangulation.'

'Exactly,' said DI James. If he'd committed suicide he would have, perhaps, sat on the branch and slipped off. A four foot drop would have caused some sort of damage. But there was absolutely no sign of that. I would guess that whoever did this nasty deed, plied him with drink, got him to stand on something like a beer crate or box, strung him up then took away the box and left him dangling there. Of course, this is just between me and you. As far as anyone is concerned, we are treating this as suicide. So keep it to yourself; actually I don't know why I've told you.'

'I have that effect on people; they find me easy to talk to.'

Nick heard Mr Allen snigger.

Nick continued, 'have you spoken to Mrs Taylor?'

'Yes, but only briefly, yesterday to tell her the bad news. I'll try a formal interview later today. Is there anything else you can add?

'Not really,' but there was something that was bothering Nick, but he just couldn't put his finger on it.

'Well, if you think of anything, let me know. You've got my number.'

DI James thanked Mrs Allen for the tea and biscuits and was shown out by Mr Allen.

When Mr Allen returned he said, 'what do you think of that?'

'Well, Dad, I think it's obvious, the Ol' Bill are clueless again and they want me to help; that's what happens when you are a consulting detective.'

'Oh, and how do you suppose to do that, Sherlock?'

'Well, Dad, it's like this,' said Nick, leaning forward. 'How well did you know the deceased?'

It turned out that Mr Allen was acquainted with Archie Taylor; he had met him on several occasions in the British Legion and the Farriers Arms public house.

Mr Allen, who had now stopped worrying about Nick's adventures or so he made out, told Nick all he could about Archie Taylor, which wasn't much. He was a quiet, well-spoken man, who liked his beer, dominoes, darts and cricket. He had spoken to him a few times, but could not be classed as a close friend. Their conversation was interrupted by another knock on the front door. Mrs Allen answered and Nick heard her say, 'hello Moira, he's in the living room.'

Nick stood up to greet Moira.

Mr Allen also stood up and said, 'I'll leave you to it, got some gardening to do.'

When they were alone Moira said 'just wanted to thank you for taking us to the funfair last night.'

'I didn't take you, Keith did.'

'You know what I mean; anyway how's your hand?'

'Oh, it's fine; just a little bruised.'

'Who did you hit this time?'

'Don't know what you mean.'

'You can't fool me, Nick Allen.'

'Oh, just some thug who wanted to wrap a bicycle chain around my head.'

'So he deserved it then?'

'Absolutely.'

'That's alright then. Now let me have a look at that hand.'

Moira grabbed Nick's hand, inspected it, then said, 'let me kiss it better.' She pressed Nick's swollen hand to her lips. She then slowly removed the hand from her mouth but didn't release it, starring seductively into Nick's eyes. Nick could feel a stirring sensation in his trouser region as his head moved slowly towards Moira's. Their lips were about an inch apart when Nick suddenly said, 'I bought a new record yesterday; would you like to hear it? It's *Juliet* by the Four Pennies.' Nick broke way and started fumbling in his record collection.

'He it is,' he said after a frantic search, and quickly put it on the turn-table.

'You didn't buy this one yesterday,' she said. 'It's been out ages. Anyway isn't a bit girlie for you.'

'I like love songs,'

Moira smiled.

'Oh bugger it,' he whispered to himself. Then he walked slowly towards her, put his arms gently around her waist and kissed her passionately. When they eventually came up for air she smiled and said, 'I've waited so long for that.'

'So have I,' he replied.

Still smiling at each other, they kissed some more. After a while they sat down on the settee, hands firmly locked together.

'What happens now?' asked Nick.

'Easy, I'll chuck Keith this afternoon and start going out with you.'

'Not a good idea, I couldn't do that to my best friend.'

'Why, don't you like me?'

'You don't know how much I like you. It's painful just to see you with Keith. But no, we must keep our feelings to ourselves, for the time being. Hopefully he'll tire of you, then that way nobody gets hurt.'

'You are so thoughtful, Nick. You could never hurt anyone. They'll make you a Saint one day.'

'Someone else said that recently; but I don't feel very saintly today,' he said as he put his arms around her, 'come here, gorgeous.'

Monday 22 June 1964

The sun was high in the sky with its rays beating down on Nick and Keith as they sat on the grass at the edge of the school playing field during the lunchtime break. Their dinner had consisted of a non-descript meat, lumpy mash potatoes, over boiled cabbage and gravy; they both declined the tapioca pudding. The playing field was quite busy; an impromptu game of football had just started with jumpers as goal-posts and a tennis ball.

'I suppose you want to talk about Archie Taylor,' asked Keith as he pulled a packet of Polos from his pocket.

'Don't you want to find out who killed him?' replied Nick sticking out has hand.

'Do I have much choice?'

'Not really; how's Moira?'

'She's fine, why do you ask?'

'No reason, just being friendly... ....you know how concerned I am about your welfare. Your happiness is my happiness.'

'Of course you are, but she was a bit funny when I saw her yesterday. She seemed a bit distant; like she had something on her mind.'

'That time of the month, most probably.'

'Of course; anyway, how are we going to solve this murder?'

'Well, I've been thinking; we need some background information on him. I've spoken to my dad and he said he was just a regular guy - quiet, but quite popular. I think we should start by visiting Mrs Taylor.'

'Do you think that is wise? After all, it's only two days since he died.'

'Good point, but we did find him, so it's only right we pay our respects.'

'Okay, do we know where she lives?'

'Portland Street, I looked it up in the Kelly's Directory.'

'Well done; we'll visit her tonight.'

At precisely 7.00 pm three smartly dressed youths knocked on the front door of the late Archie Taylor. Within a minute the door was answered by an attractive forty-something year old woman dressed in black. She had a round face with blonde hair tied in a bun. Her eyes were red and she spoke with a strong Dutch accent.

'Can I help you?' asked Mrs Taylor looking inquisitively at these three young boys.

'Sorry to bother you on this sad occasion, but we felt that we had to pay our respects, because it was us who found Mr Taylor,' said Nick in a solemn voice.

'That's very kind of you, please come in.'

She led the boys through to the living room and beckoned them to sit down. The room was clean but unremarkable. A few photographs were on display showing Mr and Mrs Taylor posing together at different ages and locations. A few sympathy cards adorned the mantelpiece.

Nobody spoke and Nick was starting to feel uncomfortable; then Mrs Taylor said, 'sorry, how rude of me. Would you like a glass of lemonade?

Nick said 'no thanks,' at the same time as Keith said, 'yes please.'

Mrs Taylor smiled and said, 'This is very difficult for all of us, I'll make some lemonade. Perhaps a slice of Victoria sponge will go down well with it.'

Mrs Taylor left the room and returned a few minutes later with a tray containing four glasses of lemonade and a Victoria sponge cut in eight slices. As the boys enjoyed their delicious ice cold lemonade and very tasty cake, the tension in the room started to ease.

'How long have you known Archie?' asked Mrs Taylor.

'Not very long,' replied Nick. 'Well, actually, only two weeks. He spotted us playing cricket on the green and he approached us and asked if we wanted to play for his team. We had a practice match last Saturday and our first match would have been this Saturday.'

'He was really looking forward to the match. It was always his dream to run a boys' cricket team. You see, we were never blessed with children of our own and I think he needed this. That's what makes it so difficult to understand why he committed suicide.'

'What have the police said?' asked Keith.

'Not much, really, they said there would be a post-mortem. Hopefully that might shed some light on why he did it.'

'How was he during the last week, did he seem worried about anything?' asked Nick.

'No, he was fine; as I said, he was really excited on Friday night. I told him to go and have a couple of beers to calm down. He normally goes to the pub on Fridays on the way home from work, but I sent him out again after his tea. That was the last time I saw him. He never came home. I waited up for him, but I must have fallen asleep. I woke up at about 7.00 am and when I realised he wasn't here, I phoned the police to report him missing.'

'How often did he go out?'

'He always went out on Tuesdays to play dominoes at the British Legion and play darts for the Farriers Arms on Thursdays. They were his regular nights out; other times he took me out. He occasionally popped in the Farriers Arms for a quick pint; he preferred it to the Portland Arms or the Blue Lion. For some reason he likes McMullen's beer.'

Don, who so far had not said a word, asked 'where did he work?'

'Marconi's; he worked in the warehouse. He was very happy there.'

'Your accent tells me you're Dutch; how did you meet?' asked Nick.

Mrs Taylor smiled, 'it is a very romantic story. Would you like to hear it?'

Nick had noticed how relaxed Mrs Taylor was becoming, it was clear that talking about her late husband had a soothing effect.

'During the last war, Archie was shot down over Holland. He was the only one of the five man crew to survive. He somehow managed to avoid capture by the Germans and he made his way to the coast. I lived in a small farm on the outskirts of Voorburg. I found him one morning hiding in our barn; he was very ill. I nursed him for many months until his health returned. It was very difficult because the Germans were constantly searching for British airmen. During this time we had fallen madly in love and we couldn't bear to be parted. We got married in September 1942 and Archie joined the Dutch Resistance. Then in 1947 we moved to England.'

'Has Archie any other family,' asked Don.

'No, only me; he was an only child. His parents were quite old and they both died within a few months of each other in 1950 from TB.'

There was a short silence, before Don said, 'do you have any more of this delicious lemonade?'

'Of course,' replied Mrs Taylor, smiling as she made her way to the kitchen.

'Nick looked at Keith and Don and said, 'I think we've got enough information to get started. We'll finish our lemonade and then be on our way.'

Tuesday 23 June 1964

Nick, Keith and Don had decided that their next port-of-call would be the British Legion; so straight after their tea, they cycled down Verulam Road to the St Albans branch of the British Legion. After leaning their bikes against the wall they walked through the main door into a small foyer. A small octogenarian sat at a table with a large book in front of him. He wore a smart blazer with a row of medals over a crisp white shirt and a British Legion tie. On his head he wore a black beret.

'Can I help you?' asked the old man looking up from his desk.

'We just want a quick word with the club Steward,' replied Nick.

'Are you members?'

'Do we look like members?

'Can't come in unless you are members.'

'Okay,' said Nick, getting a little agitated 'How do we become members?'

'Have you been in the Armed Forces?'

'No.'

'Are you over eighteen?'

'No.'

'Then you can't become members.'

'I've been in here loads of times before.'

'Were you signed in?'

'I came with my dad.'

'Are you with him today?'

'No.'

'Then you can't come in.'

Nick then noticed that the old man's half pint mug was nearly empty.

'I'll buy you a beer if you let me in.'

'Are you trying to bribe me?'

'Yes!'

'Okay, half of Best.'

'Thank you,' said Nick as he walked through the door to the main bar.

'I was at the Battle of the Somme, you know. Where are you going?' asked the old man, looking at Keith and Don.

'I'm with him,' said Keith.

'And I'm with him,' said Don

The three boys walked into the main hall and approached the bar where Jack Thomas, the club Steward, stood polishing glasses. Jack was a burley character with rosy cheeks. He reminded Nick of a Toby Jug.

'Hello, young Nick, what brings you in here?' asked Jack. 'And how did you get past Howard?'

'Bribed him with half a bitter, you don't mind?'

Jack laughed. 'I think you've been had. Sit yourself down while I'll take it out to him.'

Jack picked up a fresh glass and poured out Howard's beer.

'Did he tell you he was at the Battle of the Somme?'

They all nodded.

Jack laughed. 'He did his basic training, was shipped out to France on the Friday, got shot in the leg on Saturday and was back in England by Monday. Nice little weekend visit.'

'What about all those medals?' asked Keith.

'Let's just say that Howard likes his jumble sales,' said Jack, tapping his nose.

The hall was not the most inviting place, tables and chairs set around the perimeter; a small dance floor to the left and a dartboard. The walls were adorned with boring wallpaper, a notice board, a trophy cabinet and small wooden plaques with Army regiment crests.

Jack returned and sat opposite them. 'Now how can I help you?'

'What can you tell us about Archie Taylor? We believe he come in here quite often.' said Nick

'Looking into his death are you? I heard that it might be a bit suspicious.'

'We don't believe he killed himself, if that's what you mean. We're making a few discreet enquires, so this interview is strictly hush-hush.'

Jack smiled, 'so you're helping the police out, are you?'

'Not really, this is an independent enquiry. We may assist the police if they ask nicely.'

Keith cut in to join the conversation: 'we occasionally do some consultancy work for the police, but it's normally for British Intelligence.'

Jack laughed, 'kids of today, what imaginations. So you're telling me you're some kind of James Bond.'

'Don't be silly,' laughed Nick. 'James Bond works for MI6, we work for MI5.'

Suitably rebuffed Jack said, 'Okay, I'm a busy man, what do you want to know?'

'We believe that he comes in here every Tuesday night to play for the dominoes team.'

'No.'

'No, what?'

'No, he doesn't play for the dominoes team. He comes in here every Tuesday between half nine and ten, but he doesn't play dominoes. Anyway they only play her every other week when they have a home fixture.'

'That's interesting. Have you noticed anything unusual about him? Did he seem agitated, did he speak to any strangers, anything different about him?

'No, nothing like that. He always seems a bit down on a Tuesday; but other times, he's always happy; a contented sort of chap.'

Nick stood, shook hands with Jack and said, 'thank you for your time, you've been most helpful.'

Nick and Keith left the hall, walked past Howard who smiled and raised his glass.'

'Cunning ol' bastard,' whispered Keith.

Once outside, the boys sat on the small wall in the front of the British Legion.

'What do you think?' asked Nick.

'Well… …I think that Archie was seeing another woman. He tells his wife he's going to the Legion but he has to pop in there before going home to cover himself,' replied Keith.

Don cut in and said, 'my uncle Fred said "you must always be one step ahead and cover your tracks". Once he told me he'd been shagging his secretary all night and before he went home he stuck a bit of chalk behind his ear. When his wife started moaning at him and asking where he'd been all night he said that he was fed up with her nagging and he'd been with his secretary having a good time. She called him a lying bastard and said I know you've been up the pub playing darts you've still got the chalk behind your ear.'

'When does his divorce come through?' asked Nick.

'Next week.'

'No, I don't think it's as simple as that. He didn't seem the type. But somehow we need to find out where he was going every Tuesday. I think tomorrow we'll pop up to the Farriers Arms and have a word with the landlord. Are you seeing Moira tonight?'

'Yes, I said I'd pop in after this.'

'Okay, I'll ride with you.'

The boys cycled gently to Moira's house where Nick and Don said goodbye to Keith and then cycled on. Nick was feeling extremely jealous.

Wednesday 24 June 1964

Keith had asked Nick if they could visit the pub as soon as it opened as he had plans for the evening. Don was unavailable due to some after-school activity. This meant that the boys had to hang around until 5.30 pm when the pub opened. They had a ramble around the market but most of the stall-holders were packing away. They treated themselves to a milkshake at Christopher's before cycling down Lower Dagnall Street to the Farriers Arms, a small unassuming back street public house. The pub was empty when they entered and walked straight up to the bar. They were approached by an elderly man who reminded Nick of Jack Walker, the landlord of the Rovers Return in *Coronation Street*.

What can I do for you?' he asked.

'Two pints of Best and two pickled eggs,' replied Nick in his deepest voice.

'You cheeky beggars; go on, clear off.'

'Just joking,' laughed Nick. 'I'm Nick Allen, Stan Allen's son; we would just like a quick word.'

'Oh, so you're Stan's son; I've heard a lot about you. He's always telling me about the scrapes you get into. Says you remind him of Tom Sawyer; you'll either be Prime Minister or end up in prison.'

'We just want to know about Archie Taylor. What can you tell us?'

'Not much really; quiet chap, keeps himself to himself. Good darts player though, plays for the team.'

'Has anybody been asking for him or upset him lately?'

'Nothing springs to mind. ….Would you like a glass of lemonade and a packet of crisps?

'You've very kind; that would be great.'

'Okay. Sit yourselves down; potato or these new cheese-and-onion flavour?'

'Not those cheese-and-onion,' exclaimed Keith. 'They make your breath smell and I've got a hot date tonight.'

'I didn't think you were seeing Moira tonight,' asked Nick looking concerned.

'I'm not,' replied Keith, looking very guilty. 'I'll explain later.'

'By the way, my name's Reg; I'm the landlord,' he said as he threw two bags of Smith's Crisps towards Nick, before bringing the drinks to their table.

'Cor blimey,' exclaimed Reg suddenly.

'What is it?' asked Nick.

'I just remembered something; a few Fridays ago there was a stranger in here. Sitting where you are; Archie was playing darts. Big bloke he was; forearms like Popeye and he had a tattoo. Well, he sat there with about an inch remaining of his pint. I thought, is he ever gonna finish it. Then, as soon as Archie went to the bar, he downed it in one, got up and walked to the bar and stood next to him. Archie looked as if he'd seen a ghost. The entire colour drained from his face. I didn't hear what was said as I was busy serving another customer. By the time I went to serve him, Archie had grabbed his jacket and left. I asked the stranger what he had said to upset Archie. He replied: "nothing, it was just a case of mistaken identity."

The stranger has been in a few times since, but not in the last couple of weeks.'

Clearly excited, Nick said: Is there anything else you can tell us about him; for instance, did he give a name?'

'No, I never got his name, but he did walk with a limp.'

'What about the tattoo?' asked Keith. 'Can you describe it?'

'Actually, I can; I'm fascinated by tattoos. There was a big red heart with a dagger next to it and a banner wrapped around them with the name Polly.'

'Anything else?' asked Nick.

'As I said he was a big bloke, weathered face, about fifty and short-cropped ginger hair.'

At that point, two customers appeared in the pub.

'Hope that's helpful, better start serving,' said Reg, as he stood up.

'You've been brilliant, thanks a lot,' said Nick, then turning to Keith. 'Who are you seeing tonight, I hope you're not cheating on Moira?'

'Of course not, well not exactly. It's complicated.'

'Go on.'

'Well my Mum's friend asked her to ask me if I wouldn't mind taking her daughter to the pictures. There's a film that she's eager to see, but she's got nobody to go with. I couldn't really say no.'

'Are you going to tell Moira?'

'I don't think so, best she doesn't know. I mean it's totally innocent but you know how funny women are.'

'So what's she like, this…..daughter of your Mum's friend?'

'Who Brenda? She's fifteen, with an enormous pair of bazookas.'

'And that wouldn't have anything to do with it?'

After his tea, Nick was at a loose end and was bored. I know, he thought, if Keith's at the pictures with bazooka girl, perhaps I'll pop down and see if Moira fancies a walk. Changing out of his school uniform he put on his freshly ironed Levis and a crisp white t-shirt, dabbed on some of his dad's Old Spice aftershave and made his way to Moira's house. He walked past a couple of times before building up the courage to knock on the door. Mrs Norris answered.

'Hello, Nick,' she said. 'How can I help you?'

'I was just passing and I thought I'd see how Moira was. Is she in?'

'I'm afraid not, she's out with her friend, Dympna.'

'Oh well, never mind.'

'I've just put the kettle on; do you fancy a cup of tea?'

'No thanks,' replied Nick, panicking a little. 'Better get home; Mum will be worrying where I am. Thanks all the same.'

Nick quickly left and made his way home.

Saturday 27 June 1964

Nick returned from his Saturday paper round in an extremely good mood. The investigation had come to a temporary halt; they had made no progress on where Archie went on Tuesday nights or the identity of the mystery man from the Farriers Arms. Today they were attending the St Albans Beat Group Contest being held at Westminster Lodge. Thirteen groups would battle it out for the first prize of £25 and an audition with the Harold Davison Agency. Apparently, they promote the Dave Clark Five, the Applejacks and the Mojos. The contest started at 10:30 am and would finish at 2:30 pm, when the top six groups would be announced and they would go through to the finals which would start at 7:30pm. A well-known local disc jockey called Nigel King would handle the proceedings. The first session cost 2/6 and the evening session 7/6; Nick, Keith and Don were amongst the first in the queue. Moira was going to join them for the evening session. It seemed a bit strange listening to the groups at that time of the day and the venue didn't seem right; brick walls with industrial pipes running down the walls. But this didn't stop the boys having a brilliant time. There were three groups from St Albans whom the boys had elected to support, Unit Five, Peter D and the Veraiders, and the boy's favourite The King Bees. The King Bees played a mixture of Rhythm & Blues and semi-commercial music. Their line-up was Nick Holland, Terry Wade, Graham Hiskett and Simon Smith. Of the three groups, only The King Bees made it to the final stages. At the end of the first session the boys caught the 321 bus up Holywell Hill to St Peter's Street. Nick thought it was like coming out of the cinema in the daylight, not natural.

The evening session was even more exciting; approximately a thousand people packed into the hall to see the final stage of the contest, with the added bonus of seeing The Barron Knights with Duke D'Mond. The final six groups were:

The Rocking Couriers
The Dominators
The Trekkas
The King Bees
The Cortinas
The Leesiders Sect

Nick and his friends had an amazing evening and Nick had managed to hold Moira's hand without anyone noticing. In a tightly fought contest, The Cortinas from Hatfield won by just one point. The Trekkas from Welwyn Garden City came second and The Kings Bees were placed third. After the results were announced The Cortinas were asked to do the final set. But before that, the crowd raised the roof with the appearance of the Barron Knights. The highlight of the evening was the performance of their (soon to be released) single *Call up the Groups*, which was extremely well received.

Sunday 28 June 1964

'I've passed go, so I collect £200,' said Gwendolyn, Nick's cousin.

As customary, when Nick's Uncle John and Auntie Laura visited for tea on a Sunday, Nick has to play monopoly with his twelve-year-old cousin. Nick didn't mind the occasional game and he got to use the Top Hat as it was a home fixture. Auntie Laura was helping Mrs Allen in the kitchen and Mr Allen and Uncle John where in the living room with Nick and Gwen.

'What are you up to these days, Nick?' asked Uncle John.

'Not much, just trying to solve a murder,' replied Nick, throwing a four and landing on Trafalgar Square.

Uncle John laughed, but Mr Allen said, 'You think he's joking; well, I'm afraid he's not. You know Archie Taylor, the one who hanged himself? Well, Nick found him and between me and you and the police they suspect foul play.'

'Good luck to you, lad,' said Uncle John giving an encouraging nod of the head.

'So how is the investigation going, son?' asked Mr Allen.

'Only one important thing had happened in the last four days; and that is, nothing has happened,' replied Nick.

'Well, if there's anything I can do just ask.' said Uncle John as he started filling his pipe with Players Navy Cut tobacco.

'You don't happen to know where Archie used to go every Tuesday evening do you?' asked Nick casually.

'Well, actually, I do,' said Uncle John, sitting up straight and feeling important.

Nick jumped down from the table, 'Do tell, Uncle John… ….and keep your fingers away from the bank, Gwen.'

'As you already know, I work at Hill End Hospital; on Tuesdays I do a couple of hour's overtime, so I leave about 7.30 pm. Well, most Tuesdays, I always saw Archie cycling into the grounds.'

'What was he doing there?'

'I think he was visiting someone, not sure who, but he was regular as clockwork.'

'This is a definite breakthrough; do you know what ward he was visiting?'

'As a matter of fact I do; it was the Huxley ward.'

'Thanks, Uncle John, you're the best.'

Nick went back to the table, picked up the dice, threw a ten, landed on Park Lane and said 'I'll buy that.'

The best bit about the visit of Uncle John and Aunt Laura is that they always visit the Blue Anchor public house in the evening. Nick loved the Blue Anchor, a 17th century pub situated in Fishpool Street and its garden that backed on to Verulamium Park. Only the River Ver separated the two plots of land. To gain entry to the beer garden, one had to pass through a wooden arch which was decorated with fairy lights and the garden itself was illuminated with coloured bulbs. To Nick, this was his secret beer garden. Often on these occasions some of Nick's other aunts and uncles would join them, to make a real family event. As luck would have it, Mr and Mrs Harris were there along with Moira and Elizabeth, with Keith following behind. As soon as Nick had said hello to everyone, and Mr Allen had bought the drinks, Nick found himself an empty table and sat down opposite Keith and Moira.

'Any news on the investigation?' asked Keith inquisitively.

'Yes; we've had a breakthrough. My intelligence has revealed that Archie was visiting someone every Tuesday at the Huxley ward in Hill End hospital,' replied Nick. 'So that is our next port of call.'

'But Hill End's a nuthouse, isn't it?'

'So?'

'Why do you want to go there?'

'Because it is my desire; is that not enough?'

'When are you planning to go?'

'On Tuesday, of course; whoever he was seeing will be expecting Archie, but they will have the pleasure of our company instead.'

'Can't make Tuesday, I have an appointment.'

'No problem, I'll go with Don. I'm sure he would like a visit to a nuthouse.'

It hadn't escaped Nick's notice that all the time during the conversation, Moira had been playing footsie under the table with him.

Tuesday 30 June 1964

Don was not a happy bunny as he cycled behind Nick on their way to Hill End hospital. Nick had tried to reassure him that there was nothing to worry about and that all the really mad patients would be locked up; the only people walking about would be the depressed ones. Don was not convinced. On arrival they made their way to the main building. Nick was impressed by the magnificent architecture of the Victorian building. They left their bicycles outside and made their way through the arch to the reception where they asked for directions for Huxley ward. As they walked down the corridor, past the Art room and the Anderson ward, they were approached by a strange man in an overcoat. Nick thought he must be about fifty and wondered why he was wearing a very heavy coat on such a warm evening.

'Haven't seen you here before,' said the stranger, taking a close look at Nick.

'Just visiting,' said Nick, taking a step back.

'I came to visit once,' replied the stranger. 'But they never let me leave, been here for ten years.'

'But it's nice here isn't it? You must like it?'

'Are you trying to be funny?' shouted the stranger.

Taking another step back, Nick said, 'no, just making conversation.'

The stranger seemed to mellow a bit, 'It's not too bad, it's just the electric shock treatment I can't stand.'

Nick could feel Don nudging him in the back, 'Well, it's been nice to meet you, but we must go.'

The boys quickly bypassed the stranger and ran down the corridor towards Huxley ward. They entered the ward and not knowing what to do or where to go, just stood there. Nick couldn't help noticing the combined smell of urine and disinfectant. They were soon approached by a large, friendly-looking nurse who reminded Nick of Hattie Jacques in *Carry on Nurse.*

'Hello boys, can I help you?' she asked.

'I do hope so; can you tell us who Archie Taylor used to visit on Tuesdays?' replied Nick.

'You say – used to?'

'I'm afraid he's dead.'

'Oh dear, oh dear, that is sad. You'd better come to my office. I think we need to talk.'

The nurse led Nick and Don to her office. Nick noticed the sign on the door. It said, Ward Sister – Mrs Dora Williams. Sister Williams beckoned Nick and Don to sit down and she sat in her usual seat behind her desk.

'So,' she said, 'what is your connection to Archie Taylor?'

Don, who was not looking particularly comfortable, just nudged Nick, as to say "get on with it".

Nick started, 'Well, we were friends with Archie and unfortunately, we were the ones who found him.'

'Hanging from a tree,' added Don.

'Oh my,' gasped Sister Williams, bringing her hands up to her mouth.

Nick continued: 'We think his death may be suspicious and we're helping the police with their investigation.'

'They must be hard up these days,' said Sister Williams, instantly regretting the way it came out, after receiving a very dirty look from both Nick and Don.

'Anyway, we discovered that Archie used to visit here every Tuesday.'

'Something the police didn't know,' added Don, with a sarcastic tone.

'Also, his wife was unaware of these visits; we thought it might be important.'

'I'm impressed,' said Sister Williams. 'And you were right to follow it up. Archie came every Tuesday to visit his sister.'

Nick and Don looked at each other and said in unison: 'We didn't know he had a sister.'

'It's a tragic story, Archie's sister; her name is Sally and is what used to be called: a delicate girl. She was devoted to Archie. I expect you already know that Archie was shot down in the war and because the family didn't hear from him, it was assumed he was dead or missing in action. Sally had a breakdown and just as she was getting better, Archie re-appeared. For some reason, the shock was too much and it set her back considerably and she never recovered. Their parents, who were getting on a bit, were struggling to cope; so they put her away and she's been with us ever since.'

'But how come Archie's wife didn't know?'

'There has always been a bit of a stigma where mental health issues are concerned. Not the thing you talk about in civilised society. They must have somehow kept it from her. Anyway, their parents died shortly afterwards; both contracted TB, very sad; died within a couple of weeks of each other. So, Sally's with us for the foreseeable future and Archie visits every Tuesday.'

'How was she last week when Archie didn't show?'

'Very distraught; we had to sedate her.'

'How is she today?'

'Very anxious; she's in the day room at the moment.'

'May we see her?'

'I don't see why not. But don't tell her that Archie's dead. Tell her that he's busy or something.'

Sister Williams stood up and led the boys to the day room. Sally Taylor was sitting by the window starring across the grounds.

'Hello, Sally,' said Sister Williams. 'You've got visitors.'

Sally turned her head slightly and said, 'where's Archie?' Nick understood what Sister Williams meant by the term 'delicate'. She was very frail, her blond hair, turning grey, was tied in a ponytail, and she was wearing a thin, pink cotton dressing gown and pink slippers. There was more than a passing resemblance to Archie.

Nick took the lead, 'Archie's very busy at work and he couldn't get away, so he asked us to see if you were alright.'

This seemed to satisfy Sally. 'He's got a very important job, you know.' She continued looking out of the window.

Nick was struggling to find anything to say, 'What can you tell us about Archie? We haven't known him for very long.'

Nick could tell that Sally was deep in thought; then after about two minutes she said, 'Archie's got a secret.'

'Do you want to share it with us?'

'Shouldn't really.'

'I know, but I'm sure he won't mind. After all he trusts us. He wouldn't send anyone else to visit you.'

After another pause she said: 'One day he started crying, and said that he had to tell someone, he needed to share his burden.'

She continued staring out of the window.

'Go on,' encouraged Nick.

'When Archie was in the war, he was a fighter pilot, you know. Then one day, he got shot down over Holland. They all managed to bail out; four survived but one died. Archie and his friend Charlie got separated from the other two. But Charlie got shot and he begged Archie to help him, but the Germans were coming. Then Archie panicked and ran off, leaving Charlie to the mercy of the Germans. He didn't know whether he lived or died. Archie escaped and stayed in Holland for the rest of the war. He was frightened to come back to England in case he was arrested. He married a Dutch girl then waited till the war was over before returning.'

Nick looked at Don and said, 'I bet that was the bloke in the Farrier's Arms, that's why Archie was frightened. I bet he came back and … … … …'

Don gave Nick a sharp kick in the ankle and nodded towards Sally. Nick acknowledged his mistake.

'Thank you, Sally, for sharing that with us. I promise we won't tell a soul. Well I'm afraid we have to go now, but it's been a pleasure meeting you. And …. I nearly forgot, I bought a bar of chocolate, Fry's Milk Sandwich,' Nick had bought it earlier to eat tonight while watching the television. 'I'm sure you'll like it. Bye now.'

Sally took the chocolate bar and just starred at it. Nick and Don went in search of Sister Williams. They found her immersed in paperwork in her office.

'How did you get on?' she asked, looking up.

'I think we've been lucky, she may have provided the vital clue for solving this case,' replied Nick.

'That's good, but we need to make a decision about Archie's death.'

'I think it would be best coming from Archie's wife. If I paid her a visit and explained the situation, I might be able to persuade her to visit Sally. She's a lovely lady, I'm sure she would understand.'

'You're a very kind and understanding young man, but you haven't told me you names.'

'The name's Allen, Nick Allen and this is my associate Don Patrick.'

'Well, it's been very good to meet you. Do you do a lot of work for the police?' asked Sister Williams, tongue in cheek.

Don, now feeling a little more relaxed said, 'a little, but mostly for British Intelligence. We're on a special programme for gifted children.'

Sister Williams was now struggling to suppress the urge to burst out laughing and said, 'that's very interesting, but I must say goodbye; as you can see, lots of paperwork to do.'

Nick and Don said their goodbyes and once they were out of earshot, Don said, 'patronising old cow.'

Nick laughed as they made their way down the corridor towards the main entrance. They had just passed the Art room when they were approached by a scary old woman. It was difficult to put an age on her, but she reminded Nick of someone you would see begging on the streets of the East End during the Victorian period.

'Want a jig-a-jig?' hackled the old woman.

'I beg your pardon,' said Nick, feeling Don cowering behind him.

'Want a jig-a-jig?'

'I'm sorry, I don't know what you mean,' replied Nick, trying not to offend the old woman.

'Do you want some of this,' she screeched as she lifted her skirt up to reveal a knickerless, very hairy, crotch.

'Aaaaaaaah,' screamed Nick and Don, before running like greyhounds out of the traps at White City to the main building, where they jumped on their bicycles and pedalled for their lives.

They cycled down Camp Road without talking. When they reached The Crown public house, Nick said that he needed to visit the Police Station. Don stated that he had had enough for one evening and was going straight home. They said their goodbyes and Nick said he would phone him tomorrow. Nick made his way up Victoria Street to the Police Station. As Nick opened the door and glanced towards the desk, he was dismayed to recognise the Desk Sergeant A few months ago, Nick had been arrested for assault and it was only by the intervention of a friend in MI5 that he wasn't charged. Nick approached the desk, hoping the sergeant wouldn't recognise him.

'Can I help you?' asked the Desk Sergeant.

'I'd like to leave a message for DI James,' replied Nick, thinking so far so good.

The Sergeant picked up a pencil and prepared to write. 'And what is the message?'

'Tell him to meet Nick Allen in Sally's Café at four o'clock tomorrow afternoon.'

Nick could hear the penny drop.

'Oh, I thought I recognised you; St Albans number one thug.'

'That's not very nice; I was never charged.'

'No, never could understand that; thought we had you good and proper.'

'Can you deliver my message or would you like me to write it down for you?'

'I can write, you know.'

'Oh, I didn't know that.'

'Less of your cheek or I'll come round there and… ……'

'Just give him the message and tell him it's urgent; thank you.' With that Nick left the station and cycled home.

Wednesday 1 July 1964

When Nick asked Keith if he would like to accompany him to Sally's Café to meet DI James, he said that he was unavailable. He had already made plans. Nick suspected he was seeing Big Brenda, but didn't mention it. DI James was already seated in a booth, sipping a double espresso when Nick entered Sally's Café. He ordered a strawberry milkshake with ice cream and joined DI James. Dionne Warwick's, *Walk on By* was being played on the juke box.

'What's with the "cloak and dagger", stuff?' asked DI James.

Nick ignored the remark and asked, 'how's the investigation going?'

'Slowly; we've interviewed Archie's wife, his workmates at Marconi's and all his known associates at various watering holes.'

'And?'

'Nothing that's leads us to a murderer.'

Nick smiled to himself. 'Did you interview the landlord of the Farriers Arms?'

'Not personally, that would be DC Higgins'.

'Interesting.'

DI James could tell that Nick was hiding something from him.

'Okay smarty pants, what have you got?'

'I don't know why you sent along DC Higgins; he's a pratt.'

'His father is the assistant commissionaire; who is also a pratt.'

'Say no more. Well, we have a suspect; Reg Willis, the landlord of the Farriers Arms, gave us a description of a man who was harassing Archie; big bloke, short ginger hair, and a tattoo with the name Polly. According to Archie's sister, Sally... ... ...'

'Wait a minute,' interrupted DI James. 'According to Archie's wife, he didn't have a sister.'

'Tut, tut; do I have to do all the work on this case?'

'Just get on with it,' responded DI James getting slightly agitated.

Nick went on to explain how he discovered Archie's sister and all about their visit to Hill End Hospital. 'I believe that this Charlie killed Archie in revenge for what happened during the war.'

'Sounds feasible,' agreed DI James.

'What I need you to do is check it out through the war records; can you do that?'

'Consider it done. You've done really well, young Nick. I'll let you know as soon as we find something out.'

While he was finishing his coffee, DI James studied Nick, thinking what a strange but likeable boy he was. Although he was happy with the two young daughters he had, he often wondered what it would be like to have a son. Could he cope with all the scrapes he would get into or was Nick the exception to the norm? With that, DI James finished his coffee, said goodbye, and left. Nick decided to hang around for a while as he had taken quite a shine to the waitress. Her name was Anna and she had a short hair style, similar to Mary Quant. She wasn't too tall but had legs that went up to her armpits. He waited until she came to clear his table.

'Hello Anna, how are you today?' said Nick trying to sound sophisticated.

'I'm fine, thank you,' she replied and gave him a little smile.

'I was just wondering what time you finished work tonight.'

'Let me think, not sure, but it will be way after your bed-time,' she gave another little smile and walked away.

Feeling suitably embarrassed, he left the café and cycled home. Nick was feeling confused as he free-wheeled down Folly Lane. He couldn't understand all these strange feelings that he was experiencing. He missed seeing Carol, he was definitely in love with Keith's girlfriend Moira, and was infatuated with Anna in the café. Last night he even dreamed about the young girl he met in the park and he dare not even think about the dream he had the other night about Miss James, the English teacher. It was then that he remembered a conversation he had the other day with Richard Martin, a class-mate, who was experienced in these matters. He had the perfect solution to cure these feelings.

Arriving home, he put his bicycle in the shed and walked into the kitchen where Mrs Allen was busy making the tea.

'Hello dear, had a good day?' she asked.

'Not bad, Mum; is it alright if I have a bath?'

'It's a bit early, but don't use all the hot water.'

'That's okay; I'm having a cold bath.'

Friday 3 July 1964

Nick had decided to have a quiet night in; unfortunately, his favourite programme *Ready Steady Go* had been cancelled because of the men's final at Wimbledon. But he still enjoyed watching Roy Emerson beat Fred Stolle 6-4, 12-10, 4-6, 6-3. He was just reading the latest edition of *New Musical Express* with Dusty Springfield on the cover page, when he heard a knock on the front door. He heard his mother answer it and say 'he's in there.'

The living room door opened and Nick looked from the article he was reading, Cilla talks Heart to Heart with Alan Freeman, to see DI James standing there. Nick beckoned him to sit down.

'Any news?' asked Nick.

'You were right; all the information you gave us checked out. Both Archie Taylor and Charlie Davis flew with the RAF No. 77 Squadron and they were shot down. The records show that Charlie was captured and became a prisoner-of-war. At first Archie was listed as missing, presumed dead, until he re-appeared two years after the war had ended.'

'So what happens now?'

'We just need to find him and have a little chat.'

'Have you got an address for him?'

'Unfortunately not; he was recently living in Thetford but he moved out a month ago; no forwarding address. I'll keep you informed; in the meantime, keep an eye out for him; he must be close by.'

DI James stood up to leave.

'Thanks for coming round,' said Nick. 'I really appreciate it.'

'No problem; any luck with that waitress?'

'No. Reckons I'm too young; still, her loss.'

DI James just chuckled.

After seeing DI James out, Nick continued reading his magazine. *House of the Rising Sun* by The Animals was now number one and everyone was waiting for the new Beatles film *A Hard Day's Night* which was due to be released on Monday. After reading it from cover to cover, Nick then proceeded to cut all the pictures of Cilla Black out and stick them into his secret scrapbook.

Tuesday 7 July 1964

Nick and Keith were walking back to the bicycle shed after the school day when Mrs Kelley, the School Secretary came chasing after them.

'Nick Allen,' she shouted breathlessly, clearing not used running. 'I've got a message for you.'

The boys turned round, 'What is it?' asked Nick.

'You're mother phoned; can you pick up the sausages for your tea from the butchers. She got delayed and didn't have time to collect them.'

'No problem, and thank you, Mrs Kelley.'

'And please tell you mother I'm not a messenger girl; I'm the School Secretary.'

'I'm sure she appreciates your act of kindness. It's the little things like that, which will help you, get into heaven.'

'I'm sure my place is reserved.'

'I doubt it,' whispered Keith. 'She's a miserable old bat.'

'Are you riding with me to sample the delights of Stanford the Butchers?' asked Nick.

'Can't tonight, got an appointment.'

'There's something you are not telling me. You always seem to have an appointment. Are you seeing Big Brenda?'

'Define seeing.'

'You know what I mean; are you two-timing Moira?'

'Define two-timing.'

'Don't be smart. Look, I know you are my best mate, but I wouldn't like to see Moira hurt.'

'It's complicated.'

'It always is … ; explain!'

'It's not like I'm going out with Brenda. It's like this; her parents don't get home till 5.30 pm and she keeps inviting me round.'

'And you do what....help her with her homework?'

'Not exactly… …..well, she likes me playing with her tits.'

'Anything else?'

'No; second base is off limits unless I chuck Moira and go out with her full time.'

'Unbelievable.'

'I thought about it, but I really like Moira. She's bright, intelligent, and fun to be with. I could never chuck her. But Brenda; actually, she's as thick as two short planks but her tits are fantastic. You won't tell, will you?'

'As much as I'm disgusted by your behaviour and a slightly bit jealous, your secret is safe with me. Go on, bugger off and sample the delights of Big Brenda; just be careful that she doesn't suffocate you.'

'You're a mate.' With that Keith hurriedly cycled off, shouting 'think of me.'

'That's the last thing I will think of,' shouted Nick. 'My blood pressure couldn't stand it.'

Nick left his bicycle in Bushels the Builders' yard and walked to Stanford's the Butchers in Catherine Street, five doors from Headings and Watts paper shop.

'Hello young Nick, haven't seen you for a while,' said Mr Stanford, the owner of the butcher's shop.

'Nice to see you too, Mr Stanford; how's business?' replied Nick.

'Doing quite nicely; come for your sausages?

'That's right, Mums too lazy to fetch them,' said Nick jokingly.

'Charlie,' shouted Mr Stanford. 'Can you bring through the order for Mrs Allen?'

In a few seconds Charlie appeared carrying Nick's sausages wrapped up in white paper.

'Here you are, lad,' handing the parcel to Nick.

'You haven't met my new assistant, have you?' asked Mr Stanford. 'Charlie, this is Nick; Nick, this is Charlie,'

'Nice to meet you,' said Charlie, now offering his hand. Nick took a closer look at Charlie. He was a big bloke with ginger hair; he was wearing a butcher's apron with his sleeves rolled up, showing his large forearms on which the right one had a tattoo. Nick could feel his legs buckle and the blood drain from his head.'

'You alright, Nick?' asked Mr Stanford. 'You look all faint.'

'Sorry,' said Nick, trying to compose himself. 'Don't know what happened there; felt a bit giddy.'

'You best get yourself home and have a lie down,' said Mr Stanford.

Nick didn't need to be told twice; he wobbled out of the door, located his bike and cycled home in record time. Nick just dumped his bicycle outside the back door, rushed in and said, 'Hi Mum; must use the phone.'

The phone rang twice before it was answered by an attractive sounding female. 'St Albans Police Station, can I help you?'

'I need to speak to DI James, it's urgent.'

'Hold the line caller; I'll see if he's available.'

After a few clicks Nick heard a familiar voice, 'DI James, can I help you?'

'I've found him, I've found Charlie Davis.'

'Okay, calm down, take a deep breath and tell me again.'

Nick took a deep breath and said slowly, 'Charlie Davis is working at Stanford the Butchers in Catherine Street.'

'Are you sure?'

'I'm sure, he fits the description given by Reg Willis, exactly; right down to the tattoo with the name Polly on it.'

'Okay, well done; leave it us. I'll let you know the outcome.' With that he hung up.

Friday 10 July 1964

Nick was relaxed in front of the Television watching Manfred Mann perform their latest release, *You Gave Me Someone to Love,* on *Ready Steady Go.* He quite liked the track but didn't think it was as good as their previous songs. 'I think it will be a miss,' he said in his best David Jacobs voice.

There was a knock on the front door; again Mrs Allen answered it. 'Not you again; would you like me to fix up a bed? You're here more than you are at the station.'

Ignoring the sarcasm, DI James replied 'is he in?'

'I think you know the way now.'

Nick looked up and by the look on the policeman's face he could tell it was not good news. 'No luck then?'

'Not really; we have interviewed Charlie and almost everything you said was true; except the bit about murdering Archie. He said that he had no malice against Archie; he was surprised to see him as he thought he was dead. He just wanted to talk to him and catch up on old times. He said he forgave him from running away and he would have probably done the same thing. But it was all in the past.'

'But that doesn't mean he didn't kill him.'

'Unfortunately, we have no evidence that he was anywhere near the school and he has a water-tight alibi. They put the time of death at between eight and ten in the morning. Archie opened the shop at six with Mr Stanford and he was there all morning. We have loads of witnesses who saw him after the shop opened at 7.30 am. My gut feeling is that he done it, but there is no way he could have been in two places at once. We'll keep an eye on our Mr Davis, but for the time being we have to keep looking.'

Wednesday 22 July 1964

Nick was feeling tired and depressed as he sat all alone in Sally's Café nursing a strawberry milkshake. Only two more schooldays; then six weeks holiday, and how he was looking forward to a week at the Holiday Camp. The Juke-box played *Don't Let the Sun Catch You Crying* by Gerry and the Pacemakers. The last year was beginning to take its toll. Too much excitement for one fourteen-year-old; he also felt bereft. He hadn't seen much of Keith during the last few weeks. If he wasn't seeing Moira, he was seeing Big Brenda. Just good friends, he would say. More like Bosom Buddies thought Nick, knowing Keith's weakness. He hadn't seen Don either since their visit to Hill End Hospital. The patients really shook him up and his Mum had decided that Nick was a bad influence so stopped Don seeing him. Last he heard, Don had joined the Scouts and was now tying knots and doing bob-a-job for elderly people.

He had visited Mrs Taylor on several occasions, the first to explain about Archie's sister Sally. On subsequent visits he was informed that Mrs Taylor and Sally were getting on really well and Sally had made significant improvement; it had been suggested that Sally should visit Mrs Taylor at weekends with the view to live there fulltime.

He was also upset about an article he had read in this morning's *Daily Mirror*. One of his favourite footballers, John White, the Tottenham Hotspur inside forward, was killed yesterday. Apparently he was sheltering from a thunderstorm under a tree at the Crew's Hill Golf Club, when he was struck by lightning; he was 27. Even the very sexy photo of Cilla Black, on the front page hadn't cheered him up. Although he will cut it out tonight and stick it in his secret scrapbook.

The end-of-year exams had been a disaster; maths was okay- could have done that with my eyes shut he thought. Unfortunately, that had happened during the history and geography exams. For some strange reason, he had been selected to represent the school in the 800 yards race at the inter-schools competition at Clarence Park. He managed to finished third and was lucky not to be disqualified when a boy whom he overtook in the straight mysteriously fell over. Still it was nice to hear his name read out over the public address system, '... ... ... and in third place Nick Allen, Sandridge Grammar School.'

Being on his own most nights Nick had taken a greater interest in pop music. His favourite group, The Zombies had released their first single *She's Not There*. The song was aired on juke box jury and guest panellist George Harrison had raved about it. *House of the Rising Sun* by the Animals which had just been knocked off the number one spot by The Rolling Stones had revolutionised the slow dance. It was over four minutes long, nearly twice as long as other slow songs. Holding a lovely girl in your arms, on the dance floor, for all that time ... heaven.

Nick had also been watching a lot of television; his favourites were *Bonanza*, *Hancock's Half Hour* and *Top of the Tops*. He still preferred *Ready Steady Go* but that might be because he fancied Cathy McGowan. He also used to watch Emergency Ward Ten with his Mum, which he swears had nothing to do with the very attractive Jill Browne who played Nurse Carole Young.

He was also worried about his future. He would be fifteen at Christmas, which allowed him to leave school at Easter. Was he ready for work? His dad had encouraged him to leave as soon as possible and take an apprenticeship, but his Mum argued against that. She had suggested he stayed on at school and take his O levels, after all that's why he went to the Grammar school.

The reason he was taking his time drinking his milkshake was that

Ron Hart, the manager of the paper shop, where he worked, had asked Nick to pop in and see him at 4.30 pm. He had a feeling that he was in trouble and that one of his customers had made a complaint against him. He had been expecting it. It was all because of that horrible dog at 3 Branch Road. Recently, Nick had been rolling their newspaper up very tightly; then opening the letterbox very slowly and resting the paper on the lip. When the black beast jumped up at the letterbox, he would ram the paper in, using all his might. Most days he would hit the dog's nose, but occasionally hit him in the eye. A good shot would make the dog yelp and scurry away. So what if he got the sack, he could always get another paper round.

He slowly cycled round the corner into Catherine Street and left his bike next door in Bushels the Builders yard. Like a prisoner walking to the gallows Nick entered the shop. Mr Hart was in his usual place behind the counter and his face lit up when he saw Nick.

'Hello Nick, dead on time; that's what I like,' said Mr Hart, looking up at the clock on the wall. 'I've been very impressed with you since you started working here and I was wondering if you would like the job of marking up in the mornings. It would mean starting a bit earlier, at six, but there will be more pay, obviously. What do you say?'

Nick was taken back a bit, 'er, well, yeh, that would be great. Thanks very much.'

'I know you are on holiday next week, so if you could start the Monday after, Barry, our present marker will train you up, and he'll be leaving the following Saturday.'

'That's fantastic; I don't know how to thank you.'

'You don't have to; I think you'll do a great job. We'll be a dream team.'

'My Mum will be ever so pleased.'

'So will that dog in Branch Road.'

They both burst out laughing.

'I think I'll treat myself to some sweets to celebrate.'

'You do that Nick while I serve this little girl.'

Nick picked up a Jamboree Bag, a packet of Love Hearts, a packet of Opal Fruits and a Fry's Peppermint Cream.

Mr Hart had just served the little girl with two frozen Jubbly's.

'I hope they don't melt before I get home,' she said as she walked out of the shop.

Nick had just paid for his sweets when it hit him. He thought: I know how he did it, it's so obvious, and why did it take me so long to figure it out?   He rushed out into the street and ran down to the butchers shop. Charlie Davis was in there all on his own. Without thinking of the consequences, he entered the shop and shouted: 'I know how you did it; I know how you murdered Archie Taylor.

If Charlie was surprised by this revelation, he didn't show it. He just continued scrubbing down the chopping block with salt.

'And how was that?' he asked.

'You used ice, you made big blocks of ice and made Archie stand on them. You got him drunk then kidnapped him and put him in the butchers van. Then you made him stand on the ice while you strung him up. Then you burnt his hands so he couldn't pull himself up the rope.' Nick was speaking so fast he was struggling to breath. 'He must have been standing there for hours, he daren't move. Then, when the sun came up the ice started to melt and he slowly died of strangulation; you fiend.'

'Well, you little smarty pants, got it all worked out, haven't you?'

'Absolutely, you'll hang for this.'

Archie just continued scrubbing, then said, 'Maybe I will, maybe I won't, but first tell me, how you knew it was me. '

'The landlord of the Farriers Arms gave me a description of you and I recognised you that day I came in for my sausages.'

'No, I can't believe that, there must be more.'

'My Mum once told me, never to get a tattoo. If you do something wrong they can always recognise you by you tattoo.'

'Very good!'

Then Nick, for some reason said, 'Who's Polly? And why did you choose the school to kill him'

'Well, I must admire you detective work or sheer luck, so I'll tell you the whole story. I think you deserve to know. I was born in St Albans and attended Sandridge Grammar School. I used to sit under that tree during the summer, reading a book, or doing my homework or just shading from the sun. So it was ironic that Archie had organised a cricket match there next day. Anyway when the war broke out my parents decided to move to Norfolk, they thought St Albans was too near London and it would be safer there. As it happened, I was lucky enough to be stationed at RAF Feltwell. Polly, who lived in Thetford, and I became sweethearts. In 1942 my plane was shot down over Holland. Four of us survived, one died. Archie and I got separated from the other two. We hid in an irrigation ditch for a while, and then I got shot. We knew that the Germans were approaching, so Archie decided to make a run for it, leaving me at the mercy of those bastards. They shot me in both legs and I became very ill. After months in various hospitals, I was finally sent to Stalag Luft 6 where I stayed until the end of the war. I met 'Dixie' Deans; he got an MBE after the war. I also met the other two from my plane, George Hawkins and Bob Barker. Neither of them knew what happened to Archie; we assumed he must have been killed. When I finally got back to Blighty, I found out that Polly had married a GI called Chuck and gone to live in Louisville, Kentucky. After the war I trained as a butcher and eventually got my own business; I never married. But during the last five years my business was going down the pan. I started drinking and gambling and I become bankrupt. I then decided to make a fresh start and move back to St Albans. You can imagine my surprise when I walked into the Farriers Arms and saw Archie. As I expect you know, he just panicked and walked out of the pub. I popped back to the pub a few times afterwards, but I never saw him. At first I just wanted to talk to him but as the time went on I began thinking about all the suffering I'd been through and started blaming him. I thought he should pay for what he put me through. For a few days it became an obsession and I just wanted to kill him. I wanted him to suffer slowly just like I did. That's when I came up with the hanging on ice idea. Then I saw him coming out of the pub on that Friday. I told him that I just wanted a chat. You know, for old time's sake. I said I didn't blame him for what he had done. I would have done the same thing in his position and war makes a man do funny things. Anyway, we started to get on really well; he told me about his life and how much he was looking forward to the cricket match tomorrow. We went for a walk and sat on a bench in the Abbey Orchard. I had a bottle of whisky with me and we celebrated our reunion. He seemed so relieved and he got stuck into the whisky. When the bottle was finished, he was well gone. I managed to walk him back to my van and as soon he was seated, he passed out. I drove back to the shop, got the ice blocks out of the cold store and drove to the school. It didn't take much to break the lock on the gate to the field. Well, you know the rest.'

'Very moving,' said Nick sarcastically. 'But it makes no difference; you are still a murderer.'

'And I suppose you expect me to come quietly.'

Nick hadn't thought about that. Even with his training, there was no way he was going to overpower this man. Unfortunately, whilst he was thinking of his options, Charlie had slowly come from behind the counter, locked the shop door and turned the Open sign to Closed. Even though he was a big man with a limp, he was still pretty fast on his feet and grabbed Nick before he had a chance to move.

'Let me go, you brute,' Nick cried.

'I must say you were very clever with the ice, but it will be your downfall, not mine.'

With Nick firmly held by one arm, he dragged him towards the shop freezer and with the other hand he opened it.

'Time for you to cool off,' said Charlie, as he threw Nick into the freezer.

The last thing Nick saw was a rack full of animal carcasses before the freezer door shut and he was plunged into absolute darkness. 'Shit,' screamed Nick. 'Why does this always happen, when will I learn to think first. How the hell am I going to get out of here?'

'Let me out, let me out,' he screamed, but he knew no one would answer.

So this was it, the end, thought Nick. Nick Allen, born 14 December 1949, died 22 July 1964. What would they put on my gravestone? Couldn't keep out of trouble or If only he thought first, acted afterwards. Where's Keith or Don when you need them? Bet Keith will have his head between Big Brenda's enormous breasts. Don will be polishing his woggle. Would Moira cry? She was a great snogger, pity I never got to touch her breasts.

It was getting colder and Nick's eyes were getting heavy. He had nodded off a couple of times when his attention was caught by a bright light in front of him. Nick tried to shield his eyes when he realised that a man was standing in front of him. The man was tall and thin and his face was vaguely familiar. He was wearing an all-white football kit and was carrying a football. Nick then recognised him.'

'Hey, I know you; you're John White. Really upset to read that you died yesterday.'

'Not as sorry as I was,' said John, in a broad Scottish accent.

Nick laughed, 'they used to call you the ghost and now you are one.'

'Aye, very funny.'

'So, why are you here?'

'Well, they've asked me to form a football team. There's a match on Saturday against the Red Devils and I wondered if you would like to play?'

'Well, that would be nice. But does that mean I'm dead?'

'No, not yet; give it a couple of hours. But I thought I'd ask before the other team try to sign you up.'

'Well, if I die, put me down.'

'Thanks, see you in a couple of hours.' With that the light faded.

Charming, thought Nick. Not even dead yet and there after me. Nick stood up and starting jumping up and down, but it was difficult. He had no idea what the time was. The luminous hands on watch were blurred due to the frost on the face. Again, as his eyes dropped another light appeared. This time it transformed into a chubby man in a white suit with printed flowers on and wearing a hat.

'I know you; you're that cheeky chappy, what's his name? I know Max Miller, my Mum loved you.'

'I'm glad; so let's get on. Laughter will keep you alive, so here goes.'

Nick sat down, pulled his knees up under his chin and wrapped his arms around them.

'I got two books, a white book and a blue book. And by that, you can gather I got two sorts of stories.

'To test you out, why did the chicken cross the road? To get to the other side. What, no? You got to go further back than that. These are old jokes. Why did the chicken cross the road? For some foul reason.

'It says in the white book ... listen,

There was a little girl

Who had a little curl

Right in the middle of her forehead;

And when she was good, she was very, very good,

And when she was bad she was very, very popular.

'Now listen! You can't expect too much from the white book. This is the book. This is where we all get pinched! I don't care. I'll go. I've been there before, I have. I won't walk. I make them get the barrow out. I'm on the BLUE BOOK now.

She was but a village maiden,

Who's to say she was to blame?

But alas a wicked squire

Took away her honest name.

So she journeyed up to London

Seeking to forget her shame.

When another wicked squire

Took away her other...

'Ere... I got another one here.

'You heard about the Yorkshire man who came to London and couldn't get some Yorkshire pudding. He went home and battered himself to death.

Mary had a little lamb

Who acted very silly.

She plucked the wool from off its back

And smacked its Piccadilly.

'Which would you like, the blue book or the white book? You like both, don't you/

'Listen, I was in Spain four years ago and in Spain all the girls wear little knives in the top of their stockings. I found that out. So I said to myself, I'll find out exactly what the idea is so I said, "What's the idea of wearing a knife at the top of the stocking?" She said, "That's to defend my honour." I said, "What, a little tiny knife like that?" I said, "If you were in Brighton, you'd want a set of carvers!"

Mary had a little bear

To which she was so kind.

I often see her bear in front...

I'll get on to the next joke here.

Jack and Jill went up the hill

Just like two cock linnets.

Jill came down with half-a-crown,

She wasn't up there two ... 'Ere.

'I better stay on the blue book ... eh? I think so, yeah?

Adam and Eve in the Garden dwelt,

They were so happy and jolly.

I wonder how they would have felt,

If all the leaves had been holly!

Nick was laughing his frozen socks off when the light faded and Max disappeared.

'It won't be long now,' said Nick, to himself. 'No one is coming; they would have been here now.'

Perhaps I should try and leave a message he thought, but how?

He stared groping around in the dark trying to find anything that he could use. He wasn't aware at first of another light starting to appear. This time, two figures were starting to appear. The first was a man in a cape and a deerstalker hat, smoking a pipe; next to him sniffing the carcasses, an ugly, long-haired, lop-eared creature, half spaniel and half lurcher, with a very clumsy waddling gait.

'Sherlock Holmes,' gasped Nick. 'I didn't think you were real.'

'Do any of us know what is real and what is not?' said Sherlock.

'That's true.'

Sherlock made himself comfortable in an armchair that wasn't there a second ago and putting his fingertips together as was his custom said: 'I was impressed by your deduction; cunning idea that, using the ice to confuse the time of death.'

'I should have worked it out earlier.'

'I agree, you should have asked yourself: "why are my trousers wet when all the grass around me is bone dry"?'

'Silly mistake.'

'Never mind, you did well; nasty piece of work that Charlie Davis.'

'Never trust a carrot top; I read your case The Red-Headed League.

'Absolutely,' Sherlock smiled.

'Is it just me, or do all ginger people smell funny?'

Sherlock laughed and wriggled in his chair, but didn't answer the question.

'Will I die?' asked Nick in a serious voice.

'We'll all die one day. But today is not your day to die. I'm sure you'll be rescued. As you know I died once and somehow was brought back to life. I think there is a guardian angel looking over you. But I must go know, there is a bit of trouble upstairs, someone has stolen the chief angel's harp. But remember what I've always said "when you have eliminated the impossible, whatever remains, however improbable, must be the truth?'

Nick felt his hair, it was frozen, his jeans were frozen and he was having trouble to move. 'For Christ sake, come and rescue me,' he shouted.

Almost instantaneously another light appeared, and then standing in front of him, legs apart, hands on hips wearing a white vest and army fatigues, was his late self-defence teacher, Mr Campion.

'Come on, lad, on your feet. The only way to keep alive is keeping warm. So we'll start with some star jumps.' He started, Nick followed. 'One-two, one-two, that's it, keep up.'

The star jumps were followed, by squat jumps, then running on the spot. It was hard but Nick was determined to keep up.

'I think you'll win the girl, if you survive this,' said Mr Campion.

'What girl?' replied Nick? His mind was drowsy, he wasn't thinking straight.

'Moira; who do you think I mean, her mother?' laughed Mr Campion.

'That would be nice,' Nick struggled to say.

'I wouldn't mind a crack at her mum myself, fine looking woman.'

'Certainly better than the last one you lived with,' gasped Nick, falling to his knees.

Did he hear a noise? He looked up, Mr Campion had disappeared. Another noise, voices maybe. He was drifting, he could feel it, and his time had come. He placed his head down gently on his hands and curled up into the foetal position. Another light appeared; it started with a thin strip, and then got wider.

'He's over here.' 'Call an ambulance.' 'Is he alive?' 'Quickly, put your coat round him.'

Thursday 23 July 1964

The first thing Nick noticed when he opened his eyes was the beautiful face of a young woman.

'The face of an angel, I must be in heaven,' sighed Nick.

'Not this time, Nick Allen, but it is getting close,' replied the young women.

That face and the voice, I recognize them from somewhere, thought Nick. It took a few seconds for Nick to come to his senses before he also realized where he was.

'Nurse Hickey, nice to see you again,' beamed Nick.

'So you're back with us, getting a bit of a habit, this. You gave us a bit of a scare last night, almost lost you a couple of times.'

'Are you still engaged to your boyfriend?'

'I can see you're on the mend; yes I am, and we're very happy.'

'Okay, just checking,' said Nick, giving her his biggest smile.

Nick's first visitor was DI James.

'Before you start,' said Nick. 'I know I was in the wrong, I shouldn't have confronted him on my own. It was impulsive, but I was so excited at solving the case.'

'Well, let that be a lesson to you lad; you almost died in that freezer,' replied DI James. So come on then, tell me, how did he do it?'

Nick spent the next few minutes explaining about the blocks of ice and how Charlie had forced him into the cold store.

'Anyway, how did you find me?' asked Nick.

'Apparently, your friend Moira thought she saw you enter the butcher's shop. She had something to tell you, so she hung around waiting for you. When you didn't appear, she thought she must have been mistaken. Anyway, she decided to call on you; it was about eight o'clock and she found your Mum in a bit of a state, because you hadn't come home for you tea. Moira told your Mum what she thought she saw and then your dad phoned us. By the time we had contacted Mr Stanford to open the shop, it was nearly nine o'clock. What time did you go into the butchers?'

'It must have been about a quarter to five. Have you caught Charlie?'

'Not yet; I sent a patrol car round to his digs, but he had packed up and gone. We'll catch him soon. Still, look on the bright side; if we can't pin the murder on him we're sure to do him for the attempted murder of Nick Allen. I'm glad you're okay, I'll send round a uniformed officer to take a proper statement when you are feeling a bit better.'

DI James smiled and left Nick alone in his bed. Nick had just started to drop off when his parents came rushing down the ward, Mrs Allen, in her usual flap. For the next hour she never stopped talking, and when she did, she started sobbing. Nurse Hickey could see that Nick was getting stressed and suggested that they came back this evening after Nick had rested.

Nick slept most of the afternoon and was totally refreshed when his parents returned to visit; this time his friend Keith was with them. The atmosphere was a lot easier and the four of them chatted away quite merrily without any raised voices or hysterics. His Mum had brought in some comics and a small bunch of grapes, which she had consumed by the time they left. Keith thought that Nick might need something more stimulating and had nipped in the paper shop and bought him a puzzle book and a pencil with a rubber on the end. Nick never got to ask Keith about Moira or Big Brenda, which would have to wait for another time. All being well, they said that Nick should be fit enough to go home tomorrow.

It was about 9.30 pm, the lights had been dimmed and most of the other patients were asleep, when Nick noticed a doctor walking slowly down the ward. From the position he was lying, it was difficult to see his face but he instantly recognised the limp. He panicked for a moment, then slowly reached out and grabbed the pencil that was resting on his bedside cabinet. The doctor approached Nick's bed, picked up his medical chart, looked at it, and then replaced it on the end of the bed. Nick had one chance and one chance only, assuming that the doctor was who he thought he was. Nick's fears were confirmed when a voice said, 'you won't escape a second time.'

That was all Nick needed to hear; in one swift move he slung the sheets off with his left hand and with his right hand stuck the pencil in Charlie's left eye. The scream was deafening. Then the lights were turned on and doctors and nurses appeared to investigate. As Charlie fell to his knees writhing in agony, Nick said, 'that's for Archie.'

Saturday 25 July 1964

'The taxi's here,' shouted Mr Allen.

The usual pre-holiday panic ensued as the Allen family grabbed their cases; making sure that the gas, electric and water were turned off.

'Are all the windows shut?' asked Mrs Allen.

'I've checked them,' replied Nick.

As they made their way to the taxi, Mr Allen held back and collared Nick.

'Now listen here, lad, on this holiday you will do exactly what I tell you to do, understand?'

'Yes, Dad.'

'During the day you will stay on the beach and play with your brother.'

'Yes, Dad.'

'And if you are very good, I may treat you to a donkey ride.'

'Thanks, Dad.'

'In the evening, you will sit next to me in the ballroom and watch the entertainment. Understood?'

'Yes, Dad.'

'I might even let you have a few games of bingo, even though you are under age.'

'Gee, thanks Dad.'

'I'm glad you understand.'

'Just one question, Dad.'

'What's that?'

'Who's Tom Sawyer?'

As they were packing the suitcases into the back of the taxi, Nick noticed Moira running towards them.

'In you get, lad,' said Mr Allen.

'Just a minute, Dad,' Nick turned to Moira. 'I'm glad you came, I wanted to thank you for rescuing me.'

'It was nothing,' she replied trying to catch her breath.

'What was it you wanted to tell me?'

She smiled. 'Well, I just wanted to tell you that Keith and I split up. Apparently he's been seeing someone else.'

'The bastard, I didn't know, I swear,' said Nick, with his fingers crossed.

'I'm not that bothered, but it does mean that I'm free to go out with you.'

'Well, I don't think we should rush into it. It might seem like you are going out with me on the rebound. I think we should leave it for a while.'

'You're absolutely right, how long are you away for?'

'Seven days.'

'That settled then; if I feel the same in a week's time we'll start going out.'

Nick looked into Moira's eyes and said, 'I love you.'

Moira smiled back and replied, 'I love you too.'

All eyes in the taxi were focused on the couple as their lips met.

REFERENCES

[1]   Substitutes weren't introduced until 1965.

[2]   No Hiding Place was ITV's best known early police drama series and starred Raymond Francis as Detective Chief Superintendent Tom Lockhart with Det. Sgt. Baxter (Eric Lander), Det. Sgt. Russell (Johnny Briggs), Det. Sgt. Perryman (Michael McStay) and Det. Sgt. Gregg (Sean Caffrey).

[3]   Stephen Ward was one of the central figures in the 1963 Profumo affair. He committed suicide on 3 August 1963.

[4]   Christine Keeler was convicted of perjury in December 1963 and sentenced to 9 months in prison.

[5]   Yesterday was written by Paul McCartney for their 1965 Beatles album Help. Yesterday has the most cover versions of any song ever written.

[6]   Nick Allen attended Aboyne Lodge Infant school between 1954 and 1957

[7]   Arthur Martin became head of the D1 section of D Branch (investigations) of MI5 in 1960.

[8]   Peter Wright, English Scientist, and MI5 counterintelligence officer.

[9]   Arthur Martin set up a meeting with Blunt on April 23, 1964. At that meeting, Blunt admitted that he had worked for the Soviet government.

[10] The Record Room was an independent Record Shop owned by Mark Green. It was the only plausible record shop in the area. The shop moved to Chequers St. in the mid-sixties.

[11] Noam Chomsky, is an American linguist, philosopher, cognitive scientist, and political activist.

12   Chidwickbury Estate was owned by the racehorse owner and breeder Jim Joel. In March 1964, the Joel family were in Saudi Arabia looking at horses. Hamdam Al-Hamasin was house-sitting.

13   Jimmy Jewel and Ben Warris were a comedy double act. They formed in 1934 and disbanded 1966.

14   The Zombies won the Herts Beat Contest, organized by the Watford Borough Council and sponsored by the London Evening News. They won £250 and the ability to record a demo for Decca records.

15   Tominey's Ice Cream, a family run business, established in the 1930s ran until the mid-1980.

16   Gorhambury House is a fine neo-Palladian house, built in 1777 - 84 to the designs of Sir Robert Taylor. In the Middle Ages the Gorhambury estate, lying near the site of the vanished Roman city of Verulamium, belonged to St Albans Abbey. Early in Queen Elizabeth I's reign, the property was purchased by Sir Nicholas Bacon, Lord Keeper of the Great Seal. In 1563 - 68 Sir Nicholas built a new house at Gorhambury and it became the home of his younger son, the philosopher and politician, Francis Bacon (whose monument can be seen in the parish church of St Michael nearby). Francis Bacon left Gorhambury to his former secretary, Sir Thomas Meautys, who married Anne Bacon, the great-granddaughter of the Lord Keeper. The estate later passed to her second husband Sir Harbottle Grimston, Master of the Rolls and Speaker in the Convention parliament of 1659 - 60. The present house was built by his descendant, the 3rd Viscount Grimston. Gorhambury still contains the notable collection of family portraits transferred from the Elizabethan house (now ruined). The 3rd Viscount's son was created Earl of Verulam in 1806 and the family have lived at Gorhambury ever since.

17   For years television viewers in the UK would tune in to hear Kent Walton's opening line "Greetings, grapple fans" as he introduced Saturday afternoon wrestling as part of ITV's long running 'World of Sport' programme.

Thanks to Emma Leahy at thirteeneighty.co.uk for designing the cover.

Made in the USA
Charleston, SC
04 February 2013